THREE
WAR
STORIES

THREE
WAR
STORIES

BY

DAVID MAMET

Print ISBN: 978-0-7867-5560-8
ebook ISBN: 978-0-7867-5561-5

Distributed by Argo Navis Author Services

Distributed by
Argo Navis Author Services
www.argonavisdigital.com

To Art Shay, Ron Glasser, and Lou Lenart

THE
REDWING

Advanced age, accompanied by reasonable health, is generally accounted a blessing. I do not know that it is so, and I suspect that such proclamation is made solely by those ignorant of the actual nature of age. For though age awards, to most, both increased time and ability for reflection, such leisure allows or suggests the question "To what end?"

Youth, it is said, is wasted on the young, but it is not wasted. It is enjoyed, in all its terror, lust, and exhilaration. That it is spotted, that it contains periods of fear, of uncertainty, of loneliness, and of self-doubt, is only to say that it is a time of *life*; age, and that age possessing the much-vaunted time for reflection, is, in its essence, empty of these. That is the sum of this prized philosophic disposition. That such disposition might be employed in philosophy rather than rage is, arguably, not a societal invitation to share wisdom but rather to display a nonobjectionable retirement, in the absence of any other usefulness.

I could, at one time, split a playing card, turned edge-on, with a pistol ball, at twenty-five yards. What merit has this recollection? Or that women once found me attractive. They seek protection, and thus, always, the armed man. I made money by writing. And supported many people by it. That I count as a major accomplishment, and as a gift that I enjoyed this endeavor. The fires of youth, long self-described as banked, have, in fact, long been cold, and gone is the thirst for new acquaintance, let alone adventure, whether in the flesh or in those fantasies by the transcription of which I supported myself during those many years. But, in spite of this dreary stoicism, I find and am happy to find in myself what I must describe as an enthusiasm to set the record straight, to, as we say in the Navy, "regularize the Log."

This process, here, as there, may be used not only to supply that information lost in the necessity of action, or rendered illegible by battle, or the

Sea, but to reform the account, unconsciously or no, in light of an overriding conception.

I hope that such may not be found to be solely the author's self-love, or wish for approval. I do not think that this is the case, nor that he has employed the reader's time and patience to the end of that confession, which is finally but self-aggrandizement or boasting. I hope these corrections, written primarily to still the conscience, may, as an independent composition, have the capacity to divert or amuse.

.   .   .

They asked me did I want to go to sea, and I said, "No." For I saw no profit in it. But then I went to sea. I believe they were nonplussed by my lack of adventurousness, or took it for a want of spirit. And perhaps they were not wrong. For though I have done certain notable things, my great interest, then as now, was primarily to *observe*, by which, I believe, I must mean to consider. My travels, then, were, if I may, by way of being a goad to my consideration, which you may think strange, in light of the things it fell to my lot to do.

But as my exploits had to do almost exclusively with the preservation of life, and as the life was mine, I did them as a matter of course, as would you have done; while the products of my imagination always seemed to me the truer adventure.

For pirates are, after all, but criminals; and the ravenous shark, if one is its desired victim, merely the parish bull writ large.

My friends, on my return, I know, found or pretended to find this attitude preposterous, as have the various critics who, faced with the reality of the author to whom they have accorded that highest accolade, the confession of having been amused (in the odd case "enchanted"), rendered, or, indeed, *performed*, the silent verdict of having been, in my presence, bored.

But what matter, I asked them, as I ask you, if the incident of the whale were true? Would such truth make the chapter more enjoyable? I do not see how. It was my presence, then, or the illusion of the possibility of verification which made my presence, to them, onerous.

For they asked. And why should I have lied? At the first, upon the book's reception, I considered it my right to tell the truth. But which reader or reviewer, I found, would prefer the mottled or inconclusive truth to the "finely wrought tale"? None of them. And if the "truth" had been, in itself, conclusive, what would have driven me to write the book?

Curiously, a few bizarre or preternatural instances which I related as they occurred have been tagged by more than one reviewer as fantasies and a "blot on the verisimilitude" of the production.

On reflection, I concur. They are. And perhaps I included them out of a perverse desire to reassure myself that I am not, in toto, a fraud—that I have both suffered and traveled, and that, though I now support myself by the pen, I was once, to earn my bread, a sailor.

·   ·   ·

I will not dwell upon my first taking ship, nor on the trials and initiations, pertinent and merely customary, which befall any first voyager. The incident of "Crandall" is, of course, treated in the novel. That was neither his name nor his demeanor; nor can he be identified from reference to those characteristics I assigned to him for the express purpose of concealing his identity.

In life he was, and I use the word advisedly, evil; and he was intelligent enough not only to foresee the various ill results of his domination, but to work constantly to refine them.

It was not my lot in reality to have seen him actually among the castaways, for he died before the wreck, and never knew the trials of those months in the boat. Nor did I, as one reviewer has suggested, "give him a lift," a forecastle term meaning to help a miscreant over the side. Though I did fantasize his death in detail, after the flogging.

I berated myself then for my cowardice, as a better man, I felt, would have called him out and fought him there on the deck, though it meant death at the yardarm. But I considered the coward's way, which is to say a lift over the side, and mitigated, in my mind, the murder by grappling myself to and falling with him, through the air and into the deep, his eyes speaking that terror which was only increased by his vision of the triumph in my own.

The stripes heal. I have never considered the scars of the flogging a mark either of shame or honor. I have, of late, on accession, perhaps, of some distance or wisdom, or the understanding that they may be the same if one considers them so, begun to accept that, just as one is accorded honor on ship for the stoicism with which he may bear his whipping, one may acquire honor in allowing memory to heal, and in cessation of importuning either God for an explanation or the Devil for revenge.

It was Margaret who, as is her practice, in a characteristic aside, the tone of which might indicate equally a commonplace or a profound truth, prompted this suggestion of philosophy. "On ship," she asked, "after a man was beaten, was the sympathy with which the crew received him affected by their opinion of whether or not the flogging was deserved?"

For, of course, it was not. Their, I will not say "sympathy," for that is too commonplace a term, their *verdict*, rested not upon the justice of the punishment, but on the courage of its recipient.

For which of us, I understood to be the meaning of her seemingly offhand remark, does not suffer, to his mind, unjustly? And who is to say what any man deserves?

·   ·   ·

In the night watches, every sailor thinks about God.

He may, if it is his nature to name his thoughts, refer to the subject of his ruminations as The Universe, or The Nature of the World; but I am not reluctant to identify the subject of my inquiries as The Almighty.

Blake, in the novel called *Simmons,* went mad in the boat.

All of us saw its genesis, and it was not, as fictionalized, in the decision to eat the first of the dead.

Blake was mad long before then. But the cathartic event was not the onset of cannibalism (which, after all, was inevitable), but the appearance of a cloud. The cloud appeared on the horizon, which, from the water, lies at about eleven miles. Blake stirred in the boat, sufficiently to rouse us from our torpor, and we followed his gaze to the cloud, which, for the briefest of instances, *could*, in fact, have been mistaken for a sail. But only by a novice. And Blake had been at sea since a child.

So we looked back to him from the object of his interest, and saw, and wondered at the expression of hope, as clear as if he bore a placard to that effect upon his chest. And we stared at its persistence for the longest time, until we saw it vanish, and his mind devolve to that conclusion obvious to the rest of us at a cursory glance. And then he was mad.

Why should one write it one way rather than another? Perhaps it is a protective device, shielding the mind of the author from some horror—just that mechanism present in the mind of Blake. For I knew, and, if questioned I am sure the crew would, to a man, agree with me, that he would have stood the subsequent captivity well, accepting, as does any good sailor, that over which he has no control. But he broke when he saw the cloud.

Human flesh tastes much like any animal flesh, all of which tastes very much alike. Blindfolded, most would be hard-pressed to differentiate between chicken and pork—try the experiment. And the finest lamb and beefsteak, *fresh*, taste similar. It is only after they have begun to go off that their distinctiveness arises. And we ate the Swedish sailor fresh. In fact, we gorged on him. I must amend or qualify my, certainly at least partial, attempt at self-exoneration on the similarity of tastes. For when the Arabs had us, the infrequent meat we received was assumed by all—though none voiced the opinion—to have been that of another prisoner.

Many died in the Galleys, expiring from bitter overwork and a hopelessness accelerated by the scurvy, which is an interesting disease.

How profound is Nature and how beautiful her gift of the natural narcotics, chief among them lethargy. Those who have only witnessed it decry it as a horrible leaching away of humanity, but we who have experienced it know it as a beautiful withdrawal from care, and an adumbration of Death as a blessing.

·   ·   ·

Fire is a dreadful thing. We know it is "the friend to Man," and anyone who has ever labored, on his knees, to coax into being that fire which would make the difference between life and death is well aware of the origin of prayer.

The small twig fire in the Arab prison saved our lives through that first winter. It was our hearth and, in the endless nights, our reassurance, for its crackling was the only "conversation" which we heard. The wind, in its monotony, became a goad, first to short tempers, then to sullenness, and finally to that silence the only human component of which was the variousness of the fire.

On the days the boy did not come with the sticks, many of us, had we been alone, might have indulged ourselves in tears (less for the lack of warmth, although that was most essential, not only for comfort, but, at those times the weather turned, for life, than for the fire's sight and sound). The wind was, always, foreign and cruel. It was a constant reminder of one's state as interloper and captive. But fire is everywhere the same.

Nevertheless, it was the fire which strove to kill us.

In the novel, the fire is occasioned by a pipe left on the coil of stray line near the taffrail. But many believed it was set. And discussed it, if I may use that term for a whispered and tentative play of allusions, while in captivity. For could not the notional miscreant be still among us? On the other hand, what mischief, were he to have been discovered, could he actually do? We were held against no day; which day, *should* it have been accorded, could only be the day of our ransom. And how might we hope for ransom, who doubted the news of our capture had ever reached home? And so the only release possible was an end to that period marking the fulfillment of whatever they called their particular notion of justice, in the culmination of our execution.

Or perhaps, as we held in our darkest, never expressed but never long absent thoughts, we were simply to be left until death.

It was to deal with this thought I began to compose my book.

.   .   .

Some might question how one might apply oneself, over such a length of time, to such a bootless errand, the odds being greatly that we were to die, unredeemed.

I found myself on my repatriation, to my amusement, in the company of authors, many of whom raised a similar question, their particular Demon of Pointlessness, however, being not captivity in a foreign galley or cell, but the difficulty of publication.

All things are relative, use makes master, and various other truisms come to mind, and recall their like: the accumulations of the various precepts upon ship, which essential maxims operate at a level below that of both thought and speech. "Have always by you your marlinespike" not being required to've been written on a slate when you've witnessed a reefer at the end of the yard, his hand caught in a reef-point, battered to death in a typhoon.

One critic has alleged that certain incidents in *The Raven* may conceal more than they confess. I count him acute. He is correct. He did not instance, though I believe he meant, the nature of my leave-taking from Taya, neither the murder in the boat. For, alike with all humankind, I loathe discovery, and concealed the actual nature of those events with care. But I applaud the critic's perspicacity, noting only that his suggestion was needlessly cautious in tone and scope.

.   .   .

When one has ceased to believe one will live, there is a certain, I will not say "satisfaction," for it is not satisfaction, but diversion in the drama of watching another man die.

One does not wish for it; one would do much in the case of a friend (and the bonds between shipmate castaways are closer than those between mere friends) to prevent it; but when there is nothing to prevent it, and one knows oneself soon to follow, the taint of ghoulishness is absent, and one becomes absorbed by the progress of what is, after all, both natural and inevitable. It is the opposite of that guiltiest, most sordid, addictive destruction of the soul, the infliction of torture for revenge.

The Pirate Captain, in the novel, depicted as drowned trying to escape the longboat bearing him to execution, was, in truth, tortured to death, over a period of several days. In repayment for Taya's murder. I employed fire and steel.

As, first, his composure broke, and then as hope left him and he came to know himself lost, and as I saw dissolve in him his very identity, I felt myself the instrument of divine justice, released by God from the bounds other men must know; and experienced not remorse, but sadness only when, though living, his identity was gone; at which point to inflict further pain were but to torture an animal. And I was sad only that his new state had brought to an end my revenge.

.   .   .

There is nothing like dawn at sea, beside which I found even the beauties of the day to hold the potential for the garish or obvious. I much preferred False Dawn, or, as I am now told a correct Officer must call it, "First Nautical Morning Twilight."

But we called it False Dawn, the beauty of which I felt to be my particular discovery, unsullied by the praise of others.

My reading, begun on my return, revealed, of course, the broadcast devotion of the mariner to False Dawn. This, though rendering it commonplace, did not diminish my affection.

And I loved the night, and cherished the relation between the Stars. How simple the unhurried opposition of the Bear and the Chair (the Plow, that is, whose pointers indicate Polaris, the line continuing on to meet the Easy Chair of Cassiopeia). And, in the South, the immutability of the Cross. All of which may simply be to say I was a sailor.

·　　·　　·

The Morning Watch begins at four a.m.

There is a commonality between denizens of the night, a softness of demeanor and a mutual acceptance, for we, then, "are all in it together," and, simultaneously, each knows himself, in the night, to be alone and, in this state, grateful for company.

This is a portion of the magic of the first mature (which is to say physical) young love; when the two lovers, waking in the night, are linked not only by their embrace, but by their natural and, to them unique, discovery of the beauty of the night. False Dawn, thus, whether shared between two lovers or companions of the Watch, apportions the sense of having come through.

Here is a passage present in the novel's manuscript but excised from the book:

"Taya (what purpose would there have been to have altered her name?), I know, felt, in the night, that I had wakened. I do not know how she knew, and I do not know by what change I became aware she was awake. The sense of companionship and the certainty of returned desire instilled in my soul a deep gratitude. I lay in an exquisite balance of perfect peace and lust. Which balance was disrupted by her arm, softly placed across my chest.

"I thought, or remembered to have thought, I heard the particular 'swish' or 'tear' of a boat being beached on the sand. And, having been some time at sea, I marked, unconsciously, the turn of the tide, though it had occurred while I slept, and knew it to be at full ebb, and must have thought, as I half-dozed, 'They'll have a long haul getting the boat up above high water,' and I believe that I may have noticed that, to the contrary, the run of the boat up the sand was short, indicating that whoever had landed only meant to stay for a short while, and that while the sound of its progress through the sand called to mind a large, heavy boat, there was the suggestion of effort, indicating a reduced number of hands. And then they were upon us."

The further description in the novel is untrue. For the pirate did not "take her for his own" and transport us both to the now-captured ship, she to confinement in the cabin, I to the hold. Neither did he "take her then and there," as one reviewer, thinking himself both insightful as to the circumlocutions of the pen and knowing in the ways of the world, has suggested. He was, however, closer to the mark, as the pirates, of course, raped her to death, and forced me to watch.

How did they force me to watch?

Did they, as I have read in a similar tale, "coat my eyelids with pepper" or wedge my eyes open with sticks? No. They told me that were I to close or avert my eyes, it would cost me my life. And I had not sufficient courage to adopt the course.

What had they come for? In the book, I have them come ashore for the Native Princess, "who, in beauty, and sagacity. …" But in truth, they had come for the chronometer.

When we hove the ship down on the far side of the island, I'd been given the boat, the box of the ship's instruments, constituting the sextant and octant (the property of Halland and Grimes), and the chronometer, and been instructed to row around, find a path, and take the noon observation from the island's height—most easily accessible from the far side. I had done so, and stayed on, as further instructed, to take the lunar observation, and so was given leave to stay 'til dawn.

The pirates, during that night, had carried the ship, and, I later learned, tortured the ship's boy, Brace, until someone (I always believed it was Halland) divulged the chronometer's location.

For the pirates had been without observation since the loss in a storm of their instruments, some weeks before; and their discovery of our ship—presumably possessed of a chronometer—in an uncharted island must have appeared to them as what a believer would have understood as a "Sign of Grace."

So I did not and do not condemn Halland for revealing the chronometer (and my) location, though it resulted in the death of Taya.

In the first place, she (and I) most probably would have died when the pirates pulled around to take on wood and water; and Halland's actions, though one might say they resulted in her death, preserved the lives of those several of the ship's company who survived our capture. For I do not doubt the pirates would have fulfilled their intention of murdering, one by one, the crew until they found someone to reveal our location, which surmise is borne out by the summary execution of the ship's boy after Halland's confession.

Why did they kill the boy? As an exercise or display of might; or, though one might think the application of the phrase cruel or indeed heartless, from sheer exuberance.

For we all noted, during our captivity, their love of that which to us was inhuman cruelty, but which to them must have been quite another thing. One might say that they did not value life, but they, as much as any man, each valued his own. For I tried the experiment when I tortured their chief to death.

It is said such things alter us. Perhaps they do. And perhaps they do not. For by *whom* is it said? And what do they who have not done it know of the truth of it; for, as in all things, at a minimum, those who know do not tell, and those who tell do not know. To which we may add not only the tendency to self-delusion, common to all men, but the analgesic and disruptive effects of time. All men not only lose but cleanse their memories, or how should we live, saddled with both our sins and the inconclusivity of our own self-estimation?

.   .   .

I loved gambling. It is God's gift to the sailor, the soldier, and the captive. It is a revelation, after the first reluctance to play, when it is realized that even when there is naught to wager, the mind, if it must, will accept the contest for splinters of wood as readily as for gold.

The philosophic might thereby infer a derogation of play-for-sums; or reduce all gambling, au fond, to simple desire for status. I vote with them.

I note that, imprisoned, we held heated contests, some continuing for months, until one or the other player or group was bankrupted of the markers, stones or scraps of leather, to which, after a while, we ceased assigning putative worth in coin, the marker itself being recognized as a worthy object of desire.

These contests were heated as those in the clubs or wardrooms we had left behind, their play and progress suggesting to the partisan those elaborate uses and stratagems occurring to the hazarder of great sums, and calling forth imprecations both to the God we all adore and to his, to the gambler, more effective predecessors. And we only played for sticks. With one exception.

This was, of course, the Choice of the Victim. The incident, as depicted in *The Raven*, is, to my mind, a good example of the aesthetic question of verisimilitude. For though in the chapter "Sacrifice" nothing of the actual event was deleted, and everything was, to the best of my ability, described as it occurred, yet much of the criticism of the novel (in its first issuance) centered upon this "drawing of lots," and what was described as my "singular and exceptionable lack of affect" in its depiction.

What, I wonder, would these aesthetes have preferred? (My question is rhetorical, for, of course, they would have preferred overwrought prose: "The laudable brightness of the designated victim's eye, his firm step, the red bruise upon his ankle wrought by months of cruel chafing by the iron shackle ..." et cetera.)

But my sin is not restraint, but perjury. And I believe the critical establishment has found it out. By what mysterious process I cannot say. But I have observed, and others have observed, that operation whereby our faults, "concealed from all but God," somehow make themselves manifest. It has taken me years to adopt this view, but I believe it is the correct one, so, on reflection, adopt it I have. For years, I prided myself on the clean clarity with which I told the tragic tale. But my story was false.

No one liked Cottrell. He did his job well enough, and could in fact be relied upon to do it in all circumstances. An impartial assessment of his performance in emergency could not fault him, and he accomplished the small but essential tasks which fell to his lot, whether of execution or of supervision, unexceptionably. But he appeared, when an extra hand was required, with reluctance. And his accounts of the Watch and of his operations, his expenditure of stores shipped or expended, his assessments of the crew, though never found amiss, were always mistrusted until verification. And, far from an ability to frame a reason, the ship's company was, to a man, mute upon the point itself.

Seamen are very fair. We must be. For a ship, to be effective, must be happy. Anything less is hell. Such happiness depends upon cheerful discharge of duty, reciprocal trust, resolution, and a general assumption of your shipmates' worth, unless otherwise demonstrated.

Cottrell had never done wrong. But he was never trusted; and as one could neither (for he had done no wrong) be free to express reservations, nor, thus, be free with *him*, he was disliked.

One might suggest that we must, in the long voyage, have stopped to analyze our disaffection, but quite the opposite was true. In a long commission one *must* get along, and a too-strenuous introspection would have served no purpose, as, willy-nilly, we had shipped with him, and there he was.

Over the years, I have tried both to recall my observations and to plumb my feelings in an effort to arrive at what, after all, would be merely a supposition. But such could, finally, be different from but no more accurate than the animal fact: we had an aversion to him.

We shunned him; and his acceptation, on board ship, in the boat, and in prison, of his state, which, to give a word to it, was "pariah," only turned us against him the more. We tried to love him for his cheerfulness, and loathed him for it.

He was a Jonah. Though the myriad and inevitable reverses and disappointments upon ship could not be laid to him, though he was not in any way connected with any of them, yet they, or, better, the tenor of life aboard ship, when it was other than smooth, was laid to his account.

What was transpiring? I believe, at the distance of years, that we were witness, in Cottrell, to a metaphysical event.

I believe, like many, that in the fallible state we name rationality, generally we confuse cause with effect. I think that rather than having been the *cause* of the ship's several misfortunes, he was but the unhappy, unwitting prognosticator. I believe he, though unconscious of the fact, knew the ship's fate. That he alone, from the first, "felt" the curse (for such, taken as a whole, must be the verdict on the trip); and we, whose powers lagged behind but who were not devoid of that shared precognition which is found in inclusive, communal occupations, and which may be said to be mere superstition but which is honored in every conversation on the Sea, sensed in him, not the cause of our curse, but his conviction of it. We judged him fey. And I believe he was.

His bravery, then, I must judge as courage not in his exclusion from the herd, but in the face of the knowledge of death. So, of course, we killed him.

. . .

Mustapha Ali had sent to us, by the usual means, to warn us that at dawn there was to be another execution. We were grateful for the forewarning, for, though it was as much as he could do, still it was something, and a reassurance that there existed, outside the walls, someone who remembered us, and cared for our fate. It has been suggested that he was complicit in our continuous incarceration. But, though not addressed in the novel, I will refute it here.

His son died for us in the—previously unreported—attempt, in our third year, at escape. This incident I withheld from the novel as Mustapha Ali, at the time of its publication, still lived, and though his name had, of course, been changed, he might have been identified through the circumstantial nature of the story, and thus was in potential jeopardy from any Turk with access to the book.

I state it here: he was a friend to us captives, and to our Country's interests. His son, Saïd, died at the South Fortress Wall, and those interested, should the world situation change, are free to venture to the Fortress, where they will find, some ten yards from the Southeast Turret, head-height at the First Wall, the mark of the scimitar which ended his life.

I owe him my life. And my remaining years as a captive were lightened by the memory of his courage, as have been my years of freedom.

Cobb and I, being senior recipients of the forewarning, took ourselves apart from the group and sat for a while. It was he, I believe, who spoke first, and he spoke the truth at which he had arrived: that the sick man must go. The sick man was Cottrell. He had suffered for some time, as had we all, from scurvy, and it had, I suppose, weakened him sufficiently that when the fever struck (we all had had it; most survived) (I have been informed since, by medical authorities, on their assessment of the symptoms as narrated in the book, that it was Dengue Fever), he began to fail with astounding rapidity.

I think I must be rather a fool. I've always felt a fool, and my adventures, to me, seemed both rather unreal and sordid. I have talked freely with soldiers, admitted into their confraternity at times by our mutual proximity to death, and have but rarely found one who, after a length of conversation, the topics of adventure and combat leading to that of courage, and thus, inevitably, to cowardice, has not confessed himself ashamed.

The cause of this shame I understand to be, variously, having survived though others perished, having but insufficiently exerted oneself in the midst of peril, or being criminally lax in observation, prescience, or precaution, by which omission others were brought to grief.

Indeed, the prodigies of exegesis which these men employ to construe any occurrence to their disadvantage suggests a blanket, underlying trauma, which may be the irreparable fracture of a contract either with one's fellow man or else with God.

I remember love, and Taya, and the various adventures of my wandering years. I remember bagnios in two hemispheres and well-born women on three continents. I recall the joy of youth in combat, and the feeling of invincibility before a fight. And I recall its opposite, when the bowels loosened and one could not still the limbs. Of my dealings with men, I recall chiefly distance.

Though I have read of the various emotions comrades bear for one another, I do not recognize them as having occurred fully in myself. I know, of course, the difference between trust and lack of trust. And have been both aided and imperiled by my faith in my opinion of men. I recognize trust as an essential component of any communal enterprise, but as for the fine feelings pertaining to men, I do not think I have felt them. I would suggest I am a monster but for my love of women who, although I do not share their assessment, were so decided in their affection for me as to incline me to consider (though I cannot quite adopt) their conviction that my life must have had some worth.

An obvious concomitant supposition would appear to be a belief in God. I do not know if I believe in God, though I have given it some thought, and have been variously moved or confronted by the basic precepts, as I understand them, of theology. For who can know the unknowable? None can, though all but the depraved recognize the existence of a mystery.

The feeling of this Presence pervades life at sea. So, perhaps, my life has not been totally without Religion, and as I feel that creditable, perhaps this not only implies an appreciation of the Artifice of Creation, but suggests the existence of some conscious Instrument of Instigation, which may be what is meant by "a belief in God."

I heard a man pray once. I was moved, and I told myself I had been moved by his prayer. But was I moved by prayer? And have I, in some mute way lauded, as I understand it, by "new philosophers" in my inchoate musings, indulged in a kind of prayer, or only in another wretched exercise in self-consciousness?

Many's the night, and day for that matter, I've wished myself dead.

Other than in animal acts or contemplations, I have understood happiness mainly as a post facto appreciation of a momentary prior state in which I did not loathe myself.

Here is a fragment written on the first night of our release. I remember, more than the food, the drink, the cleansings, the fresh clothes, two things: the absence of a sense of freedom, and my happiness at the quality of the notepaper supplied by the Consulate—the embossed seal, and the paper's thickness, almost a card stock, really, taking the black ink perfectly.

"I am safe. The Expedition coming to the aid of Jemmal al Har reduced the citadel of Bisra, which, though its name and its location were withheld from us during our stay, was, it seems, the site of our incarceration."

The Note, for that is all it was, achieved fame after its release by Mrs. Simms to *The Times*, and, thence, to the world at large.

It was this paragraph, so self-conscious and proud in its adoption of the tone and diction of the day, which prompted Gerald Brown to commission my memoirs. It was *he*, not "the Board of Brown and Mayne," for, there was, in those days, no such group, but only Mr. Brown, his perception, his capital, and his will to back the first with the second.

It is the fashion, currently, to decry the Individual in any field. But the celebrity of "teamwork," or "team Spirit," or, in the most unfortunate phrase, "organization" presages, to my mind, both a decay in the individual, and lack of understanding in the Mass, of that process whereby any new thing occurs.

For "the new," though it is celebrated, can only be celebrated *by the Mass*, which is to say, in its broadcast accepted, which is to say, dated form. The call for novelty on the part of the public is not a demand for titillation; it *is* titillation itself. It is a drug.

The Mass, I have observed, is charmed not by the new, but by the commonplace presented so as to allow the self-congratulation of discovery. Novelty is brought forth, and, in the main, succeeds as a sop to the public's discernment. But the Mass has no discernment. Witness the furor over my dispatch.

I applaud Mr. Brown for his business acumen. He saw in my paragraph not the promise of an artist, but the promise of gain. He recognized and invested in a phenomenon.

Would he, equally, have adopted a castaway such as myself, who (he was assured) could actually write? No doubt; or, differently, had an actual writer of talent been marooned, captured, imprisoned, and so on, would Brown and Mayne have published his memoirs? Of course, though such a coincidence, the Writer mired in actual adventures, would not perhaps have made so promotable a story. For the charm of the thing, to the public eye, was the intersection of the fact of our adventure and the naïve, therefore obviously "true," nature of the recollection.

I was ashamed of the dispatch after I sent it. It is melodramatic, and though such melodrama might be excused in one overwrought, I was not overwrought, but (and this, I have found, is a common reaction of the newly released) angry, or, say, irritated.

·   ·   ·

For, to begin, my world had changed (though for the better) violently. It changed on that instant when the West Wall was breached and the jailers ran down the stairs. They were screaming.

As a matter of survival, we learnt Arabic during our stay, but the sound of the breaching charges and the continual firing had both deafened and disoriented us, preventing our interpretation of the jailers' cries.

It is not impossible that they were descending to set us free, and so win some concession from our liberators. And it is possible (we thought so at the time) that they were coming down to kill us. I, had *I* been a savage (and I believe my shipmates share this view), would have desired, at such a time, to dispatch my prisoners, if for no other reason than the certainty of their indictment of their captors for torture.

In any case, our troops cut them down, keys in their hands, some few feet from our cell doors, and we will never know, nor would I care to know, were it given me, the true nature of their errand. I would have killed them myself, and I'm glad they're dead.

I have described my reception at the Consulate, and my brief description of the sentry, it has not escaped me, has become a staple of the after-dinner speech, and, I suppose, a part of the language.

It would be disingenuous to say I am not proud that my words are so remembered. I am proud. It is a great distinction. For the odd phrase, adopted into the general speech by, as is the only course, such general consent that it persists 'til both its author and its antecedents are forgotten is a truer immortality, or, say, a more extensive memorial—for all things die—than any conscious endorsement of art or the artist.

.   .   .

When the sentry finished his watch, he came down to the kitchen. It was just at dawn, and I was still sitting there.

I was unable, of course, to sleep. What my shipmates were doing, I do not know, for we were all housed separately, in a nice appreciation, by the Consul, of, in each, a desire for privacy.

It was our first night in the protection of the Consulate. I'd come down to the kitchen looking for liquor, and I found some. The cipher aide, holding the night watch, had, as an additional part of his duties, administration of the kitchen, and any consular requests for refreshment during the night.

I asked, and he was pleased to open the liquor store. I sat and drank with him, and had been drinking with him, at the long preparation table, through two bottles of whiskey. He'd risen to open a third, when the Marine came downstairs. He walked toward me, at the table, loosening his stock. He unbuttoned his tunic and removed it, and draped it over the back of the chair, revealing a small commercial pistol stuck in his belt. I remember thinking, "Surely that is against regulations," and "Surely it is an addition both wise and, probably, usual in a sentry's accoutrements."

The aide brought the new bottle, breaking the seal as he came, and an extra glass. The sentry looked back from his whiskey being poured, as he'd felt my gaze, and saw I was looking at his pistol.

He removed the pistol from his belt, placed it on the table, slid it toward me, and continued the motion, his finger now pointing at me, indicating, "It is yours now."

We drank 'til the morning crew came on to prepare the Consul's breakfast, when the sentry shrugged himself into the tunic and left.

I have the pistol with me still.

Alcohol I have found to be an attractive analgesic, and have employed it in that capacity at various times in my life. My return from captivity began a period of some years in which, to my shame, I was often affected. I have found this is not uncommon with returned combatants. This drug, of course, became a habit. Its imbibition, in increasingly large doses, was attended by less and less visible effects; so I congratulated myself, as has many another, on my harmless "habituation," more accurately perceived by the nonafflicted as a deleterious dependence.

That alcohol is, in the West, the near-universal social emollient is like most things, both good and bad. In stilling boredom, remorse, fatigue, and, indeed, diffidence, there is much to be said for it. Its increased consumption, however, will magnify those very conditions its beneficence is proposed to address, and open both the physical and moral character to the fact of or the temptation to ills to which it theretofore was ignorant.

The panaceas of the East I enjoyed as and whenever they were offered to me. Ignorant of the societal norms, prohibitions, and anxieties associated with these, my Epicureanism knew neither the possibility nor, thus, the apprehension of addiction, and I partook of these as one would of any delicacy, with delight at the experiment, and with no thought of making it a permanence. Perhaps, then, my episodic instances of an overattachment to or a difficulty in separation from alcohol were, in part, a sociologic rather than a somatic difficulty.

In any case, it was the sailor's friend and the companion of many a night or morning coming off watch. It loosed the inhibitions of those with whom I dealt in the service of my government, and comforted or dulled my conscience at these interchanges' conclusions.

That I, like many, personify the substance, imbuing it with personality, and that personality, in the main that of a friend, must speak greatly to our human need for solace—for alcohol may be a friend, but it is, after all, a friend who may weaken and kill.

What would we not have given, in our various trials, for spirits? And how we strove, on our release, to overcome the natural barrier to their consumption wrought by those years of enforced abstinence. For, irrespective of the part of spirits in burning the ship, and of their role in the inattention of the Watch which led to our capture, still we held liquor as our friend.

A better-tuned mind could draw a parallel between this and other, ineradicable delusions. For example, the "goodness of Man."

I long thought Man was Good, and explained all evidence to the contrary either by reference to this or that circumstance or institution which warped his Nature or to my inability to behold clearly.

Age has brought me to the opposing view, for what are the various institutions—State, Royalty, Government, Industry, Religion—but the works of Man in his attempt to supersede his Nature, and, were they abolished tomorrow, would they not grow again in the night, their names changed, but their natures, as untempered by tradition, even more virulent, crass, destructive, and false than their contemporary counterparts?

These institutions differ superficially in form and tone, but they are everywhere essentially the same: Man craves security; Man craves dominance; he creates institutions in search of the first, and corrupts them in search of the latter.

This is our nature, and it is jejune to indict anywhere the institution for the faults of any individual—it is not our forms which fail, but ourselves. And it is, I fear, the uttermost error to instill in the young a myth of human beneficence.

It was the fault of ———, the Midshipman of the Watch, to excuse, on his first acquaintance with it, the fault of Croft's dereliction. For he knew the man to be a drunk, and discovered him drunk on watch, and pardoned him.

And it was Croft who had the fire watch the night the ship burned.

I have heard theories of the Innate Goodness of Man, but, though I have encountered instances of high morality and courage, these I lay to the triumph of the individual will over a nature cowardly and weak. They were not the emergence of an Essential Goodness, but acts contrary to a nature which, taking myself as best-known subject, I must judge essentially bestial and vile. The sentimental view, of course, is more acceptable—I always found it so, and began to doubt it only upon realization that much sentiment hides cruelty, and that I never met an actually cruel man who was not sentimental.

Alcohol dulls the senses, alcohol soothes the soul; Man is a monster, Man may be courageous and good—both alcohol and Man may be exploited. I did so over many years.

One might think it odd (indeed, I thought it odd) that, having dedicated my life to the Navy, I spent the bulk of my career on land. But it was so, and though many have fared similarly, it was, in the main, their lot to be involved with the direction or administration of that force, interlarded with occasional duty at sea, while for me, it meant virtually continuous active service. I had been recruited into that group which never names, nor need name itself, but lies beyond though salient to Naval Intelligence.

On my return from captivity, it was suggested by preamble, that my state and my wounds perhaps unfitted me for further service at sea; but I required no preamble, and acceded at the first suspicion in my mind of the identity of that occupation and group to the existence of which my docent was gingerly alluding. Who was he? I will tell you, for he is long since dead, and no possible connection, could his identity be deduced from these words, might be followed from his name to that organization to which he (and then I) belonged.

His name was Herbert Burgess, whom I had known at college. He became my companion, teacher, instructor, and comrade-in-arms, on various missions in various parts of the world, over the nearly twenty years from my recruitment 'til his death.

.   .   .

I saw a levitation once in India.

The few times I have told the story, men have suggested I was drugged, or under mesmeric suggestion. I don't discount either theory out of hand, for I have both known of and employed the same expedients, and have seen, particularly, the effects of that suggestion which I understand to be the root of Mesmerism.

There is no force more powerful in battle, when men may be convinced to the hazard of their lives or honor by a word, a gesture, a mood, or indeed a suggestion the basis of which is nowhere to be physically observed, and must originate in the mere transference of thought.

The Sophists of old were known for their ability to "make the lesser cause appear the better," which is the essence of suggestion in battle. Or, put differently, the gifted or inspired leader, whether so placed by rank or the spontaneous effect of afflatus or example, may rouse exhausted, hopelessly outnumbered troops not only to attempt, but, in the attempt, to be assured of the conquest of what, to the uninvolved, must appear with certainty to be an invincible opponent.

This suggestion, transmitted not man-to-man but from one spirit to the whole, may also communicate itself to the enemy, causing their devolution to uncertainty and, thus, to panic, greatly swelling or insuring the chances of victory of the "weaker" side.

The opposite, of course, is true; as men, in that state before battle, are of infinite receptiveness and sensitivity. They may be spooked as a horse is spooked by an innocuous word or occurrence—the unspoken assurance of doom communicating itself from one to the whole by instantaneous contagion.

And I have seen several times the well-documented instance of the combatant assured of this impending doom. I saw it first upon *The Redwing*, where a foremast hand confessed himself visited by a premonition of his death in the next engagement. He was well liked, and his shipmates attempted reason, Religion, humor, and cajolement, none of which would amend the man's conviction. And, indeed, in the next engagement he fell.

One might say that, perhaps, cause and effect have been inverted here—that a dispassionate observer might construe the case thus: a man grown despondent has lessened his decision and alacrity in all things. In most of them, his mood is of no consequence, but in battle, depression may prove fatal.

One might say further that many (perhaps all) men in a martial career have premonitions of their deaths—what else, in the mingled boredom and apprehension which are the gist of such a life, would they think about—but we only remark those few whose vision, in the event, has been uttered and has proved true.

I say to both: granted. But the foretopman on *The Redwing* foretold his death by a ball, passing just below the tattoo on his left arm and, thus, through his body, left to right, and pointed out the foreseen place of entry to his shipmates. And this was indeed the place where he was struck.

If courage or cowardice, assurance, nay, certainty of victory or vanquishment, can communicate themselves at the speed of thought and by no known or recognized mechanism, perhaps it is possible, after all explanations, cavils, or objections, that there exists in the human being the power to foretell the future.

Perhaps this power cannot be bidden. (I dismiss the fairground hacks, and storefront mystics, for, if they could foretell the future, why would they toil for the odd coin?) But perhaps, unbidden, I say, men may be visited by, or, better, come upon, a disjunction of those processes which we incorrectly understand as immutable.

I have seen men stride through battle unscathed, unaffected either by fire or fear, assured of their invincibility.

I have seen the Kril, of Africa, apply to their bodies a paste concocted to turn the point of a spear, and I have seen it put to the test and proved. You will say this is prestidigitation. Perhaps. I will not discount the possibility—for the trial was assembled specifically for our enlightenment, and so must be open to the suspicion of possible conjuration.

But I saw a man levitate. In Lahore. I was accompanied by Burgess.

As to hallucinations induced by drugs, we had eaten nothing that day but our own rations, and had drunk nothing but the contents of our own canteens. And we could not have been "suggested," for we came upon the scene by accident.

We were seeking a house in the Parsee quarter. We had lost our way, and, having turned into what we found was a cul-de-sac, began to retrace our steps to the main street.

As we did so, we glanced into a small side courtyard, in the middle of which was a fakir, seated, cross-legged, on a rough mat.

Around the edges of the courtyard were some twenty people, very still, and watching him intently. So Burgess and I stopped to look.

The fakir attracted us, I believe, by that air common to the master of any craft or art; a surgeon, for example, silent and still, gathering himself before his commitment to the first incision; or, say, the virtuoso, perhaps pausing between the movements of a concerto. These moments are not "rests," but an ingathering of energy or spirit before exertion, and shared with the look on the fakir's face that mixture of submission and resolve.

He rose from the ground, still seated, cross-legged, slowly, and straight into the air, some three or four feet, unassisted, with that odd silent rhythm common to the game animal, which appears in the watched field on the instant, having made no visible approach. Now the field is empty; now it is not. And now the man was floating in the air.

And neither Burgess nor I nor the crowd reacted as if witnessing a revelation. Rather it was as if we were participants in a religious observance, whose place and honor it was merely to observe.

I have felt and seen similar behavior at a Catholic Mass. They, I am told, believe they witness a miracle in the transformation of bread and wine into Christ's Body and Blood. I saw an irrefutable suspension of natural law, and I felt what I now can imagine the Catholic Believer feels at the Mass: a sense of thanks.

Burgess and I, though we were friends 'til his death, never afterward discussed the incident.

And what of the instant transmission of thought and intention between the sexes? Surely the most important—some philosophers would say the sole important—human interaction must consist of and display that adaptive mechanism superior to all others. And if, in effect, all human life is nothing other than a pretext for transmission of the germ plasm, would it not be sensible scientific thinking to search, in the sexual interaction, for manifestations of its supreme power? And do we not confess to our understanding of this superpowerful state in adducing, as explanation or defense for the otherwise incomprehensible, "I (she, we, he) was in love"?

No. We suppose the hidden existence, between states and powers, of interactions screened both by necessity and by habit from the public eye. Must we not suppose such between those two moieties, female and male, who, though now linked, now ostensibly opposed, are united in ways inconceivable to the rational mind? There is a bond between woman and man, and an instantaneous communication, which, though it may depend upon proximity, may be said barely, if at all, to depend upon sight. And I believe, after discounting, in their operations, the influence of scent, sound, "current of air," and whatnot, there will remain an irreducible remainder which might be called "a mutual interrogation of spirit." For if it is not God's deepest, it is certainly his most discernible wish that the Race continue.

I am told of some sects which, in fact, worship Death. But I am not sufficiently conversant with such, beyond that knowledge, which is essentially gossip, which relates their names.

I had seen enough of the world long ago to learn to withhold judgment, and am grown sufficiently old to have progressed to a further state of what might appear wisdom but which is, if not apathy, then a distrust of my perceptions coupled with a decrease in curiosity.

I have seen "a substance" issue from a man's head at the moment of his death, and it was a sort of mist, rising and dissipating as he expired. Was it his soul?

I heard a voice call to me, once, in an empty alleyway in London. It called my name. At a time when no one in that city knew my name. There was no one there.

On leaving the alleyway, I, distracted, found myself barring the progress of two women on the street. I raised my hat and said, "I beg your pardon," and made way for them to pass. But one of them, as she passed, looked back. And that was my first vision of Margaret.

My years in government and the nature of that service supplied to me that which is most necessary to an author: anonymity. And, after *The Raven*, I never published another book without thanking God that I'd issued the first under a pseudonym. Did no one know I was the author? Burgess knew. Though I never told him.

I will tell you how he discovered my secret.

Let this be as a sign to those who engage in secret works, either in spying or, indeed, in adultery: be not too proud.

It is said that three things cannot be hid—money, illness, and love: but the pride in one's duplicity, in the ability to lead a dual life, in being unremarked, or incorrectly understood, this godlike feeling of invisibility, this pride has been the end of many, living the life, as they feel, of an unremarked, and so invisible, being.

I had lived a life of action. Now that life is spent in a comfortable retirement. Sometimes I want "to go away," although I do not know either where I would go or what I would do on my arrival. My life, since my first days at sea, has been one of constant travel. But I do not know as my desire for retirement has for its location, any of the places I have seen, nor any of their like, the nature of which I might be able to extrapolate from my experience. To wit: mountain, desert, forest or wood, seashore, island, city and town.

And I have known the Llamaseries of Tibet, and returned rested, and something beyond, having experienced that peace induced both by the beauty of the country and the nature of the people and their practices. But I do not desire to return there. That would not be the fulfilled object of my fantasy of rest, for fantasy it is.

I desire, in the ultimate most frank refinement, freedom from strife. Which I believe must mean I long for death. The truest approximation to the indicated state for which I long was the year of convalescence after my repatriation.

Though I was very ill in body, I remember to have felt, or, retrospectively, I would now describe myself as having felt, that my soul was free.

For I had been absolved of all responsibility. Whatever I may have thought myself bound to do, I was incapable of accomplishing it, for I was, for most of the year, barely mobile. More importantly, there was no reason on earth why I should be alive. And so I enjoyed a general sense not merely of holiday, but of incorporeality.

It was during this period that I began to transcribe, which is to say fictionalize, those "adventures" I had rehearsed into myself, as fantasies of revenge, during my imprisonment.

.   •   •

There has always existed a link between the Sea and the Secret Service. Which, is, on the face of it, odd, as the open love of the first might be supposed to prompt a detestation of the other. The love of the Sea is a pre-Christian (though it is not an un-Christian) understanding of the world.

It is not the god Neptune, or Poseidon, who rules the Sea, but, in our Western minds, the survival of those entities the East knows as Shiva and Kali, the Hindu gods of Death.

Though one is offered, in the words and acts of Christ, both forgiveness and some latitude of Divine Judgment, the gods of Death will neither be mocked nor appeased, and every sailor knows it. That is the beauty and the sway of the Sea, upon which life is a constant dialogue between Man's understanding and the unfathomable nature of the World. Intelligence work, on the other hand, is an exploitation of the sordid pretensions, sinfulness, biddability, and error of Man.

A moderately well-brought-up youth, (I offer myself, for example,) on his first acquaintance with those commercial aspects of sex attendant to a nautical life, gains in perception, part of which perception is the conviction that any woman is potentially corruptible.

He has gratified desire at the expense of an ideal, and he covers his sorrow at the loss with a knowingness it will take time, shame, and experience to dispel.

The Intelligence Officer—in operation if not in intent a criminal—has, similarly, been taught that men are not what they seem. He, like the soldier or sailor combatant, has had the veil rent. They, however, though forever after disillusioned with Man, are saved the final ravagement of a contempt for *men*, for they have suffered with their comrades, and have seen, both in them and in the enemy, some virtue. While the Spy, for his very survival, must both believe in and work to bring about the reduction of all with whom he deals to a state of treason.

But many leave the Sea for Secret work, and not a few—some who are known to fame, some who are not—pass from the first to the second through literature. For what is writing but the desire to confess?

.   .   .

I am told various dictatorial entities, on capture of an interloper, or upon the expressed desire of the disaffected to convert, request or reward his production of a life-history. The interrogated, whether specifically instructed or not, comes to realize that the production is to be a *confession*—not only of sins against the new political entity, but of *all* sins. The purpose of the exercise is to create, in the Writer, self-abasement, and, so, a submission, born of shame. I have employed the technique, retail, in interrogation of prisoners.

Physical torture is the most despicable and sinful exercise known to Man. Further, it reveals, finally, only that which is already known: that men are cruel, and that we are all subject to pain, to withstand which every man has his given capacity beyond which he must, of course, break.* But that every man may

---

* In torture, one must, finally, know or be able to deduce, before the fact, the answers to the questions put. "Where is the bomb?" must issue from a knowledge that there is a bomb, and that the subject has knowledge of its whereabouts. The same train of thought that began with the supposition that he must possess the answers will, if continued, most probably reveal the device's location.

be reduced through the mere expedient of self-examination is a profoundly disturbing revelation. I had taken to the hospital bed three scant days after my repatriation. My body and mind, released from the constant effort of the sustenance of life, collapsed.

In the year of hospitalization, I was left with my thoughts. The stories I created for my diversion while imprisoned were, as I have said, fantasia of revenge. For that is what a prisoner does. His days are empty, but his mind, as the poet has told us, is "a raging fire," its *exercise* the only mitigation between his urge for retribution and his impotence to effect the same.

I say the mind's *exercise*, and I use that term specifically to indicate that operation not unlike the shifting of weights for maintenance of physical health. Here his thoughts, like the weights, are inert, and the exercise to no purpose other than retention of those powers which may someday be expended toward some concrete object.

For he *thinks*, but there are no conclusions at which he can arrive. He has been captured; he is enslaved. There is no justice in the world, and *then* what? For, if *he* had been the captor, would he not be treating his current tormentors in much the same way that they treat him? Indeed, having actually suffered their depredations would he not, likely, treat them worse? Of course he would. Thus his mind runs upon the theme of revenge, in which his cause is just, his motives pure, and his capture due not to his martial weakness, but to a flaw in the regular fabric of God's rational plan.

These fantasies instill in the prisoner a sense of secret power. That is, they allow him to retain a fragment of autonomy, as if (though he will not confront the fallacy) he were actually engaged in constructive *plans*, rather than just dreaming. But, more importantly, these reveries pass the time.

.   .   .

How does one learn to write? In this pursuit, one is not unlike the prisoner of the tyrant, who, pressed to recount his sins, will, at some point, become disgusted with both the content and the effort of his dissimulation, and, in fatigue and shame, begin to bring forth some truth.

In the hospital bed, the mechanical, repetitive, pointless rehashings of revenge, no longer appropriate since my liberation, were pressed into a different service. Here my experiences and dreams were again reformed, now as an entertainment. These fictions, in *The Raven*, and then in the subsequent tales, were superior to my prison fantasies in this: they had a plot. Each, that is to say, had a stated premise, and, thus, a foreseeable end, at which end the fictional Hero, Captain Marrion, was triumphant, released, or honorably discharged from his participation in that particular pursuit. His efforts, that is, were recognized, he had achieved his goal, and he was granted rest.

Burgess found out the secret of my authorship.

He did it on a summer day. At a lawn party. We were at the home of Admiral ———. The Admiral's wife had laid out a sort of tea on the back portico, or veranda. I, Burgess, and the Admiral's son (who had just entered the Service) were amusing ourselves with desultory shoptalk, and enjoying our lassitude. We heard the tennis being played, on the court to the house's side, and the occasional shout or banter of the players.

One of the Admiral's daughters lay in a chaise longue in a corner of the veranda. She was reading a novel, and the novel was *The Raven*.

I watched her from the corner of my eye. For I noticed the portion of the book she had reached, and I wished to see her react to the revelation at the end of her chapter. She turned the page, and I saw her eyes widen. I felt myself smile, and as I smiled in triumph, I felt someone's gaze upon me. I turned to find it was Burgess.

It was evident that he had been watching me for some time, for his face bore the stamp of one who has been working at a puzzle. I saw him glance from me to the Admiral's daughter, back to me, back to the novel, and back to me with a slight smile—not solely that he had found out my secret, but that he had just learnt one more thing about the world.

I was debating such-and-such an action recently, and Margaret asked me if I hesitated as I feared one of the choices might cost me some friends. I was surprised to find myself responding, "I have no friends, and I require no friends." I was pleased with the apothegmatical aspect of the response, a cheap pleasure, yes, but one to which authors are susceptible; the better authors (or authors when in league with their better selves) are aware of the easy tawdriness of such pronouncements, and, being forewarned, may then—at least in their work—salutarily excise them in a second draft.

My second draft, as it were, was, here, the contemplation of the statement on friendship, which I found, to my surprise, to be true. There was Burgess, who, during his life, was my friend, and Crawford. But since the death of one and the apostasy of the other, I have been content to invest my affections where I find them safe, which is to say, exclusively within the confines of my family.

I have been so often disappointed both in men and in myself, as partaking of all the faults which I decry, that I am happy to have lost the habitude of confidence, reposing it, now, solely in and with my wife, and, as the reader may have observed, with my readers. But this latter is not friendship; it is the discharge of an excruciating tendency to introspection. Could not this be dealt with by first the delineation and then the destruction of my observations? In a better man, perhaps. But I am not a better man, and, it seems, seek fame both for the status and for that ratification it suggests itself able to supply. Put differently, I am at bottom, as are most men and, I fear, all writers, a fraud; and, at my late time at life, I feel there is nothing I could gain from the joys of friendship which would not be offset by either the reality or the fear of exposure.

It was Crawford who betrayed me that time in the snows. The sequel to *The Raven* situates him as part of the longboat's crew. But this is merely invention, appropriating the character of the man for use in a sea tale. He did not serve with me in the Navy. I met him upon government service in Egypt.

It is a commonplace that one learns a man's true character in circumstances of shared danger, and there is in this much truth. Shorn of pretense, or refuge in rank, wealth, or privilege, a man, there, will generally be seen for what he is. But in the secret world, the necessary assumption of mutuality, and the attendant suspension of judgment, may allow the most otherwise blatant and continual practice of betrayal. Which was the case with Crawford. And we had been friends.

In Egypt, upon my first mission, it was he who adopted me. I see now he did so, of course, not out of a recognition of my native gifts, personality, or character—that is, from friendship—but from a desire to have such recognition imputed to him, better to betray me. He was, that is to say, a most excellent Spy, and, retrospectively, instructor; though if I may permit myself the conceit, the tuition was rather high.

.   .   .

I do not understand that discipline called "Ethnography," which seems to me the validation of a prejudice by means of an excursion.

One can no more understand the operation of other cultures from observation than can one so understand the sexual act.

Observation, in the case of each, is missing the point, and Ethnography, or "Anthropology," rests on a false assumption: that one may be free of prejudice. But one is not. And here "scientific method" rests upon the fallacy that there exists some "norm." But the norm, if stated, must, if examined, open assumptions (themselves dubious) about one's *own* culture; it, therefore, remains unexamined.

For it is no more scientific to laud the noble savage than to extol, meaninglessly, one's culture's own practices. Both observations are tainted—from the prejudice of one's ineffable partiality, in the case of one's own culture, for status as more advanced, and in the case of the undeveloped, for status as appearing the more benignant, natural, and humble.

What greater sin than false humility, for which Man will sacrifice not only his own interests but those of his dependents?

I instance the phrase "I come in Peace," which should *never* be uttered without overwhelming superiority of force. (Indeed, the only two possible meanings of the phrase are a declaration either of hostile potential or of surrender.)

The combatant, the policeman, the lawyer each must suspend human feelings in service of his profession, which has subjugation as its desired result.

Will this power to subjugate be misused? What power will not? It can be misapplied either through intent or through error. But the fiction of its happy abrogation has brought about more human misery and enslavement than can be catalogued. Not only the scouting party, but the city, the city-state, and civilizations have voted themselves out of existence by an overreliance on "goodwill among men." We note that after Christ was betrayed and killed, His adherents took care to spread His gospel by the sword. This is not to detract from their sincerity, nor the worth of their cause; it is merely to applaud their foresight.

Our vastly superior force was taken by the pirates because of the credit given by a first voyager to their impersonation of helplessness, and their appeal for aid. I thank you, Lord, that that first voyager was not myself.

The incident as abstracted in *The Raven* is much prettified. Were I to begin it today, I would write it as a report rather than a romance; for though I have spent most of my life reading and much of my life writing fiction, I do not know whether the costs of such entertainments may not be too dear.

Perhaps these fictions are, as the more stringently religious suggest, the tool of the Devil. For they do, indeed, cloud the senses, which is, after all, their purpose; and we may understand the phrase to mean "inducing a euphoria in the enjoyment of unreality." We speak of novels as a "distraction"—that is, as a salutary lack of occupation. Perhaps the cost of this euphoria is an enervation of the power to discriminate. I believe it was so in the case of Blake, the Midshipman first voyager and Officer-of-the-Deck, when he departed from the Standing Orders and welcomed on board four men posing as castaway mariners.

His Standing Orders required him, in such circumstances, to call out our Marines. What would such compliance have cost him, or, indeed, the "castaways," if such they had been? The expenditure of the two or three minutes necessary for the alarm.

But the projected cost was not to the castaways, but to the Midshipman's self-esteem. It would have injured his self-image to withhold the exercise upon the instant of his obviously treasured capacity for mercy, which exercise cost twenty-seven mariners their lives and the remainder of the crew (myself included) their freedom, dooming us to twenty-two months in the Galleys.

Discipline exists for the protection of the whole. Its cost is the momentary or intermittent discomfiture of the individual. Such chafes upon the neophyte, until he has, not first through conviction, but through habit, come to obey. This habit is often inculcated, in whole or part, through punishment or its threat. For what is leniency to the individual may be cruelty to the mass.

At times one will disobey; and yes, at times one *must* disobey, it being a truism in all armed forces that the exceptional act is as likely to earn a decoration as a court-martial. In a deviation from martial order, not only the *motive* of the actor, but the actual nature of the act must lie outside the realm of human certainty.* The Hero is rewarded for the same reason the miscreant is punished: for the effect of the response upon the whole.

.   .   .

A man was shot because he carried, as a good-luck piece, a decoration won by his father. He was in civilian clothes, behind enemy lines. He spoke the language of the enemy with perfection, having spent, in his youth, part of each year in that country.

Not only his speech, but his manner, his papers, his fabricated "story," and the ability to present it without raising suspicion were perfection. He was unmasked *solely* as there was, in his coat pocket, an object the possession of which could bear but the one explanation.

He died because his government had considered it good to reward his father; or, to inspire others by such an award. The Captain of the firing squad, in an excess of gallantry, or drama, (the reader may choose which,) asked the condemned if he would like to wear the decoration, which offer the man declined, stating, as a matter of course, that it was not his to wear.

Did he feel regret? I cannot think so, though the talisman, I was about to write, "had brought him anything but luck." But who is to say that its possession, or his *comfort* in such, did not carry him safe through unrecounted, or unnoticed, perils; and is it not as likely that such is the case, as that it somehow exerted a malignant influence?

Further, the man *was*, in fact, a Spy; which, I believe, may well have been the light in which he understood his capture. For to be a Spy is to survive almost exclusively upon the charity or inattention of the Fates, and every Spy knows it every waking moment behind enemy lines.

And so he died, who, had he lived, would, today, be, like myself, an old man, and who, likely, would have added his own decorations to those of his

---

* Though a report may be given of a *static* situation, the report of the actual progress of an encounter can only be, *at best*, likely—the observers being at too great a distance to form, or too small a distance to consider, any "overall picture," and the actual combatants being engaged otherwise than in analysis. The metaphor has doubtless been employed "as a game of chess played in the dark." When the illumination is renewed, the position of the pieces may be clear, but the process by which they became placed, though it may be conjectured, can seldom be ascertained.

forebears, and entailed them upon *his* son. For we must inculcate martial virtues.

This is a part (some might say approaching the whole) of that process called Civilization—there being ever that boundary beyond which the Law of the Tribe does not apply, upon the other side of which lie those who are not of our kind. And sometimes they, as we are not of *their* kind, harbor, and sometimes exercise, the desire for conquest of their subhuman, or detested, neighbors. And sometimes we do the same.

I felt that part of my friend's decision to carry with him his father's medal was a protest against complete submersion in duplicity. Perhaps he feared loss of honor; perhaps he feared madness.

Before his execution, he was permitted to write to his wife, the Captain of the firing squad enclosing, as part of the packet, the decoration which brought about his death. Both are displayed today in the museum of the Regiment from which he was seconded into the Secret Service.

We are told, "Old men forget, and all shall be forgot," but the deeds of the men referred to, and their import, are of no interest today, other than as they may lead to a fuller understanding of the poem. There is a lesson in this, but it lies outside my ken.

It is the universal notion of those who have survived battle that they are, unaccountably, the beneficiaries of a series of inexplicable aberrations of statistical certainty. Such men do not describe themselves as "lucky," for we regard our survival neither as a result of our own personal excellences, nor as the whim of a superior power, but as the operations of the unfathomable. And when we think of our continued existence, we do so, now and again, with thanks, but more regularly with awe. Perhaps this is the meaning of "a fear of God."

· · ·

Am I Captain Marrion? That was the question I was asked, repeatedly, upon the revelation of my authorship. What can it mean? Was he my creation? Of course. Did he differ from me, and if so, in what respects?

He differed from me in that his adventures were *contained*, and so a meaning might be inferred therefrom. Only those things were reported which advanced the story, which was, formally, the depiction of a Hero. My intention, thus, was, in the Marrion novels, an opposite of my intention here, for this book is a confession.

This is not to say that I have not, at times, acted with courage or honor. I believe I have. It is merely to point out that life, mine or that of any other, cannot be encapsulated, or apostrophized in the creation of the illusion of human consistency.

The novel and the drama exist to create the fiction of human comprehensibility. This is why we enjoy them. But they may harm us in suggesting that a man who falls short of such consistency is therefore dismissible or, say, contemptible, in spite of actual heroic or, indeed, moral acts.

For no man is consistent. And those few perfect masters of thought and behavior, the masters of ethical and spiritual discipline, to which discipline they devoted their lives, and who succeeded to a perfection of thought and deed, were, to the estimation of many a regular man, insane. Their teachings reveal a closeness of God (or "perfection," calling it a different name) which, to a man concerned with the workings of the world, immersed in the world not only for his pleasures but as his responsibility, might appear risible nonsense.

We credit the attainment of Grace in such men because of our predilection to do so. Were their same wisdom proffered by a beggar in the street, we would think him mad; or, by a stockbroker, inebriated. This is not to say that such wisdom is false, nor that the apparent insanity of the Yogi is not, in truth, misnamed and both the result of and a testimony to the existence of a mystery. No, I write with respect of those mute ascetics upon a mountain, exempting their brethren of a lesser caste, who move in the world, *professing* enlightenment, and whom I have found, for the largest part, to be mountebanks and frauds.

The human capacity for credulity is boundless, viz., the periodic adulation accorded this or that politician; which, unlike the public's relation to a famed artist, even a personal connection curiously cannot dispel. The love of Him Who Simplifies (and what else is a politician?) reaches its perfection in the adulation of the Dictator.

This adulation is transformed, of course, as he, or that cabal which has displaced him, reveals the inevitable reverse of the medal. But in the early days, which lie each to one side of his accession to power, not only his lies but his *person* are lauded as the perfection, one of reason and insight, the other of grace and beauty. He has suggested himself as a demigod, and his audience, in the name of reason, accepts him in joy, lamenting only the lateness of his appearance.

Both the politician (perfected in the Dictator) and the mystic profit from a proximity (in the first feigned) to the Meaning of Life.

Captain Marrion expatiates upon the subject in the third book. The first part of his speech has been suggested as my own view of the world. Is it so? If it were, what would it matter? And why, claiming one thing rather than another, should my assertion or opinion be believed, which, after all, must be self-serving, redounding, perspectively, either to my credit in the world, or to my own self-estimation. For the mind of Man is "Evil, only Evil, all his Days," we are told in the Bible. Which inspired the section in the third book, beginning "Sick at heart and sickened in mind, I beheld the ship brought to ruin by my Pride."

This, critics have noted, is the only time in the novels when the Captain indulges himself in what, they are correct, is soliloquy. I was unaware of its exceptionality until the critics brought it to my attention, their characterization implying, I believe, an error of taste. Why, they seem to ask, this self-referential monologue, the discovery of which was to them as that of a dear friend in a low quarter, walking with a trollop?

Here, I believe, is the answer. The chapter's beginning in the *manuscript* (this excised from the published book), ran thus:

"I believed I had gone mad, and questioned myself as to the *truth* of the belief; such questioning, at first intermittent, then near-incessant, became, in my increasingly rare moments of clarity, recognizable as madness."

.   .   .

In the Galleys, we were forbidden to speak, to gesture, or to communicate in any way.

As we were, to a man, upon our capture, ignorant of any word of Turkish, this admonition, the first we received, was communicated to us by the slaughter of the seaman Croft.

The Odibashi, or Sergeant, for such, we learnt, was his title, directed his underlings, or "ship's corporals," to seize the most convenient of our crew. The nearest was Croft, who, to his credit, displayed a brave front, nonetheless shivering. As indeed were we all. For we had been kept standing, on the ship's forepeak, in the cold the entire night. I should add that it is a near-universal reaction, in any man, to come down with the shakes after combat. For then the body, once electrified by fear, endeavors to dissipate the toxin. In defeat, this effect is heightened by both shame and rage; by attempts at resistance to the first, and at control of the latter.

Those new to conflict require (and will not be disappointed in) the counsel of the more experienced, barring which the tyro is likely to interpret his shaking as cowardly, superadding his horror at what he supposes to be a display of weakness, to the shame of his defeat.

The new combatant, I say, is, and always has been, *comforted* by the tutelage of those whose ranks he has just joined. But in our silence, there was no one to comfort Croft. And we stood, and had been standing for the most part of a day, without water, food, rest, or instructions, beyond the occasional blow signifying that we were not to move.

The appearance of the Odibashi was, apparently, that event for which we waited; for, on his progression over the eyebrow, and onto the boat, the ship's corporals drew themselves into that attitude which, even their lowly imprecision could not disguise, was an attempt at attention.

The Odibashi gestured to these men, who took up the nearest captive, who was Croft. One moved behind him, pinioning his arms; the other, at a nod from his Commander, took Croft by the face, and manipulated his mouth in a manner which we understood to illustrate the concept "speech." This man then raised an admonitory finger toward us and wagged the finger, indicating "do not." He held the finger still, which we understood as the conjunction "or." Then, the man pinioning Croft bent the prisoner's head over the gunwale while the interlocutor drew his sword and removed Croft's head, thus completing the instruction.

The armorers then came on board the galley, sharing the load of a heavy basket, which, we found, carried shackles which they now began to fasten on our legs. Croft's headless body was tipped into the bay, we were chained to the oars, and our day began.

.   .   .

Madness may be the attempts of the soul, sick of consciousness, to place itself beyond care or consideration of all things, including a concern for the nature of the balm itself. Free from both fear of ridicule and concern with reason, the madman and the mystic join in a godlike omniscience made possible only by a curtailment both of all mental variables and of the possibility of action.

In age, a diminution of abilities is accompanied, soon or late, by the diminution of desire. This, I believe, is true of all things but greed.

The miser, curiously, projects or wishes to project his power even beyond the grave; sure (if mistaken) in his posthumous control through legal instruments of both the gratitude of his beneficiaries and the rage of the disinherited. But this, though he might feel otherwise, is but imagination. Where is the joy, and what is it? That sparked by the thought of the excluded relative, is not a product of his revenge, but of his contemplation of it, as is his glow in the notional gratitude of the employee awed by the deceased's generosity.

In the two cases, the joy is prompted not by a display but by the contemplation of a display of the reaction of the powerless to power. The miser, then, it may be said, is addicted or habituated not to *gold*, but to certain *thoughts*. This, I believe, is the thesis of those Alienists whose practice is among the Neurasthenics. Their view, curiously, mirrors, though their practice differs from, that of the Eastern Mystic, for whom, equally, joy, sorrow, and grief are delusions.

Such, to the young, do not feel like delusions. The young man asks, for example, what is more real than desire—the rest of the world and goods and experiences beside it, paling to nothing? What can compare to it in virulence? Nothing but the urge to kill. And the prepotent admixture of the two is Jealousy.

I saw a man, in Cantonments, who had just murdered his wife and her lover.

He'd come upon them on his early return from a scouting expedition which he and I had made to the Northwest. On our return, we separated, each to his lodgings, agreeing to reconvene at the Club. I preceded him there, and waited, wishing him happy, as was I, in the return to cleanliness, rest, ease, quiet, and the absence of anxiety, coupled, here, with the rare assurance of our mission's success.

Its aim was limited: the inducement of a certain Chief to "accept the hand of friendship" and so signify by his endorsement of a certain document. This we had done, and returned, ourselves and the document intact.

Here are the analgesic benefits of rank: his duty toward subordinates will supplant, in the conscientious Officer, concern for his own convenience and safety. But submission to superiors, which is to say devotion to the ordered task, frees one from anxiety for any success of the operation wider than that of the immediate task with which one has been charged. The passes might close, and the Tribes rise, in contravention of our treaties, and in despite of our interest. But we had brought our slip of paper as ordered, and presented it, intact, and our mission was successful and complete.

I was moored bow and stern to the long bar at the Club, when I got the news. Here is how it came.

The club steward entered, and approached Colonel L———, who was in the card room, and to whom, in fact, we had delivered our report and prize a short hour previous. He rose and turned to survey the club, disseminating the communication, known to all who have known battle, that something had gone amiss. And when his eye met mine, for he had been searching for me, I knew, if not the particulars, the essential outline of the tale.

For I knew when I saw the Colonel that my colleague had come to grief, and I wondered how such could have come in the scant hour of our return to the security of the Cantonment. And in the specific set of the Colonel's jaw, I saw we were involved in a tragedy. My first thought was "Oh, my God: she's *killed* him."

I did not know that I knew of his wife's infidelities, but in that moment, in the Colonel's glance, I discovered that I did, and that the knowledge had lain dormant in me. How had I become aware, if not quite consciously, of her adultery? I believe it was on seeing her feign an inattention, at a Regimental dance, to that young man with whom she would be murdered.

I was newly arrived at the post, and my colleague, my liaison with the Army, introduced me to her by the name and fiction which had been constructed to disguise my purpose and affiliation.

She was a stunning woman, black-haired and ivory-skinned, small and finely formed. And she exuded a sense of, perhaps not "power," but, more vitally, a *contentment* with power. That power was her sexuality.

On meeting the women, wives, and occasional companions of armed men, one exercises a finely honed sense of deportment. Any gentleman, of course, will behave with finesse and gallantry on being introduced to *any* lady.

But one's introduction to the woman of one's comrade-in-arms, or, indeed, of colleagues or acquaintances, if these are men-of-arms, has not only a sentiment, but a *performance* of restraint—the performance superadded as a compliment, not to the woman, but to the man. This woman must never be complimented by even those seemingly innocuous gallantries one awards to the young girl in short skirts and to the grandmother, but by their absence.

My colleague's wife, when she was presented to me, smiled, and was about to suggest some conversational commonplace or inquiry, the thought just framing itself on her lips, when a group of three Officers entered the club. They hailed my colleague and made to join our group.

I was introduced to each. Each then paid his respects to their friend's wife, and she was charming to the three, but more charming to two than to the last, in whose arms she now lay naked and dead, slain by her husband.

It is an ancient adage of the Sea that if you are to return from an extended voyage before time, tarry in port, and write to acquaint your wife of your return.

Great wisdom of the world descends in jests and apothegms disguised as jests. "Marry in haste, repent in leisure"; "After battle, tighten your chin strap"—these, of course, brought to mind by the above-related occurrence.

For perhaps, as I stood at the bar, awaiting my friend's return from his home, I should have paid attention to a sense of alarm. For it *was* an alarm. For how, to the combatant, can the phrase "I am in a place which is perfectly safe" be anything else? it cannot.

And there *was*, of course, hidden and unconscious, in my invitation for him to accompany me to the Club, an attempt to keep him from his home. For I had asked him to come with me to the Club, and he had intimated, shyly, that he thought first he would see his wife.

His happy though shy demeanor—a healthy young man separated, for some weeks, from his beloved bride—forbade, in politeness, a reiteration of my request. But I reiterated it.

And he demurred. And returned to his home, and slew the girl and the other man with the stiletto he carried in his sleeve. For he was a careful man.

.   .   .

My first thought, on hearing the thing described, was "What a waste," and, wretch that I am, I did not mean "of human life," but of the astounding sexuality of that young woman, who, on her discovery as an adulteress, had released me from the Code of Gentility; and though my lust was released only in fantasy, and, then, only toward the dead, I marked in its virulence the strength of what was revealed as repression.

There is that, of course, in being armed, which not only regulates the *display* of lust, but increases the *fact* of it. For two thoughts, then, are coupled: the first, the penalty for coveting your comrade's woman may be death; the second, I could kill him and take her.

As a chess player, in his mind, skips past the first obvious moves to halt at the crux of the problem, I, prompted by the Colonel's look, understood the woman had been taken in adultery, and violence had ensued. But why, then, did I think, "My God, she's shot him?" when the more likely act would have been the opposite? Because, in my lust, I wanted her, too. I felt it was not my *assessment*, but my *wish*, that my colleague were dead. For, then, I could take his wife. And why would she accept me? I give the answer of the combatant down through time: because she was without protection, and because I was armed.

But, in the event, my friend had killed them both. He was hanged for it. And I still lust after his wife, absent opportunity or possibility, like the miser, the slave of my fantasy, the slave of desire.

I attended the man's hanging. I was asked by my Department to make a report. But there was nothing to report. I told them I did not attend.

.   .   .

Much is gained by reticence in sexual affairs. This was explained to me, on my first voyage, by a bosun; and I have abstracted and applied his wisdom in a wide-ranging series of difficulties.

We were in port, the various liberties arranged, and only an anchor watch kept on the ship. I had the duty.

I saw one of the ratings coming aboard with what purported to be a "drunken comrade," but which the briefest second glance, or, indeed, suspicion, revealed as a young woman in sailor's clothes. How romantic. And quite fetching. Is this the homoerotic urge, which finds women in men's dress so provocative? Perhaps. And perhaps it is the outlining of their limbs, nor may we discount the mere suggestion of *license* in travesty; for if license is once begun, who (as we are ever hopeful) may say where it will end? Which is the subject of this homily.

I saw the young woman, attention being drawn to her both by her lovely form, and by her companion's wretched portrayal of a concerned shipmate helping a drunk friend aboard. He would have done much better just to've walked on with her, and trusted to his luck.

The much-vaunted, much-published, and much-posted rule upon ship was that under *no* circumstances were unauthorized person to be allowed aboard. The force of the rule was understood by all to indicate "women." Here was the sailor, breaking the rule, and here was I to put a stop to it. He and his friend found the companionway and started down, and I was stepping off after them.

The bosun came up behind me, said, "May I be of any help, sir?"

I explained my errand with what, I hoped, was a healthy mixture of umbrage at the flouting of the rules, and knowledge of my duty—not untempered (though undeterred) by the shared realization that rank and age may differ, but men will be men.

I stepped off, I say, to discharge my duty, and the bosun said, "With respect, sir, might I suggest something?" He suggested that when the young courting couple came aboard, I might have been involved in duties which prevented my observing them. I explained that, as I thought I had made clear, I had no objection *whatever* to a sailor "having his fun," and neither did I, between men, feel much harm was done by having the odd woman aboard for a visit, but that laws were laws, and regulations sacrosanct, *however* youth and lust might try to subvert them.

"Do you, then, think, sir," he asked, "that the lads will, *whatever* the regulations, attempt to smuggle women aboard?"

"I think they will attempt it, and I think," I replied, "in many a case, they will be successful."

"Then, with respect," he asked, "what is the point of the regulation?"

This brought me up short. I was sufficiently young to be ignorant of Man's right, let alone his ability, to come to an independent conclusion, and searched my brain for an answer which would fit my station, my duty, my rank, and the circumstances. I could find none beyond "We must have laws," and rested there content; for its opposite could not, to my young mind, be other than that each incident should be decided on a case-by-case basis, trusting to the discretion and understanding of the Officer in charge. This, though grateful to the anarchist or free-thinking delusions common to one of my age, I understood would have, if adopted, put, even I knew, an intolerable strain upon the time and judgment of all. Which left "There must be law," and the corollary "And what good is a law which is not enforced?" Which rhetorical conclusion I shared with him.

"Since you ask, sir, I will tell you," he said. "The purpose of law, as I understand it, is *restraint*. This particular law cannot be enforced. For youthful desire will thwart oversight as sure as any certainty in life.

"The *permitted* admittance, on board ship, of unlicensed females *will*, loosing the bonds of order, result in horseplay, jests, and bawdiness, which must, eventually, progress to insult, jealousy, and, not infrequently, to murder and rape. The regulation was created to spare the ship these results. But lust is stronger, as we know, sir, than law. The young will transgress, but the regulation will cause them to do it in *secret*. It will restrain them from promiscuity, and fear of discovery will cause them to be quick about their business and get the young woman back ashore."

I thanked him sincerely for his wisdom and his time, and left the young sailor and his young friend to their hour of bliss. I saw him, near the end of my watch, shepherding her back ashore, she happy with the success of her deception, as most women are, and he, now sated, anxious of discovery; and I felt I had made an accession of that wisdom necessary to the conduct of a Naval Officer.

There is no unmixed motive—save perhaps the preservation of life. All motives are not only mixed, but their predominant nature unclear, most times, both to the observer and to the actor. Perhaps this ends my disquisition on Lust. What of Courage?

The novels were said, upon their first success, to be, among other things, "an Ode to Courage." Do I think it the highest of virtues? I think that an answer would or could be no better than an aphorism. And I have been privileged to have seen enough of and to have profited from the display of this virtue as to count my acquaintance with it, worthy of more than a verbal flourish.

·   ·   ·

The life of the Sea, and my life in Government Service, were a life of action which, however high some of its costs, did not include a corrosive slavery to words; which is why, for my sins, I have augmented penance by my subsequent choice of occupation as a writer.

Starvation, thirst, brutality, both received and practiced, and constant fear leave little room for self-loathing. For the engine of the martial life is *shame* rather than *guilt*. (I exempt the guilt of the Commander, which I will treat of here.)

In the case of the adultery and murder I testified in camera, as my position as an Operative allowed me to exploit the plea of anonymity. My testimony was that the Lover, "A," had said, and I had overheard him say, to my colleague, "B," "You ———, I will take your wife if and as I please, and should you intervene, I shall kill you." I will not say that I was asked to "swear upon my honor." I could not have been asked to do so, as my testimony was not admissible in evidence. It, therefore, had no judicial weight, though it retained the *force* (I believe) of the word of an Officer and a Gentleman.

I lied. Everyone knew I lied. The penalty was, you might suggest, shame at finding my (perjured) testimony disbelieved, the evidence of such lack of credit being the verdict against my friend.

I was prepared for the open or unstated calumny, which I felt must accompany the dismissal of my tale. I was unprepared for the unmistakable though silent approbation of the Court. For it was clear they thought I had done "the right thing," and applauded the act, and what I took as the endorsement of my perjury as courage.

But then, I wondered, why, if they felt I had acted correctly, did they condemn that man whom I had lied to save?

My lie was licensed, I think, as, although the circumstance as related never took place, it was, after all, a logical if unfactual expression of what the Lover must have meant or felt. And, though I was not there to see it, his contempt for the brother Officer whom he was cuckolding, *might* have been communicated from the seducer to the cuckold by the mere expedient of a contemptuous glance.

Who is to say it did not occur, even at that very moment I described? For had not I, a stranger, descried in a glance the ongoing infidelity without dif-ficulty; and, in the same instant, the identity of the two partners to the crime?

Of *course*, my friend knew of his wife's treason. This, likely, was his reason for the immediate repair, on our return to the Station, to his lodgings. He meant to discover her. And he did.

It was some time later, at another post, I heard the incident discussed, my part in the affair being, of course, unknown. The question was raised, between those Officers, as in these pages, why had the Court, in possession of the obvi-ous, irrefutable plea of the Unwritten Law, chosen not admonition but death?

A wag opined it was because my colleague, rather than adopting the tradi-tional Christian expedient of the revolver, had dispatched the couple by means of a previously concealed knife. I told the man to shut up. He asked me to identify myself, and I said that I was the fellow that was going to send him to Hospital. But I cannot say I could, at the time, completely discount his theory.

To return: my efforts to release my brother Officer by perjury having failed, I resorted to secondary expedients. For it is an axiom of the Secret Service, which is, after all, merely a State Apparatus for Betrayal, that the social fabric is at all points permeable, and most human bonds easily sunderable if the op-erative will simply think like a criminal, which, I suppose, I was, though in the service of a State. And, as a Naval Officer, the case could be made that one was, after all, merely a killer licensed in that same service. But these are the quibbles of the schoolboy. I am aware it has amused various Jacobin commentators to indict now this and now that mechanism of Society as evil: property as theft; employment, slavery; government, coercion; and so on. These, of course, little recognize, or discount, the certainty that any form of government overthrown will be replaced on the instant by another. And that all the goodwill and good nature in the world will not ensure that this new thing, based upon "human goodness," or "eradication of forms," will not be a worse arrangement than that based upon a more mechanical attempt to mediate between the irreconcilable fancies of men. I do not equate espionage, morally, to crime. I did not and I do not find it criminal to serve the State; I merely note the similarity of methods.

The fear of the inhuman must be inflamed to inculcate in those no ban can completely dissuade, restraint, or caution. I found this useful in my contem-plation of the expedient of torture.

May a State break the law? I once in France heard a clergyman discourse upon that topic.

He called the attention of his listeners to a division, in his city, between the classes of people, the division being their relative wealth. He called them "rich" and "poor," and there existed, he informed us, an eternal enmity between the two, the rich hoarding their wealth, the poor alternatively starving in silence or entreating the rich for bread.

This conflict, we were told, sometimes matured into violence, by which now one and now the other side would dramatize its position. When the démarches became demands, a fight would ensue which was called a "Revolution." How much better, he suggested, to hear the requests of the poor, as we had been instructed to do in the Gospels.

I found his argument attractive, for it spoke, each man, to his self-interest: better for the rich to consider the poor, and by a simple subvention at least to forestall the depredations to which that class must otherwise devolve. For, we learned, in the dialectic between the two classes, *requests*, on either side, always failed—requests by the rich inevitably escalating into demands, the nature of which was oppression; and those of the poor, similarly availing naught, progressing to the end of the Revolution.

We know of various Unwritten Laws. In diplomacy we attempt to both deduce and adduce them in support of a position—the search for and support of such laws is the first step toward any possible *rapprochement*.

In warfare, the strategist, conversely, aims to discern mutually held suppositions in order to subvert them. This, in fact, is a good definition of tactics. Its most profound practice consists in the violation not of common *rules* (this is obvious) but of unconscious *assumptions*, about the physical and the moral world; e.g., it is impossible to take cannon over that mountain range; or, one would never approach with wounded under a flag of truce, in order to distract, while executing a flanking movement.

In war, it is almost universally the less scrupulous who is the victor. He, then, on his accession will attribute the victory not to that guile and savagery which are the only means by which war may be won, but to moral superiority. This victor will, then, construct new rules, condemning both war as such, and those particular new means of his late discovery, whose use he attempts to bar from future implementation against himself by an appeal to Humanity.

This attempt to codify is a profound mistake, for it serves as an advertisement of vulnerability. From his newfound self-awarded position of moral superiority, the victor dictates those laws which, in torpid self-regard, he assumes will ever afterward govern the conduct of those who hate and envy his success—he announces, in effect, that he no longer wishes to fight.

It is one task of the Spy to convert to his use this complacency which, more frequently than force of arms, has brought about the downfall of the Great.

How comes it that the State, then, does not fear the Spy more than armies, and the subversive more than both? And how curious that such a figure is a staple, a beloved of our literature.

My particular Iago, Doctor Brandt, plagues Captain Marrion through the novels. More than one reader has informed me, with asperity, that his presence ruins three otherwise good books. I count this quite the highest compliment.

I was pressed, upon the completion of that trilogy, to continue the tales. I often considered it. For the tales brought me enjoyment and financial reward. But, try as I might, neither in my imagination nor in my experience could I find another in me.

To decry this lack, or to force the effect, seemed to me rather a blasphemy against that power of inspiration which had given rise to the tales in the first place. My inspiration having come from nowhere, that is, it seemed to me neither unjust nor unremarkable that it should thence return. I did, however, seriously consider a book with, as its Hero, Doctor Brandt.

Here is the story I would have liked to have written: the Doctor is a young man. He pursues his studies in Dresden, Edinburgh, and London. He falls in love with a serving girl. He gets her with child. He vows to marry her. She disbelieves his vows, and leaves him and weds her employer, who has been importuning her. The Doctor murders them.

This is a harsh tale. And in delineating it, I realized that my joy in its exposition came from a desire to *destroy the form*. Having tired, that is, of the Adventures, I was interested in taking them up only to violate my understanding with that public whose need, flattering though it was, I found oppressive.

For it was *not* a good story, to see their beloved Doctor, essential to their enjoyment of the Marrion Tales, revealed *as a true monster*—which is to say, as human. He existed in their fantasy, finally, as that ever-thwarted force who, by contrast, and in his defense, allowed them greater enjoyment of the Captain's successes. He was the Bear Beneath the Bed, and I was considering conclud-ing my bedtime story (for that is the nature of the books) with the Bear eating the child.

•   •   •

Bravo the critical mind. It is capable of two distinct insights: that all a writ-er's production must stem either from experience or from imagination. Such mind, further, is happily constructed to indict either as the spirit moves, saying of the Experienced, "It is merely a *recicative*," and of the Imagined, that it never actually took place.

Some wag, when consideration of my works had progressed from the nec-essarily slapdash consideration of the Daily to the more reasoned enormities of the Monthly press, suggested that the Captain's amour with Mme. Lacombe was but, if not a mirror of, then a reference to one of my own.

Let us consider the dismissive "but."

Some men have done more than others. The experiences of some are more interesting and exceptional; further, some are more capable of arranging their experiences for the interest and the understanding of an audience.

The critics taking against a part of my work—an extended part, indeed, cat-aloguing, through the fugue of battles and excursions, the Captain's particular amour, through courtship, conquest, and Marriage—dismiss by employment of that simple conjunctive, my efforts both as raconteur and fantasist, suggest-ing that my work cannot be passed as either, as each contains the preemptive taint of the other.

To grow philosophic, what is there in Memory unsullied by self-deceit, self-aggrandizement, regret, or self-justification? Nothing.* Where is the fantasy which is not constructed upon or inspired by Experience—if only the experi-ence of desire? The starving man fantasizes about food, the frustrated swain, of necessity, about Love.

But the critics must write something, for they, like the rest of creation, must eat; and the natural world presents no known instance of a life which does not feed upon some other.

---

* Note the experienced Jurist's contempt for the "eyewitness."

.   .   .

There was a woman in Bombay who claimed to exist upon air, requiring neither food nor drink for sustenance.

She became the subject of a bet between two Officers of the Garrison. She was, at her direction, sealed in a cell into which there could be no possibility of the passage of food. Contained, she thrived for the stipulated period of five weeks, and emerged not at all frail, though, as I recall, somewhat irked that the passage of time had cooled the ardor both of the participants to the wager and of the world at large. But emerge intact she did.

The wager, I believe, was paid; and contemporary clippings relate that, on her release, she sat down with the contestants to a celebratory meal—though why she should have chosen to do so, her professed preference being to live upon air, escapes me. And I was further baffled by the lack of similar comment at the time.

But I came to understand that lack thus: that the wagerers, having lost interest in the bet, were recalled to their stated positions by the woman's emergence, which, like the appearance of a long-invited, long-forgotten, and now importunate guest, must be greeted with a compensatory (if factitious) jollity, the importuned taking comfort in the knowledge that it will soon be over. I construe the various awarding of Honors at the end of a literary life similarly.

How did the woman "live upon air"? She did not, as one cannot. Friends in the more technical reaches of the secret world, those dealing with the mechanics of concealment and allied deceits, inform me that the difficulty in this esoteric ruse is not the secretion of nourishment, but, begging the pardon of the squeamish, the concealment of excrement.

.   .   .

I do not believe in deathbed confessions. I have seen many men die, but have heard few. For most die suddenly, or drift, unconscious, away. Some few die conscious, but from them I have heard little remorse.

As the body has its natural opiate, it seems the mind and soul have, too. I particularly praise the Roman Catholic practice. At death, their Priest, I believe, inquires if the afflicted is truly penitent, rather than requiring an actual catalogue of sins. For I believe the sinful die in sin, and perceive that the beneficent Catholic rite is one of Grace rather than of judicial catharsis. I applaud them for it. For the doctrine that Grace, though it may be awarded, may not be earned. For all men die in sin.

One dying man revealed to me, on shipboard, however, terrible crimes. I found his recital both an imposition and an impertinence, for what, I wondered, did he expect of me? It was not mine to pardon or forgive him. I thought his acts loathsome, and his reference to my rank, as one fitted to receive confession, a presumption.

This sufferer had obviously struggled with his guilt for many years. I pitied him, but I did not know that I could find it in myself to say that I forgave him, or suggest that "it was all one in the eyes of God." Neither did I feel, plumbing my shallow reserve of theological opinion, that such a man, should Hell exist, should be spared its torments in exchange for a late and cost-free confession, the very fact of which catharsis must have been to him, a pleasure.

But, on the other hand, he was dying. And he was a human being. And I, as an Officer, had a duty in comforting one under my command.

"What would a Priest say?" he asked, and I told him I supposed a Priest might allude to the presence of God in all things, and left those, I hoped soothing, sounds to be accepted or interpreted in that way which might both bring him comfort and allow me escape from my position.

I had no sympathy with him. A better man, I thought, might have taken his sordid secrets to the grave. And if there *were* a Hell, such a stoicism, I felt, might have better served to mitigate his sentence than would the lugubrious and sordid recitation which, like his original crime, was, finally, but one more wretched absence of self-control.

In the Naval Service we are schooled to stand and die, preferring stalwartness to dishonorable self-preservation.

In a rout, the warrior's chances are increased by stout defense and attack, and ruined by panic, flight, and fear. A certain inversion of the social mathematic ensues: defiance here accounted better than negotiation, brutality than sympathy; a love of victory supplants love of life, and a life without honor is scorned above all things. I considered the man's deathbed confession an act of surrender, less worthy than defiance—or let him, I felt, make his silent peace with God and end it as a man.

Further, I have known criminals, and spies, and convicts, and have lived a part of my life as each or as its close simulacrum. The first lesson each learns is that speech is a tool only to be used to exploit—it exists neither to express nor to communicate, but to obtain—by misdirection, deceit, or suggestion—that desired from any opponent sufficiently naïve to believe in the sanctity of speech.

And so, in the man's confession, I recognized the desire not to *reveal* but to *distract*—which is the essence of the plea of *any* apprehended. What, I wondered, was the crime which he would *not* confess, and from the existence of which he strove to distract his confessor?

This though occurred to me in my cabin, whither I had repaired after our interview. And I returned to the sickbay to put the supposition to him.

I found him as I had left him, starting, sweating, frightened, and distraught. I sat by him. He held his hand out to me, and I held his hand. "What have you *not* confessed?" I asked. His face took on the sudden, pinched, sly, withdrawn look of the criminal, and he gave me a small, approving grin.

.   .   .

I believe in physiognomy. The sea captain's eyes are deep set to shield them from the sun; the musician's face is immobile in placidity; that of the criminal is quick, and his mouth disdainful or smiling. The face of the convict is stolid, the energy of his life force recessed; that of the warrior is still and sad.

There exist also monstrous variants of humanity, some born without conscience, and insusceptible to, though capable of miming, human sympathy. I believe these, in truth, do not possess souls.

How to account for this variation? For it is obvious that differing dispositions and confirmations of the human mind and body offer, through interbreeding, possibility for endless beneficial adaptation, natural selection ensuring that the helpful variant will thrive and breed, improving the race. But how or through what mechanism can it be that beings may be born without a soul? To what end?

Neither may the lack be considered an oversight or accident, which would reflect upon the Omnipotence of God, and on the basic tenet of all Religion, that we are put here for a reason. Such reason, at its most reductive, to acknowledge the Greatness of God. Why, then, would God create men without souls? And yet such is the case.

These monsters I have seen like the lantern fish, attracting their prey. They are, to that end, when they cannot be vicious, charming, sympathetic, friendly, and of such an easy and immediate assumption of intimacy that this may, in fact, be relied upon as a diagnostic symptom of their actual state.

This easy transgression of social bonds they share with the criminal, for whom it is a matter of policy. But to the true monster such is not policy, but irrefrangible mechanics: to control, to inflict pain, to destroy. Such is the essence and the totality of their lives.

I devoted much thought to the abilities of the psychopath in my years as an Intelligence Operative. For my job, like his, was to subvert and undermine the human capacity for discrimination—this, while not an attractive, is, I feel, an accurate description.

Many have difficulty overcoming an initial reluctance toward deceit. I was one of those. But in Intelligence work, as in warfare, the previously learned must be unlearned, and scruples supplanted by notions of duty, patriotism, honor, and esprit de corps, these lessons finalized, in the field, by the great master, Self-Preservation.

The healthier man maintains some aspect of both systems simultaneously, the civilian and the warlike. His failure to maintain the first is characterized by guilt, the second by shame. Those who are not convinced that life is struggle are the real or potential victims of those to whom it is the central fact.

Captain Marrion is portrayed as periodically assailed by scruples. The ensuing hesitation or lack of decision is responsible for his capture and torture by the pirate Brock.

Brock has been taken by the Captain, and sentenced, out-of-hand, to death. About to be shot, Brock pleads for "one last moment of reflection." The Captain nods; Brock turns away and kneels; the Captain, in deference, half-averts his gaze. The kneeling Brock pulls the secreted pocket-pistol from his boot, and shoots the Captain in the breast.

This passage provoked, in military men, a fairly universal objection. Among these the books had, most gratifyingly, found much currency. But here they felt themselves betrayed, and the Captain's behavior inconsistent with both their experience and common sense. Several denigrated it as "romantic," that is, as false. In which indictment they were most correct. For spies and pirates are, were, and will always be—whatever the public is told—executed out-of-hand. Why indulge them? For to the military mind, if their horror of death unshriven indicates their assessment of a Supreme Penalty, why not inflict it upon them?

The Captain, thus, lost some credit with the military reader, which loss I greatly regret. And, perhaps, had I the passage to write again, I would act in a more realistic manner, e.g.,

"May I pray?" the pirate asked.

"In a moment," the Captain replied, and shot him dead.

This, the astute reader will note, is neither less romantic nor contrived than the existing version; it is merely more abrupt, ending the antagonism many chapters too soon, and would have thus constrained me to invent another stratagem to round out the book, which, like any novel or confession, to close the conceit, is a romance.

.   .   .

The Captain's courtship of Mme. Lacombe has this in common with my early association with Margaret: both began as an immediate overwhelming conviction of mutuality, and both continued as such, throughout many years and trials, none of which marred the revelation of the first encounter.

There are many bad things in life, and every man commits bad acts, the good man being he who repents, repairs, and desists. There is no perfect man, but there may be perfect actions, and, independently, moments of Grace. These do not suggest nor convince of the possibility of Sanctity, but are, independent of Sanctity, unearned Salvation.

As I have always, and with reason, considered myself a bad man, these moments of Grace, the love of my wife in particular, constitute to me a proof of God.

Those things which preserve us will, of course, be construed into a catalogue of Deliverances, through which one may perceive the operations of Grace—the fellow killed by accident will have his recitative terminated, the long-lived, find his attenuated.

Many, however, structure their history as a list of grievances. Among women, such is called a shrew. Does the type exist among men? It must, human attributes being generally distributed with a laudable impartiality. But, as the congruent word does not leap to mind—"shrew" standing alone—I suspect that such behavior in the male may—as the physicians say—present differently.

A man may be querulous, petty, self-pitying, and so on, but these, and their like, do not seem to convey the totality indicated by the former word.

Perhaps Society, being, in the main, conjugal, excoriates this behavior in a female with greater vehemence, as it expects from her better performance. Why? As, in a marriage, such behavior is more destructive in the female than in the male. It is true. We expect more of women. And it is true our expectations are, in the main, rewarded.

.   .   .

Another instance of a spousal murder. An officer in the Caribbean shot his wife in public, indeed, at a Regimental ball. And the community strove for a way to exonerate him—for he was beloved, and she abhorred—the assembly settling upon that fiction usefully employed to mask both murder and suicide: the accidental discharge.

Why had the fellow brought the weapon to the ball? It was explained. It had malfunctioned in the sear—that part communicating the motion of the trigger to the hammer. The sear had worn, making the pistol dangerous, and the fellow had brought it to another Officer, to pass on to his gunsmith.

The blunt obviousness of this fiction functioned as the noted fig leaf which at once conceals and announces the presence of the objectionable. But function it did. The malfunctioning gun shot the woman who had made his life, and, in fact, life in the community, unbearable. This coincidence the community dealt with through the most efficacious of means—immediate amnesia.

The murdered wife was, on the instant, remembered as a Saint, their marriage as one of happiness at least sufficient to allow expressions of grief indistinguishable from the real, and the man condoled with as one who had lost a Treasure.

A similar situation exists in battle. The obtuse martinet risks his life to a shot from behind, his killer or killers known to all, and any guilt shared out by mutual understanding of the act's communitary benefit. As in the case of the murder of the shrew. A somewhat less apposite instance is that of the officer utilizing the fog of war to cleanse from his contingent a dangerous coward or fool. For he can share his private guilt with no one. His case is congruent with that of the autobiographist, who must mitigate shame and guilt within himself—his creation only secondarily that defense or apology which is his Work, and, more to the point, the imagination of a notional audience composed of the well-disposed and credulous.

Men die in battle. They are maimed horribly. And every combatant knows the fear of torture and mutilation surpasses the fear of death. Death is an end, and comrades are sworn to end each other's pointless agony; thus mutilation is reduced to the first case. And death, though regretted, may be accepted as the end of pain; but where is the philosophy to still the fear of torture? And who is unwilling to discharge a debt in a debased coin?

War and sex are, in essence, savagery.

Nothing is fair in Love and War, but many actions otherwise shunned as uncivilized are here reasonable. And what ruins the soul of one may, perhaps, by another be quite simply forgotten.

.   .   .

We all know the look in the eyes of very old men. In some it has the tinge of confusion, in some of resignation, in some of peace. But all are characterized by an unmistakable alteration which seems not to be wrought by consciousness, but by imposition from above.

Perhaps this change, like the desiccation of the leaves, may be adduced as a proof, or the beginnings of a proof, of the existence of God; for we are certainly born with a soul—it is observable in the newborn infant; each appears with a disposition and the light in the eyes of that individual's particular consciousness. At the announcement of the imminence of death, that light is changed. Now that which seemed a possession is revealed as a gift or loan. Those who have appreciated this gift, and used it in humility, are at peace, others are reduced to confusion or remorse.

But if the soul goes back—for as nothing may come of nothing, so, we may reason, nothing, though it may be changed, may be completely destroyed—perhaps it is possible that, as the Orientals teach, there is a wheel of continuous life. In this wheel, they say, the soul will be reborn, for punishment or purification, into another body—this essential soul different from the individual consciousness as an actual object differs from its depiction on canvas.

The Buddhists, I am told, suggest a progression of the reborn soul toward enlightenment, each new incarnation advancing—through reward or castigation—progress toward the goal.

This is a comforting doctrine, containing, as it does, immortality—that insuperable human desire. But note that though some essence continues, the *personality*, which is to say the consciousness-of-self, is shed, until the Being is, through the pain of its various lives, cleansed of the wish to continue as discrete. And then it is merged with the All.

It is the fulfillment of this process which one sometimes sees in the eyes of the Saintly, when the turn is made toward death: it is the absence of Desire. This, the Buddhists teach, is the freedom of the soul to dwell in gratitude, which they call Nirvana.

With the erosion of the sexual impulse, the frantic operations of Youth become incomprehensible; they become as the attractions of a lethal quarrel in which one has no stake, the fine distinctions and the causi belli of which are, to the uninvolved, a pointless expense of spirit.

But Remorse, which I will characterize as a passion, is most difficult of conquest.

Some believe in the power of confession, some in the transformation of the soul by Profession, water, or fire.

The Islanders engaged in rituals of great barbarity to signify or induce the reception of Grace. These, though they outraged the Western sensibility, seem to me, on reflection, an expression of a sophisticated intuition: that the state brought about by physical trauma and the fear of death, is so like that of the anguished sinner that the change wrought about by his unconditional plea for salvation may be *mimicked* by the pain and fear of ritual—the result being the same: a conviction of transformation.

I observed the Islanders' rituals and cursed myself, for I had the desire, but I had not the will to be transformed. I see now that the transformation would have been effected not by their knife and fire, but in that instant in which I chose to step forward to accept them. I see this with such clarity now that I wonder how it could have been obscure to me for all those years—that Grace would have come not in or through the flesh, but through the *soul* of him who willingly surrendered to the exchange of remorse for submission.

Sailors tattoo their flesh, for they, in truth, have no possessions; those few rags or trinkets they call their own are, they understand, theirs but at the sufferance, whim, or inattention of the Sea, which will, most certainly, eventually reclaim them. These tattoos, then, are their mementoes and, like all of these, reflect their individuation, their status, preferment, and pretensions to taste, quite as much as do another man's tailoring, drawing room, and equipage.

I understand the attraction of these markings, and would have so indulged myself but that, in the beginning of my life, I was debarred by my status as an Officer, and, in my second career, by my work in Intelligence. For in this second career, the acquisition of an indelible identifying mark would have been a potentially lethal indulgence.

Who is the excellent Intelligence Operative? That man who is not there; he who, in a room of twelve, will be the last suspected as a threat; who will escape all notice in a crowd; that man over whom the eye of the border guard, sentry, policeman, will pass, who will in no way awaken that unconscious martial suspicion of threat known to all who have known combat.

To pass unnoticed, a Hostile in a hostile place, requires both courage and arrogance, for it is a sort of superhuman suppression not only of *fear* but of intent; and the reward for its accomplishment is a feeling of godlike omnipotence: "I am not what I seem; I am working for your destruction, free of the laws of both your Country and mine. I have found the New Thing; I am *the New Man.*"

All men return from combat in an altered state, which, could he understand or experience it, the noncombatant might call Madness. This state, in the majority, is weakened over time and through the necessities of a daily interaction in the normal world. Here it is like, though of a greater virulence and duration than, the transition from bachelorhood to Marriage—some practices and habits must remain, but they will grow attenuated.

Few men, though we may remember the thrill of battle, would, given the choice, freely return to it. The case of the Spy is different, for the solitary sense of invisibility, and the power of deceit, is not easily relinquished. Many a denizen of the Secret World has, on return to civilian life, turned criminal. The two careers differ only in that one has the endorsement of the State.

I do not intend this as sophistry. The murdering fiend and the surgeon both employ the knife and a knowledge of anatomy. The first serves the Devil, and the second Man. Both take pleasure in the act.

How can the retired Spy, however, exercise, beneficently, his powers? He may not; thus, many turn to crime, or to those operations of sharp practice between which and crime lies only the carping of attorneys.

And some resort to brutality. It has been written, by another claiming experience in Intelligence, that effort was made to weed from the ranks of applicants, any displaying an "unhealthy" taste for violence. Nothing could be less true; why not, then, debar from the Law those with a taste for sophistry, or from the Military those of aggressive bent?

Intelligence is brutal work, assaultive to the spirit and, at times, to the body. One must frequently act with such brutality that the act and the actor, were they known, would be abominated by all decent folk. And some enjoy it. They are not chosen for this trait, but neither does it debar them.

But what to do with the returned, now-unfrocked practitioner who has taken his skills to an unlicensed market? Will I confess that one man was shot? Many men were shot, or otherwise disposed of, by a Government which was, or thought itself to be, imperiled by the depredations of its onetime servants.

There is harsh precedent in War for the summary extinction of both the coward and the mutineer. For in the press of battle, all—inspiration, courage, panic, and fear—is contagion. It is for this that all armies have divided themselves into the leaders and the led. Men need to be led. The act of the mutineer, coward, or traitor is a bid, at that time when the mind is regressed from intelligence to chemic response, for a change of leadership. The good officer, feelings apart, *must* act to preserve his command.

The execution of a traitor or recreant—absent the possibility of contagion—still partakes of this precedent; it operates, however, differently upon the executioner, for here he acts in cold blood.

One man, guilty beyond cavil, pled for his life. His grounds, after the exhaustion of the specious, were Human Sympathy: which is to say, he prayed to be allowed to live because he was alive. But it was the job of his executioner to alter that state, which could only be done with brutality. Might he cleanse that sin, if it be sin, or memory, if it be not?

Just as unlicensed sex warps the potentialities of marital conjugality, war, and, particularly, espionage, destroys the practitioner's view of Human Nature.

I have seen virtue on the battlefield, and my success as a writer derives, first, from my reputation as a delineator of virtuous strife. But these fantasies, like all fantasies, are a wish for power: if only my Carpet could fly; if I possessed Seven-League Boots; if I were Beloved of the Daughter of the King.

The martial fantasy which formed the basis of my fame is, essentially, the tale of Jack and the Beanstalk: there exists another world, and one may venture to it, obtain Treasure, and return unscathed. It is not true.

And what of the ongoing battle between rich and poor? I have witnessed a Revolution, and I do not wish to see another. I do not believe in "the people." I have seen them formed into a mob. And their eventual adoption of uniforms did not excuse their savagery.

And the Mob may also be convened as an Audience. He who possesses the power to so convene them, we call an Artist. The audience which enjoyed my fantasies has cushioned my years and provided for my retirement, for which I am grateful. I enjoyed my years of action; I have enjoyed my years of repose.

·   ·   ·

My colleague who was hanged was a religious man, though I doubt he would have described himself as such. All sailors are religious, and I recognized in him that attention to the hidden world which we all learn at sea. I saw it in his eyes, at dawn, on the Northwest Frontier. And he turned, and spoke to me about the Bible.

I am aware that it is not only the Devil who can quote scripture to his own purpose, but also his superior in perfidy, Man. But my colleague, that morning, spoke of Solomon's wisdom in exhorting us, here below, to do our work, strive to do good, enjoy our strength and the wife of our Youth.

And when he killed his wife, after my efforts at his judicial release had failed, I went to him in his cell with a plan for his escape. He rejected the plan, as I supposed he would.

I had brought a pill which would have *ended* (though I told him it would only have dulled) his sufferings. He thanked me, and accepted it, and told me he would take it after my departure. But he did not, and he died on the gallows.

I knew he would reject escape. But I thought he might accept what I presented as the Opiate. And I hoped, in taking it, to have spared him the agony of that last trial to be suffered: the trial of his courage. But he rejected my attempts.

I believe I passed him the drug to curtail that which, had it been myself,

I would have found intolerable, that is, hope. For I thought that he, as would I, in similar circumstances, held on to a hope of a pardon, or barring that, of reprieve. But I knew, though I did not tell him, that there would be no pardon. For the Colonel had so informed me.

The Court-Martial Officers felt that his conviction was sufficient to deter a growing sentiment among certain indigenous groups, of disaffection with our Government. It was said, at the Club, that the swift, sure, disposition of Justice by our forces to our own, would reassure the restive of the contrary of that which they described, in various pamphlets, as our "high-handed lack of accountability." That being done, we all opined, the man under sentence of Death, could be removed back to his Native soil, "there to await execution."

The General Staff, however, in cognizance of what they felt to be "the tenor of the situation," gave us to understand there would be neither pardon nor reprieve. That the situation could stand neither the revelation nor the *suspicion* that a sentence issued would, at home, have been, judicially or circumstantially, abrogated; and that the sentence issued would and must be imposed at once, and publicly—thus to forestall a disruption in that new realignment of forces initialized, in fact, by my colleague's and my actions on the Northwest Frontier.

"A veil between Thee and Me."

·   ·   ·

Who is more persistent than a prisoner? Who more inventive?

Though a subject, he must acquire and employ all Man's ancient and accumulated instinct and wisdom as predator. He must watch and learn while in concealment. He takes for his blind not the cover of the natural world, but his understanding of the mind. For he must mime subservience and vacancy, servility and passivity to that degree, but not beyond that degree, which will convince his captors first of their safety, and, then, of the needless folly of rigid adherence to the practices which have ensured it.

He brings his captors to this state not through their consideration, but by the most subtle degrees of misdirection; so that at no time are they conscious of the alteration in their tendencies. And so, over the months, over the years, his hand is permitted to stray ever nearer to the club, the key, the jailer's throat.

His fantasy and his machinations and consideration are to the one end of escape. A bar may be weakened, and any captor may, theoretically, become a confederate. Why not? For all men are human. We work for gain, and there are few loyalties which may not be suborned.

How, then, if a poor wretch, sentenced to life as a guard in the Galleys—his life differing but minutely from that of his prisoner—how then if he is shown or induced to believe in reward for a mere moment of inattention?

Over the months, we reasoned with the one Corporal of our galley's guard; but did not call it reason, but rather "reminiscence." Our beginning acts of transgression were the whispered references to home, and a life of freedom and ease. His first dereliction was a failure to suppress us, his curiosity leading, over time, to his inclusion in the conversation, and to his wonder at the bounty of the world which we described.

The crux and truth of our escape were not, as fictionalized, "the signal to the Warship by the improvised heliograph," but our pitifully ordinary seduction of the guard.

This is a far from pretty story, being a record of the manipulation of blunt instruments (curiosity, cupidity), and the subversion of trust. And it ended with the thole pin with which ——— battered the guard to death, after he had loosed us from our chain.

I asked him, later, why he had killed the man (the agreed-upon plan being merely to knock him senseless, effect our escape through the short swim of the harbor, and, upon the guard's appearance at our Embassy, to hand him his reward).

"It was a bad plan," he said.

"Why?" I asked "Because the Turks would never have believed his story?"

"Yes," he said, "that's true, but the plan's true defect lay in its lack of an incentive to our fellow captives' silence."

The escape encompassed but me and him; he was my benchmate, and to him I was chained. The short chain ran through my manacles and his, and to the staple set in the gunwale at my side. Its release freed but the two of us. We had bruited the possibility of a general uprising, and discarded it as an impossibility, as the necessary movement and noise of the chains, being drawn from bench to bench, would certainly draw the notice of the Watch below.

This left the still-imprisoned forty-some, of which one, to improve his state, might likely have called attention to our escape. Unlikely, you might say, to which I respond, as a prisoner, more certain than unlikely, for in prison as elsewhere, one finds distributed the brave, the average, and the craven; and any group of forty men, in whatever situation, must contain, mathematically, the same proportion of the treasonous and criminal as the populace at large. Into which equation one must co-add envy. For we were to go, and they to stay, and all, by that instant process by which prisoners share knowledge, were awake and watchful, who, by our act of individuation, became potential enemies.

Why did the Corporal not propose to come with us? The fellow could not swim. So he allowed himself to trust his eventual fate to the credulity of his fellow guards, when his true danger, of course, lay with us, whom he had freed, but who he had left with no incentive to keep him alive.

He may have thought, "But what motive have they to kill me?" whereby we see, as in many another coming-to-grief, that the error lay not in his logic, but in the unconscious underpinnings of the question. For it supposed upon our part a benignity a clearer mind must have questioned.

We killed him as a warning to any potential traitor among our fellow prisoners. And ———, after he had struck the blow, swept the boat with his warning gaze, before joining me in the water.

•   •   •

Readers have asked where I obtained medical knowledge sufficient to delineate the work of Doctor Brandt. Especial mention has been made, among the admirers of the books, of the scene of the amputation in the longboat.

Here, again, the profession of the Writer and that of the Spy converge. The unschooled might consider good preparation for an excursion in disguise behind enemy lines a training for withstanding interrogation—the Spy's assumed identity, thus, an extended fiction, any point of which he must be prepared, on the instant, to defend. But his life hangs not upon his ability to survive, but to *avoid* interrogation. His life is forfeit not to failed questioning, but to *suspicion*.

The Spy's job is to avoid suspicion, and all the coaching, false papers, rehearsal of intent, and so on, (and here I reveal a secret of that trade,) are not to support him in interrogation, but to calm him sufficiently to decrease the possibility of his drawing attention.

It is, in all aspects of life, the guilty man who defends himself with specifics.

The innocent are cowed or outraged. And, should he be apprehended, these are the two avenues open to the Spy—a frightened or awkward subservience, or that repressed anger so gratifying to any official, all of whom know that a reasoned, prepared, and cogent defense is the recourse only of the guilty.

Likewise, the Writer, to succeed in an explication of the technical, must engage in misdirection. A close reading of the amputation scene reveals its content as, in the main, chance detail, or, better, description of the nonsurgical. Its success, or acceptance, may be attributed to some mastery not of the art of surgery, but of the rhythms and the sound of prose.

I count it a great, and ever-gratifying compliment, to have praised, "the chapter of the amputation," for it is not a chapter. It is contained in one page and a quarter. It is an illusion. It succeeds not through "accuracy," nor even verisimilitude (for how many have seen or indeed imagined an amputation?), but through a sort of poetry—to use a perhaps curious word.

The art of the Spy is never to be noticed. I have seen an operative enchanted at the work he has done on his jacket cuff—fraying and singeing it to approximate that state to which it would have been brought were its owner in truth that blacksmith he pretends to be. This is a great work of imagination, for see how the Spy thinks: the blacksmith has, of course, removed his coat for work at the forge. He banks his fire at the end of the day, and dons his coat. But he looks back at the last ring he has turned, and sees lacking in it one final blow—that last loving touch of any artist at the end of a good day, and he takes up the tong and carries the ring back, and stirs up the fire, and one final blow leads to the next, and he singes his cuff.

Or he finishes the one ring, the one buckle, or hinge, and lays it aside, and is inspired to redress another. He reaches for it with the tongs, with that same reach he employed fifty times that day, but now his unaccustomed sleeve drags low over the flame, and so on. This is the fantasy of the Spy, borne out in preparation, and it is this investment, this physical preparation, more than all the detail capable of being retained, which may protect him in enemy lands, for, by it, his fantasy has become memory, and, so, consigned to the unconscious, and the policeman's eye sees and passes over a blacksmith.

•   •   •

Women lie with more ease than men. It is rare to encounter, among men, an accomplished liar. This may be laid, perhaps, to the opprobrium which, in our sex attaches to the achievement. Women, we know, must lie, for they are, in most things, powerless, and the great treasure of their sexuality they, from earliest youth, correctly conceive, in its disposal, to be the concern of none but themselves, their ability in prevarication stemming from the early, continued, and legitimate experience of its defense.

Iago is circumstantial, Desdemona has no defense but a confused innocence, the failure of which might, perhaps, injure my thesis, were I not to enlarge it to observe that Othello, like the border guard, like you and I, believes what he wishes to believe. We are credulous creatures. I know nothing of medicine, but enough of the world to be assured that I share this deficiency with many a man in a white coat.

Here is a story, which in fact is true, which I gave to Captain Marrion in the third book. It was excised by the publishers, as too provocative, which I understood to mean "obscene."

The Captain has come ashore in France to make contact with Dussault. The contact is to take place at the Austrian Embassy, at a ridotto. The Captain is in civilian garb. He plans to enter the ball and receive from Dussault that envelope which he has just abstracted from the Embassy's safe.

Dussault is delayed, and the Captain, having foreseen but a momentary presence in the enemy hall, is marooned. He cannot leave, he knows no one, and, indeed, his singularity attracts the notice of a woman. She is found on the arm of the French Minister of Police. She is a woman of some forty years, quite beautiful, stately, and charming to the men around her. The Captain's eye falls upon her, and she feels his gaze. She turns from the men she has been entertaining, and they turn, with her, to find the object of their interest: a man none of them know, who has been staring at the Minister's companion.

The Captain, caught out, advances to the group and addresses the Minister in French. "I wonder," he says, "if I might presume to have one moment, sir, with your Companion." He draws the woman aside. "Madame," he says, "I am not *your* physician, and if he has already advised you, I apologize for my impertinence. Are you aware of that to which I refer?"

She says that she is not, and he asks her if she would step closer to the light. She does so. He looks at her eyes, pulling down now one lid, now the other. And he shakes his head. "What is it?" the woman asks, and he responds,

"Madame, I believe you *know* what it is. It is what you fear." The woman begins to weep. "I am sure," he says, "that you have adequate medical advice, but ..." He hunts in his waistcoat, as if for a card. The woman shakes her head, and returns to her Minister, and his group.

He sees that she has explained his presence, and the Minister turns toward him with a bow, which the Captain returns. Dussault appears, et cetera.

The publishers found the passage, as I understood it, both too suggestive, and too cruel, casting the Captain in the light of an irremediable cad, who would ruin the woman's peace of mind for his self-preservation. I rewrote the passage, with, as its Hero, Dr. Brandt, at which they objected to his violation of the Hippocratic Oath, and I agreed with them, gratified that these two fictions, the Captain and the Doctor, had achieved, in their minds, the status of person-ages, each with characters which must be preserved. Theirs were preserved; mine, in the publisher's eyes, was perhaps injured. So be it. The story was true, but the setting was false; its truth was no defense. They had engaged me not to tell the truth, but to create a cohesive fiction.

The aging man and the old civilization dream of a return to an unchang-ing time or Paradise. This may be named the Tribe, or Childhood, or the Unspoiled Land. The Bible mentions it as the Garden of Eden, which, as it appears as Man's oldest memory, must be his deepest wish. It has two compo-nents: abundance and peace.

But, of course, there must have been abundance if the entire world held but two persons; and though we have observed unhappy marriages, we admit that, politically, the largest number of persons theoretically capable of living in absolute peace is two. For these two would contain the fewest possible per-mutations of opposing or irreconcilable desires.

·   ·   ·

The essence of the state of Being in Love is the absence of strife.

Here the humors of the body overcome the capacity of the mind for dis-satisfaction—that capacity without which there would be neither civilization nor material progress.

The ancient, savage Tribes were depicted by romantic travelers as dwelling in a state of peace. But these pacific Aboriginals dwelt no more in peace than you or I—those Adventurers who retailed their languid existences merely chanced upon their subjects in the interregnum between bloodshed.

The erosion of our desire reveals the existence of a pleasant, unexamined, and false intuition: that there exists between human beings a perfect relationship, free of strife. That strife may be obliterated by perfect repletion is an error similar to that of the victorious warrior, surveying the battlefield stilled, as all his foes are dead, and concluding that Man is a creature of peace.

Man is a creature of strife. We seek it and find it, we shun it and find it. We preach peace, and preach war against those unresponsive to our teaching. Our most godly and pacific thoughts are the occasion of doctrinal wars spanning millennia—the rich grind the poor, the poor revolt, and their leaders become the new and worse oppressor.

Where is this history absent? Nowhere. And yet each sect, Religion, polity, and cabal thinks to have discovered anew the secret of peace: it is called unanimity, and can be brought about only through the extirpation of the infidel.

In prison in Africa, we watched the Faithful called five times a day to prayer. We were not the first Christian captives to perceive that this periodic distraction might offer us an avenue of escape, and, further, that our captors, to whom one must grant, inter alia, a natural sagacity, had equally perceived it, and taken precautions against such possible effrontery.

For the Fort made its obeisances toward the East, and our cell was on the Eastern side of the Square.

But the mind of the captive is devoted, in each conscious moment, to consideration of escape. His jailers have, of course, taken precautions both to contain their charges, and to free their minds from the constant enervating considerations of surveillance.

These precautions are structures and procedures which, however well-thought-out, must hold, at their core, the exploitable fault of *regularity*, which observation, daring, and imagination may uncover.*

---

* One might consider this in application to the securement of our homes, in accession to which we may, over the years, devote some minutes' thought to the provision of latches and locks, the defeat of which occupies the burglar in every waking moment of his life.

The Arabs had formed the only opening of our cell facing into the Square, and there they knelt, five times a day, toward the door of our cell. These devotions, as they pertained to the Fort's routine, might be considered a *disruption*, or a *regularity*, and it was this ambiguity, which suggested to the captive mind, the possibility of exploitation.

The religious among us called to our attention the story of Simeon and Levi. Their sister, Dinah, we will recall, was ravished by a Hittite man. The ravisher fell in love with her, and pled to be allowed to consecrate his crime by Marriage. Her brothers insisted that he signify his remorse and resolution by adoption of the Jewish faith, demanding both the man and all his Tribe be circumcised. And on the third day, following circumcision, we are told, when all the Tribe "were in great pain," Levi and Simeon went among them, and slew them all.

We intuited that this tale might hold some clue or suggestion of the possibility of our escape.

The difficulties in such escape were these: to defeat the lock on the door. To make our way across the Square to the arms the Arabs, I will not say "stacked," but set aside during their prayers, then kill the sentries on the battlements, who, we all assumed, were given special dispensation to forgo the prayers; and, forcing the gates, to make our way to Acca, to our Consulate, and Freedom.

This is the progression depicted in the book: a picklock is fashioned from a nail wrenched from the dungeon wall, the lock (observed in detail at those times when the door was opened to admit our food) suggesting the probable confirmation of the key fashioned from the nail; the most agile and long-limbed of our crew practicing to fit his arm through the barred grate and pick the lock; and then our rush across the Courtyard, past our recumbent, praying captors. How to add credibility to this rush?

The touch I employed in the book is an ancient martial strategy: the creation of a moment of hesitation in the attacked.

Captain Marrion, whose idea this was, characterized the Act of Prayer as a withdrawal from the everyday world, and a momentary devotion to the world of Spirit. How to maintain the guards, that extra half-instant, in the other world? He advised the captives, as they ran from the opened cell, to shout, as if in friendship, "Alla Akhbar." The captors, reemerging from a devoted state, might, at this unforeseen development, remain in a state of inaction just sufficiently to increase the chances of the crew to seize their weapons.*

So it was written in the novel, and, I believe, as a tactic it might have had some success. But it was never employed, as the cell door, in the event, had neither grate nor lock. It was, when closed, barred and bolted from the outside, in a way offering no possibility of defeat. And the cell walls held no nails, being contrived exclusively of sunbaked brick, mortared with bitumen, which sets harder than rock.

We captives, in truth, returned to the story of Dinah. It tantalized us by suggestion that it held a hidden clue. The clue came to light at last through an affinity and a betrayal.

One of our foremast hands, DaSilva, was a Portuguese, and, thus, assumed to be, and indeed practiced as, a Roman Catholic. But he was in fact a Jew. His family was of that Tribe persisting in the centuries since the Expulsion through the underground continuation of their Faith. The name of this subsect, "Marrano," or "Converso," I had understood to mean "one who, to preserve himself, conceals his Judaism behind the deceptive embrace of Christianity." But this understanding I found incomplete. For DaSilva revealed to me that his coreligionists were also to be found behind the veil of Islam, and that one of our Keepers was of that group.

By what sign or omission DaSilva divined this connection, I do not know. Nor would I ask. For it is not impossible that it was the Keeper who perceived his brother first, and, perhaps, in offer of release or friendship, made the first approach.

However it was, like recognized like, and DaSilva came to me with the

---

* Each man *envisions* an action before he performs it. The skilled prizefighter or brawler induces his opponent to commit to receive a blow at a place where his opponent has no intention of delivering it. A scout I had dispatched, in my second career, found himself forced to eliminate an enemy picket who had interposed himself between him and his safe return. The picket was turned toward our lines; the scout drew his bayonet and advanced on him. The picket, however, sensed the attack and turned. There was room and time for the picket to fire, but not enough for the scout to close with his knife. The scout became still, and raised his finger to his mouth, indicating "quiet," approached the picket with a conspiratorial grin, and stabbed him to death.

information: our Keeper, passing as a Mohamedan, was, in fact, a Jew. The knowledge put his life into our hands. I spoke to the man and threatened him: contact our Consulate at Acca, and bear them my message, or I shall denounce you, and you and your family will die.

What can be worse than irreconcilable loyalties? For I believe the jailer spoke first, offering his brother escape, and preferring this religious duty over his martial vows. And consider our co-captive, offered the choice of betraying his brother or betraying his crew.

The note was delivered to Acca, we were freed, and the Arab Garrison destroyed. How terrible to be a Jew.

· · ·

In writing these memoirs, I came across an address book. It had slipped behind the drawer of a bureau long-stored.

It was vest-pocket-sized, and covered in pale blue Morocco leather. How long had it lodged there? I do not know, but it dated from some four decades since; and must have migrated from its original place of rest or storage, during some move, when the drawers of the bureau may have been removed for transport from some lodging to the warehouse. Or perhaps it had been displaced during some cleaning of the drawers, or I had secreted it there, though I have no memory of having done so, nor do I retain a sentiment of having considered such a spot other than ludicrous as a place of concealment. But if I had not placed it there, what had prompted me to remove the drawer?

The first entry to which my eye fell was of the abode of ———; a friend who had died in a duel. He died for a witticism.

It was uttered at a common resort of Naval Officers in Portsmouth, at the conclusion of my first or second cruise, in which cruise he and I had been shipmates.

We were but one day returned, which is to say, we had enjoyed that modicum of refreshment and rest, (after the wild debauchment of our first night ashore), to prepare us to begin our leave and dissipation in considered earnest.

We had begun drinking, awaiting that critical mass of friends, or onset of inspiration, which would give a theme or direction to the evening's romp. As others came, we caught but the tag-end of a conversation, one saying, "... which is to say she takes everything lying down," to which my friend, his face happily signaling the onset of a witticism, replied, "What is she, a prostitute … ?"

But the reception of this jest was not the expected peal of laughter he anticipated, but silence. For the jest's recipient's face had, and I assure you it is not a figment of speech, turned ashen-white. And he began to tremble. He then mastered himself, nodded to his companion briefly, and walked out of the pub. His companion bowed to us, frankly, and asked where we could be found later in the evening, and I discovered myself the second in a duel.

It is the second's primary job to dissuade his principal from continuation of the quarrel—sparing no effort short, of course, of a breach of Honor. It would, that is, be impossible to suggest that the principal lie, flee, or conspire to subvert the rules or to alter the instruments of the duel. It was the job of the second to ensure, both as appurtenant to his principal and to their opponent, that the thing came off with Honor—or, for those who might find the term archaic or the concept ironical as applied to premeditation of murder, that it proceeded fairly.

Direct apology being suggested by myself and rejected by my friend, it was my task to meet with the other second. This I did. Could it not be, I ventured (as my friend and I had decided), that the offended party might accept a general statement of regret over the horrible but accidental conjunction of his statement and my friend's bon mot? No, I was told; it had been decided such would not do. As no countersuggestions were forthcoming, I proceeded to my first, and then my second prepared retrenchments; first, that my friend, unaware that one had been speaking of his wife, had made, perhaps, an error of *taste*, but not of *Honor*, and that he would confess the same to that party which had witnessed it or, indeed, to any group which might approximate the same.

This, too, was rejected; the only acceptable alternative that my friend confess, in the place of the affront, that he had, at the time of the utterance, been drunk.

I returned with this démarche, but it was, as I knew it would most probably be, rejected. For my friend had *not* been drunk. And he reasoned that such a false admission could be employed only to defraud, and, so, to escape danger.

This was the Officers' code: that it was acceptable to lie to a woman, to be vague, or, indeed, *misleading*, in matters of business, but one could not lie, by commission or omission, to a fellow Officer.

Do these Talmudic rules and customs seem absurd? Are they absurd? They are, *in petit*, a reduction of the laws and customs of diplomacy, and their purpose is the same: to attempt to mediate in the shadow of the ultima ratio regio: to prevent violence.

The French progression of propos, démarche, avis, bordereau, et cetera, leaves to the entity both armed and jealous of its autonomy, space and room for maneuver, and consideration; and, like the progress of a seduction, time for assessment of the other's intention, and the ability, should it be necessary, to reform one's own whilst preserving face.

It is a healthy process, and necessary in the affairs of State, in those of the boudoir, whose fluctuating balance of power mirrors that of diplomacy, and in the Code Duello, which, unsurprisingly, treats of the concerns of the two. For most duels deal with sex, or aspersions against Honor, which, again reduced, may be found to be but accusations of unmanliness.

Was the affair absurd? Certainly. At least to the extent that sex is absurd, and in much the same way; as, though to those uninvolved the actions might seem risible, to the participants it was, in both theme and form, a matter of pomp and weight. Which is to say that of course it was absurd. And it was tragic. Was there that about it which was noble? Yes. Courage is noble. Though in a bad cause it can be tragic, it is not the less laudable as a victory of will. Which is, of course, why the duel was countenanced, though unofficially, in the Navy.

The choice of weapons fell to the injured party, who elected pistol; the choice of the ground to me. After a night spent in negotiation and preparation, we four, the two duelists and their seconds, convened at a waste space beyond the Naval Hospital which had been advised as a safe recourse for affairs of this sort. This triangular field was shielded from the road by a high wall, and from the Hospital by a thick stand of birch. The third side gave upon a view of the harbor.

In the duel, does the necessity of furtiveness mirror that of the sexual act? In each, we find the attempt to mask shame or to ensure privacy for indulgence.

Why was the other officer intent on taking offense at a comment of which, in truth, the worst that could be said of it was that it was boorish—of that boorishness which must have deserved some mitigation, as all understood it to be the product of the unbearably high spirits of one returned intact from the War, a comment the offended might easily have elected not to have heard?

But lust, desire, and self-love are not reasonable. And it is generally not these defects but the mistaken belief to the contrary which brings us to grief. For there is, I think, usually, an instant of warning feeling, counseling, if not restraint, then that best advice of a friend, a moment for "reconsideration," allowing the blood to cool.

We seconds stood, each on one end of the line in the earth we had previously drawn. We bowed to each other, and returned, each, to our principals with the formal last request for resolution, which, in each case denied, signaled the moment for the principals to come to the line, and receive their pistols and instructions. The duel, ensuing, unfolded as described in the first novel, as between Captain Marrion and Flechette, diverging only that in the actual event both participants died.

.   .   .

My father was a country lawyer. He tried to instill in me the virtues of thrift, conservatism, and respect for property.

This study was, to my young self, oppressive. I have decided that such experience is not uncommon, for the young, though perhaps accepting on faith such verities, can find in them no fascination. How great was my joy, then, to find, as I have found in my several endeavors, not only license but the necessity of the opposite view.

This is, of course, the criminal view. He is not ignorant either of the laws nor of the general benefit of their implementation. He is happy both that such laws, in his estimation, do not apply to him, and that their general observance by those under the conviction of their sway, makes his job the easier.

How much more applicable this description to the military man, whose profession is, in sum, to kill or destroy. The nice may cavil that our task is, more benignantly, to project the *threat* of force, and by so doing, to keep the peace. This suggestion, though supportable, is to the mind of the combatant an unwonted sophistry.

"The plenipotent cry of 'license,' whereby the penultimate whispered pleas of conscience may be stilled, is known to be sometimes heeded by the criminal mind; not so the clarion call of Duty." So begins a feuilleton passed to me through my publishers, upon the reissuance of my novels. The attached note suggests that my "romanticization of war" has "corrupted the fibre of the impressionable reader," which I understand to mean the young.

But Man is a fighting animal.

My father's profession of attorney is but a pacifist reduction of physical combat; for which all Honor. For any conflict which may be actually resolved short of a trial of arms should be so resolved. It is to that end and by that means that civilization has progressed.

But after all such possible resolutions as by law, diplomacy, negotiation, patience, or plebiscite, there rests that unresolved remnant of disputes which may be concluded only by the surrender or death of one of the litigants.

When to fight? When to warn? When to restrain? These deep questions rest, in our modern world, upon the shoulders not of the wisest, nor, unfortunately, of the best of men, but upon politicians.

Our political life has veered, over the last age, toward the Democratic. Concomitantly, the Political Profession has attracted, increasingly, those possessing both the power to sway the mob and to delay the discovery of their essential careerism. I am not unaware that this is and has been the plaint of the Military since the dawn of the profession. One may long for the councils of Ancient Greece, where the electors themselves were the combatants, and no war was fought but that which they had deemed worthy of endorsement with their own blood. But the lot of the professional soldier and sailor is, no less than that of the politician, a fact of our modern life. And in the two careers, we see a bifurcation of that tribal ideal—for today the man who fights is no longer he who decides to fight. And just as the profession of politics will attract (inter alia) the demagogue, the sophisticate, the temporizer, so that of the warrior calls the aggressive, and the bellicose, for one must want to fight. And these essentially competitive men may improve or display their skills only in war. How then may they, in truth, be supposed to pray for peace?

Thus, the warrior is possessed of a secret unsharable with those outside his clan, and, therefore, seeks out his own. This he must do just as any profession or group insulated by experience from the general sententiousness.

The surgeon, at a supper, shies from new acquaintances, who may be fascinated, as are we all, by the forbidden and unknown. They are too apt to quiz him about hidden, morbid aspects of his craft. He is happier among his own. As is the Officer.

The experienced combatant will consider the gap between his conduct and the aphorisms of his youth. He will weigh his behavior against the principles of his Church, and the unreasoned cant of the noncombatant, and will find their scholism impertinent. For his problem is deeper and more interesting than their polar reductions, good and evil; wise and unwise; self-interested or noble. It is not enough for him to hear that he fights for Christ—if he should, that is his own concern; or that he fights for Duty or for Country—though he may in total faith and truth fight for all these.

Both the reductionist questions, and those assurances which are merely their inversion, are, to the combatant, an affront. For he makes his pact not with the Church, or Christ, neither with his Country, but with an older god. He gives this life in secret bond. He has paid the price for circumspection. The particularities of his bond are sealed to the uninitiated. They may be shared only with the similarly sworn, who, like the similarly grieved, are the sole possible source of comfort.

·   ·   ·

What is the Organ of Apprehension? We say it is the mind, but what is the mind?

What are the processes which can be known—which is to say, which are predictable? For everything rests, at some level, on our acceptance of a mystery, beyond which point we are incapable of or uninterested in further explanation.

The mechanical predictability of the process whereby heat may boil water is sufficient for both the householder and the savage; the thermodynamical principles sufficient for the physicist; and the invocation of God, sufficient to the mystic or philosopher celebrating the final unknowability of all things; which last might say, "What do we *mean* when we assert that 'water boils'?"

The sophist and the chemist each has his sticking point, and the assertion that so do we all, is merely the exercise of his particular discipline by the Cynic.

What "can be known"? Empirically, only those things the operation of which may be *predicted*, which is to say "already known." Pursuit of anything in excess of this is generally called folly and occasionally prophecy.

What is the Organ of Apprehension? It is the Mind. This is tautology.

The Writer is engaged, better, *locked*, in a dialogue with his mind. Is the mind, then, two things? All common speech proclaims it: "I was of two minds"; "I could not make up my mind"; "I was out of my mind." Here we find the opposed, "I" and "my mind," and, further, the adjudicating principle, which frames (if it does not control) the conflict, for the benefit of a *fourth* entity, which is the ever-present audience for which we perform our miserable play. And I will go no further. For what is the mind? It is that organ with which we think. And what is thought? That most precious adaptive mechanism separating us from the beasts? Perhaps (though the interested, hunters, horsemen, et cetera, are all, in our hearts, convinced that the animals share with us some mental ability) one might characterize the same merely as "instinct," but I would suggest that the same proviso is equally supportable applied to Man.

My life, in my various careers, has been an occupation with folly. In my service to my Government to capitalize upon or to induce such in the enemies of my Country; as a writer to mold my experience of such into several entertainments.

I have seen a man, demonstrating to a group of Cadets, the correct operation of a Mortar, in attempting to discern the cause of a hangfire, stick his head into the Mortar tube, and have it removed.

I have seen colleagues chain themselves to partners, paramours, and spouses the unsuitability, nay, the outright vicious malevolence of whom was evident to the most casual observer; I have seen wise, excellent women link themselves, time after time, to the dissolute; and a friend wager the fruits of a decade's labor on the turn of a card, which all *knew* to be marked. I have seen my beloved Country squander life, treasure, and reputation in halfhearted attempts to accomplish goals which neither those then in power nor History could describe with any clarity.

·   ·   ·

We are soothed by it, we are nourished by it, we are enchanted and provoked, we are killed by it. But we are neither bored nor disillusioned by the Sea. And we account all errors in our mutual intercourse with it as our own. For what was unknown? Nothing save the new revelation of our own powerlessness, inattention, weakness, or folly.

Captain Marrion, like many of the men with whom I was privileged to

serve, and unlike myself, never complained; further, he, again in contradistinction to myself, never philosophized (which may be but an attempt to
diplomatize confusion or affront *within* the mind). He was depicted as bluff,
hearty, and all the adjectives attendant on a virile, laudable self-image, and, so,
intended to appeal to the Reader. He appeals to me. Had I my life to live over,
I would *be* Captain Marrion. The vehemence of this wish accounts, I believe,
in large measure, for the success of the novels.

My gift and its cost are one: a long life. But I do not complain; I merely note
the co-identity of the two, the conviction of which increases with age.

.   .   .

Upon my emergence from anonymity, I was asked, by the Press, what, in my
experience, had I the power, I would change. I found the question provocative,
not as it pertained to history, but in its ability to reveal my understanding of
the nature of Power. For my review (not vouchsafed to the Press, but conducted in seclusion, and over some time), discovered to me that I would, had I the
power, change not those occurrences of fortune, but only my own behavior.
Thus, I found, I was, (at least as pertinent to the Past), a stoic. I conveyed my
discovery to Margaret. She smiled, as at the beloved folly of the young—not
for their *choice*, but for their occupation with the otiose.

.   .   .

The Southern exposure of our home gives on the Sea.

My study, which Margaret had built, soon after the acquisition of the house,
has the Southern view; so that, should I turn from my desk, I would see the
Sea, the location of which my wife pointed out to me. For "I have never seen
you," she said, "turned away from your desk, and its prospect of the paneled
wall."

My "prospect," I explained to her, was not the wall, but the notebook before me. To her credit, she accepted her rebuke with an appropriate spirit of
humility, for the half-second before erupting in laughter, which, after some
intervening moments of umbrage, I could not but share.

.   .   .

My study cannot be accessed from the house, for my wife had so instructed the builder. She left its decoration, as was only right, to me. I have adorned it with my sword, and with three Maritime paintings.

Many have painted the sky and its various conformations and moods; and many have painted, with equal accomplishment, a ship—a ship at anchor, a ship in a storm, on a beach; an action, or a shipwreck; but few have *accurately* painted the water. I do not mean the breaker, the wave, the surf, or the swell, but the Sea itself.

Many asked why I had chose to conclude the Captain's adventures with the third book, and why, having so chosen, I closed the novel with his death. The answer to the second question is, of course, to ensure my resolution in the first case.

Why, I was asked, not, then, leave the reader with some more romantic, if less conclusive, termination? Why not, for example, have the Captain marry? But, lest we augh, let us observe that though the suggested conclusion, as applied to one's actual existence, must be construed as an unpleasant sarcasm, it is an accepted, in fact, universal, resolution of the Romance.

Now, to invert these observations, and so, in the words of Heraclitus, "to discover, thus, perchance, some more essential relation," is it not clear that the standard fictional resolution of Marriage, is, with Death, an equally abrupt and irreversible conclusion to the genre? It must be, for it implies, and all know it implies, "And there ensued no further adventures."

This, of course, is women's view, evident to them from childhood, their universal task, in Marriage, to disguise or make palatable to their mate the captive nature of his newfound state.

"And they lived happily ever after," the fable concludes. And, indeed, some do. I am one who has. I have enjoyed, with my wife, connubial bliss marred only by those naturally occurring changes lightened by our partnership.

But, in fiction, the phrase, as a termination, is employed to mean "Wish for no more—the tale is done."

I was also entreated, during the series' course, to allow the Captain to wed—suggestions for a spouse running heavily toward the Comtesse LaCombe. I demurred. For the art of fiction must be, again, compared to a seduction, which flourishes most healthily in being thwarted, and in which conquest must result in that disappointment attendant upon the completion of any ardent task. This is the difference between a seduction and a courtship.

.   .   .

A magical effect is a seduction. The viewer pleads to be taught its mechanics; but should the magician be persuaded, the trick, he, and his profession fall forever into scorn, and will be recalled but with disappointment. More neat for the Captain to marry. More cleanly for him to die. And better. And I will tell you why: consider two beloved friends, one who has married and the other passed away. Of whom does one think more often?

There is nothing interesting in Marriage. If happy, it can entertain none but the conjoined pair; if otherwise, it is to the observing world boring and sordid, and they to be at all costs shunned.

All things must die. I, and you, if we are of an age, recur, at intervals, to this or that dear friend, forever gone, and find them fixed, and unchanged in memory. We remember as the golden youth that friend who, had he lived, would, my coeval, find himself at the end of life bent and altered by its course. Or we recall that mentor, or preceptor, who formed us, preserved in our thoughts as a perfect Sage, at that age which is to us now, that of a very young man; who, had we known him better, must have been found to have contained any variety of faults. And what of those memory preserves as generous and perfect young girls, whose youth and beauty exist now but in our thoughts?

But this is too lugubrious. Let us stay only to answer the question: Why did the Captain die? All men die. He is thus preserved. Death is cessation of change. Only the dead do not change.

.   .   .

I will not confess that the pipe which burnt the ship was mine. It was not mine. And it was not I who skewed the drawing-for-straws when our captors required a victim; nor I who made the first cut into the body of the Swedish sailor. These, however, rather than the many acts of which I bear the guilt, haunted me in the Galleys.

They speak dismissively of delusion who have not experienced it, and of the odd duality of believing a thing to be true and knowing oneself mad.

I heard a speaker in the Park one Sunday proclaim his self-confected gospel, which, in reduction, was "People are Everywhere the Same." Youth love the radical doctrines, as such are, in contradistinction to the nature of the world, comprehensible. But even in my youth, absent experience, I dismissed the speaker's doctrine as unlikely.

My first voyages confirmed my insight, and I concluded that not Race but Culture will determine, if not a foreign group's morality, then, say, its acceptability in our Western eyes. With some groups we were friendly; with others not. It is not the job of the Navy to make friends, but to act upon orders issued (rightly or wrong) in our Country's interest. This group, then, was avaricious, that sullen, and the other tractable. Not, again, in general, but in light of our objects, and why reason further?

This view, though historically decried by that aspect of the polity fashioning themselves, variously, Whigs, Social Thinkers, Humanists, or the good-at-heart, was accepted by the readership of my novels, some of which second group must have contained members of the first. For novels are accepted as they accord, on some level, with either our consciously held, or our more basic, understanding of the way of Life, which is that Our Life is a story, and that stories have a Villain.

In *The Raven*, the despised villain, for all the intermittence of the Corsairs, the Arabs, and the French, (and even more than Doctor Brandt,) is, finally, the "man of no known or discernible nationality," La Frenette.

Why is he so described? Or, rather, how, taking an analytic view, might one account for my spontaneous (for such it was) characterization of him as stateless?

I believe it was to indicate that he was without that factor mitigating actions of *all* men—connection to the Group. His lack of loyalty afforded him scope, both in object and operation, for he was limited by no National interest (for, as the novels are historical, they must either conform to political facts or plausibilities, or risk rejection as false) nor convention of National *character*: Dutchmen being placid, the French womanly, Germans warlike. But the Man Without a Country is free of all restraints—much like the Writer or the Spy.

As I have said, it was suggested, when my identity became known, that Captain Marrion was my self-portrait. This I understood to be an expression of thanks from a diverted readership. Later intellectual dissection of the novels (for such, for a time, existed) held that the author must be an amalgam of the Captain and his Nemesis—a bold application of the truism that No Man Is All of a Piece.

But I believe I am more of a piece than most. After years of review and self-examination, I have come near to concluding that I have no conscience, and I hold short of the complete, unadorned admission from fear not of hell but of self-dramatization.

.   .   .

I was tortured, in confinement, by a dream.

In the Bible, God admonishes the Israelites, warning them that, should they reject His teachings, they will be so afflicted that "during the day they will pray, 'If only it were evening,' and at night, 'If only it were day.'" This description could only have been written by one who had been mad.

In my dream it *was* I who left the still-burning pipe upon the faked-down line. It was I who killed the Swedish sailor, and I who gave the captive to the scimitar. This dream became a delusion, that is, an incradicable, consciously held belief demonstrably in variance to reality. The dream-delusion occupied me, through the various years of my imprisonment, 'til I began to shrink from Human contact. The experiences narrated of the kind interactions in the Cell, of conversations, reminiscences, of the age-old expedient of the imprisoned teaching, each by turns, his skill or knowledge to his brothers, these, as related in *The Raven*, did occur. But I did not participate. For I was mired in a mixture of terror and self-abomination which is both suggested and recalled by the words of the Scripturalist.

.   .   .

One reposes full confidence in the accuracy of one's watch until the force of circumstance convinces one of the contrary. The cuckolded husband, similarly, is brought to the conclusion of his wife's guilt, not through her behavior—it is axiomatic that he will be the last to know. This is to say that absent the suspicion of guilt, those actions which will later be adduced as glaring proofs will not present themselves to the attention. Inversely, the suspicion of guilt once inculcated, the most neutral behaviors will be understood as criminal.

This is the subject, of course, of one of Shakespeare's plays. It is also the effective mechanism of our Trial by Jury. Here, the prosecution, whatever the law may state, exploits the presumption of guilt, supporting its position by the particularization of circumstance which, absent that presumption, would possibly escape the eye. The Defense, however, like the slandered wife, is reduced to reliance on the Presumption of Innocence, which presumption, though touted in our laws, has been abrogated by the accusation.

Thus, the Defense, in a trial, as in an actual contest of arms, is constrained by the very mechanism upon which it supposedly relies (the defenders of a Fort may exploit nothing but the Fort); and the disadvantage of the wrongfully accused is greater than that of his guilty brother, for as defenders of a Fort are tied to that Fort, the innocent accused is tied to the truth; while his guilty brother, the Prosecutor, and the fort's attackers are gifted with the freedom to improvise. These are free not only to pick and choose among the facts, or even to color, slant, and organize them to their benefit, but, should these stratagems prove insufficient, not only to suggest, but also to invent circumstances happier to their cause. There is a theoretical limit beyond which they may not go in their dramatizations, but the line between actual truth and perjury is so broad as to have both spawned and, for millennia, supported a complete profession dedicated to its exploitation.

With what do the Attorneys deal? The inculcation, exploitation, or refutation of suspicion. I have both witnessed, and participated in, many terrible, sordid, and tragic things; but the libel trial, attendant on the publication of *The Death of Marrion* taught me to understand the phrase "It broke his heart."

This is not to say that I learnt from it self-pity (of which accomplishment, I fear, I had long been a dedicated student); for what, in fine, is a Writer, save he be a Poet Laureate, if not a master of complaint?

A Sad Tale, we are told, is best for Winter. And as the Howling Storm calls for strong, sympathetic liquor, so complaint eases the ancient heart. But the gross insult of the libel suit was its injury not to my self-esteem, but to my estimation of the World.

.   .   .

I have not often encountered, nor often expressed, gratitude. I, like each man, value my own deserts too high. I believe such is universal, save in those neurasthenics who delight in self-abasement. Bravery I have observed and wondered at—its appearance so common as to suggest a reassessment of the worth of man; and Piety, which often expresses itself not only in physical courage, but in submission and forbearance, which, in the catalogue of excellence, must rank, if not Bravery's equal, then something much like it.

But these, courage, forbearance, and submission, may be understood in reference to an Abstract Idea, viz., the State, or One's God, whereas Gratitude must have as its object, finally, a mere man like oneself, its discharge, therefore, suggesting, reciprocally, a lack of worth in the recipient. (I do not speak of the Performance or Impersonation of a sense of indebtedness, but of its actual conviction. This I find rare to the point of being near the stuff of legend.)

The antiquated libel laws of my country, an acquaintance with which I have gained at some cost, prohibit me from methods more direct than allusion in relieving the reader, should he possess such, of ignorance of the more major facts and personages of my Case. I hope the circumlocutions here implied, coupled with that which I understand to be the current state of my onetime persecutors, may render this account harmless to myself. For the spiteful weak, once having discovered litigiousness, are not unlike that horse which has learned to kick—neither will abandon activity productive both of amusement and a sense of power.

In any case, here is the truth. The causus belli, that which both occupied and diminished my treasure, my time, and my health—the first recouped, the second and third now beyond recovery—that which marked and precipitated my withdrawal from the production of literature, from that time to this, may be found in the third and last Marrion novel, in the tale of the Reduction of Mont-Michel. Here I employed, as has many another author, the device of the Tale on the Eve of Battle.

There is this in the writing of Historical Fiction: the impulse grows upon that which it creates, sparking diversions, divagations, and fantasia of days different not only from the Present of the Writer, but from that in which the novel's primal fantasy is set, the Writer becoming intoxicated with his power to abrogate Time.

So I, on the eve of Marrion's Engagement at the Straits, picture him listening to the story of a still-more-ancient war, told, as it has been since the time of Homer, by the Old Soldier—here appearing as "The Bosun's Tale," which, though the speaker was not, in the novel, described as of that rank, is the name by which the story became known during the Trial.

The Captain's thoughts are occupied in consideration of a stratagem which might allow him to force the Straits. He walks the quarterdeck. The Old Sailor is yarning in the gangway below. His voice carries to the quarterdeck, and Brown descends to beg him to be still. But the Captain, whose peace Brown has been protecting, intervenes, and asks the Old Sailor to continue his story.

In the book as revised, which is to say in all except the first edition, the Old Sailor pulls his forelock and replies that, rather than disturb the one man "whose conjectures alone might, nay shall, enable us to Take the Straits, I would as lief ..."; here he supplies several oaths, attesting to his belief in the powers of the Captain. In the first (suppressed) edition, however, the Old Sailor continues:

"There was a lad from the marshy country to the South of Essex. He'd heard the Drum as a lad, and had been with his Colonel since that enlistment, which was, one year since, as the Colonel's servant. In that time, the lad had never spoke a word, save: 'Yes, sir,' 'No, sir,' or, 'By your leave, sir,' which were the three responses taught him at the drum head. And no one knew whether to credit their exclusive use as the boy's totality of speech, as love of duty, fear of punishment, or, indeed, mere stupidity. For that is all he said. But his work was good, which is to say the Colonel found it unexceptionable.

"This Colonel had been ordered at all costs, to take the hill before which they now found themselves encamped. This hill was dominated by the enemy's cannon, which were situated in an old Church. This, by its height and setting, was impervious to our own fire; and as our cannon could not be brought to bear, our infantry could not advance, and there the matter stood.

"The Colonel could settle upon no scheme alternative to the crossing, under plunging fire, of the field beneath the Hill. Here lay the problem: skirmishers might, in darkness, cross the field, but the reduction of the Church could only take place if our cannon might, similarly, be brought across the field, and, so, to bear upon the Heights. It might be possible for these few skirmishes to cross the field in stealth and to subdue outlying pickets, but how, (this was the Colonel's sticking point,) might one, in stealth and silence, move the cannon?

"The lumbering and creaking of the cannon was the point. Various remedies of improvised carriage were suggested, each, of course, resting on the fallacy that an elaboration of machinery might move the thing more silently than those two wheels which were the inspiration of the engineers of old.

"Here the boy spoke up: 'Lash a crate of frogs to the limber,' he said, 'and conceal the one sound with the other.'"

Readers of the third novel not in possession of its first edition have not read this page, as, after having been excised from subsequent editions, the first printing was recalled as part of the settlement

I would have thought the passage inoffensive, but my views were not shared by that gentleman who found in it an oblique reference, he thought, to his behavior under fire.*

The passage was in no way intended as a reference to his courage. The incident to which he convinced the Court it referred, while prominent in his memory, was absent in mine from the time of its occurrence (onboard *The Redwing*) 'til its excrudescence in the lawsuit.

He brought suit. I remembered, then, his behavior on the brig. He was, in fact, a coward. I state it here, and regret, only, that I did not proclaim it at the trial. I was advised—to employ those saddest of words—that the issue at stake was not the man's behavior, but *mine*, and I accepted the advice; the fault, upon its acceptance, becoming mine.

I learned, and I paid for the lesson, that the weak, too, must live, that they live upon the strong, under our protection or sufferance, and that just as a martial opponent, or indeed, any animal, will lie in wait to exploit an inattention, those of the weak who yearn for Power, will wait and scheme, and, lacking the martial virtues or the animal abilities, will, as they must, exploit the weaknesses which their opponent does not understand as such. I would like, in my case, to name such "Honor." The lesson of the case, however, taught me to name it "Inattention."

A prisoner schemes, fantasizes, and remembers. He recalls past amours, he reimagines the circumstances of his capture to a happier conclusion, and he plots revenge. These, in totality, are the mental play of the child, and, indeed, the prisoner becomes a child—his danger, in reposing in his captors, as does the unhappy adolescent in his parents, that dual sense of hatred and indebtedness which will link him to them forever.

---

* At this writing, I am informed, this man is failing; at the publication, I have been assured, he will be gone.

It is to avoid this that a prisoner's Code of Conduct is found in every modern force of arms. This code, which we Officers strove to enforce, and our captors to break, might be reduced to this: the loss of the ship, and capture, in no way whatever lessens the force of the Articles of War.

I hope this was a comfort to those men over whom, though a fellow captive, (in the galley, and on land), I strove to maintain discipline. I know my lot was easier than theirs. For they, in accepting that which, after all, was, though a useful fiction, still a fiction, were held in that same thrall which characterized their service upon ship; such, though, I believe was comforting.

Yes, the crew might find death at the hands of the Turk, but they could find it equally in battle—the lash was the lash, whether applied by friend or foe; and the ultimate horror, torture, might be avoided by a recourse to Death.

The sailor, then, might be comforted by a belief in a continuation of our original Hierarchy—and his belief made it so. But we Officers knew it to be a fiction. We continued the same for the benefit of the men, and, in so doing, I suppose, found comfort in performance of our Duty. And, we of course, continued in the satisfaction, common to all Officers, of the superiority conferred by our Commission. (The more worthy, down through time, have, inspired by this low thought, supplanted it with an increased sense of duty. But the thought itself is there, pursuit of superiority to one's own nature replacing, in the good Officer, the Martinet's celebration of his autocracy.)

.   .   .

There are aspects of the lives of martial men which, though on first acquaintance might appear odd, a protracted intimacy will reveal if not as a usual, then at least as an acknowledged variation of the type.

I speak of the transformation from a man of war to a servant of God.

I do not instance that near-universal enlightenment attendant upon the fear of death. A time under unanswered bombardment will occasion impassioned confessions, as does another impassioned activity occasion oaths— such understood to be other than binding (absent the provocation) not only by the confessor, but (though she may deny the knowledge) by the oath's recipient, who, in the case of Woman as with that of God, may be presumed to accept an impassioned vow as mere song, and without belief in its fulfillment.

There are vows, however, which are made upon consideration, and are pleas not for intercession, but for acceptance.

All men are changed by war. Some, I will not say "for," but "toward," the Good.

A friend from my Naval days was as complete a specimen of warrior as one could hope to meet. He spent his life in pursuit of mastery of the various aspects of his profession: seamanship, gunnery, navigation, strategy, and a deep perusal not only of the operations of the winds and tides but of their relation to the movements of men, which last study served him not only in his first, but in his second career, which was that of a Priest. The Good Commander, he said, must master the mechanical in order to free his mind to contemplate the ineffable. He cannot approach either tactics or the psychology of command, until he has mastered seamanship. Just so the Priest, by application to practical skills,* prepares his mind for dealing not only with the vagaries of man, but for contemplation of the Divine.

"It was of the greatest aid to me," he said, "that I had been, until an advanced age, a convinced sinner."

"Do not we all sin?" I asked.

He said of course we do, but he had taken the task seriously. To this I attest, presenting in evidence my recollection of a night in an Annamite Seraglio.

This word, in the East, has not that sordid connotation which assaults our Western sensibilities; for the practices which with us are furtive are, many of them, indulged elsewhere as a matter of course, their practice occasioning neither shame nor comment.

We were in port, and granted leave. The wisdom of the Gun Room suggested the establishment in question, and thither my friend and I repaired—our brother Officers still occupied aboard ship, in discharge of these last harbor duties from which my friend and I, by reason of seniority, had been excused.

Previous visitors to the port had advised us to place both our affairs and our purse in the hands of a Docent or Dragoman familiar to the squadron. And this, coming ashore, we did. His attitude had nothing about it of the procurer, and neither by an assumed air of confederacy nor by a sur-politesse did he convey to us a sense of our errand's singularity. This gratifying frankness,

---

* He instanced theology, doctrine, homiletics, and exegesis.

I must say, I have found in so many another Turk that I am tempted to understand it as a National characteristic. Such, like many another trait both national and personal, may be understood as good or bad depending on its application. I remarked it in its other form when, in captivity, I detected in this same group, now my oppressors, neither remorse nor consciousness of viciousness, although they tortured me.

This Dragoman, hearing the name of the establishment suggested, seconded the Gun Room's endorsement. We entrusted him, each, with our funds, and received his offer of a receipt with what our demurrer revealed as a, to him, usual if nonetheless appreciated gallantry upon the client's part.

He explained to us the customs of the house to which we were bound—that we had but to instruct him as to our desires, and he would, then, both communicate them and negotiate their price with the proprietor. Or, he suggested, we could leave the evening's entertainment entirely in his hands. For which suggestion my friend and I were both grateful.

The evening marked my first experience not only of opium, but of various practices I would suggest best left to imagination, were I not convinced of that organ's inequality to the endeavor.

Our "evening" occupied, in the event, eleven days, being both the whole of our stay, and a superaddition to our leave. It exhausted not only our cash, but that of the party of shipmates who eventually discovered us—and much of their credit, too.

We were returned to the ship in disgrace, having only through the silent exertions of the Quartermaster, been carried on the books as "present," and, thus, spared the disgrace of indictment for desertion.

My friend ended the adventure with a fine scar on his forehead, and with the blood on his hands of a local Gendarme who had been enlisted to aid in our attempted transportation to the Ship. He was removed from the ship and held at the house of our Consul, for a promised castigation by that man upon his soon-expected return. A threatened prosecution for mayhem was forestalled only by a further tax upon our fellow Officers, and a precipitously accelerated date of departure. This advanced date of sailing truncated our provisioning, and left us short, notably, of that spare chronometer the possession of which might have satisfied those buccaneers I have alluded to.

.   .   .

My memories of opium are happy; my second experience was of the anesthetic, for which gift I thank the gods. And my first is forever linked by my experience, whether extraordinary in itself, or only through the heightening effect of the drug, (I cannot say,) of the Seraglio, and, thus, with the man whom, decades hence, I rediscovered as a Priest.

I remember him, that night in Hanoi, his eyes blazing, his naked skin covered in sweat and oil, wrapped in a yellow silk shirt, lit by the many low candles burning in red glass, shouting his release from all strictures and cursing God, cursing God.

He did not share in that continued cruise which eventuated in our capture. There were, in fact, twenty-five years and twelve thousand miles between that night and our next meeting.

I would never have recognized him but for the scar. There was a stooped, thin man in late middle age, a Roman Priest in a much-worn black suit. He turned on his examiner, he beamed, he held out his hands and called my name.

The evening which we spent together was occupied both by my joy in our mutual rediscovery and my curiosity as to his transformation.

When the meal had been taken away, when we had lighted cigars, he leant back and shrugged, as if to excuse a necessarily insufficient explanation. "I found God," he said.

.   .   .

I will tell you that even those ignorant of and uninterested in Astronomy must come, after a lengthy stay exposed to them, to an extended study of the Stars. One observes, over the month, a correlation not only between the Moon and the Waters, but between the Moon and Man. For Man does grow restive or docile in conjunction, if not in response, to the movements of the Moon. And incipient Madness, if it shows itself, will do so at the full.

Human life, likewise, ebbs with the tide, and a man, however near death, who survives the morning may be counted on to persist at least until the evening ebb. The creatures of the Sea arrange their migrations according to the quarter of the Moon; and the infinite conjunctions of the Moon and Stars, ruling the play both of water and of wind, the path of the fish, and the moods of Man, may, I believe, be at no great leap said to control even our fate.

This encapsulation I was surprised to find first put forth not by an Astrologer or Necromancer, but by my friend the Priest. It was these observations, he said, which led him to God. For men, he said, like the Stars, are predictable, and it is the same Power that makes them so.

"Most," I suggested, "call upon this knowledge but to manipulate."

"Yes," he said. "Men being predictable, some exploit this knowledge for various ends."

"And do you not?" I asked.

He shook his head. "A man fallen overboard," he said, "will swim toward a thrown lifeline. Would you indict the man who throws it as manipulative?"

I asked if he could tell me what had brought him to his conviction. It must have been a matter of sudden revelation. Was it not? He thought for the longest while, and then, with infinite politeness, shrugged in a manner compounded of courtesy and pity, which I on reflection recognized as having last seen in the Dragoman.

•   •   •

The girl Taya practiced that Religion endemic to the Islands. I do not know its name, nor, indeed, what such knowledge would signify should I possess it. The Islanders' attitude toward worship was much like their attitude toward sex—it was a simple part of life. How different from our practice, which strives to demythologize the first, while making of the last a mystery.

But there was that most provocative about their observances. I will relate what I saw, though I can, I fear, contribute but little to its understanding. Its essence seemed to be the custom or practice of "Taboo."

This was the systematic exclusion of an object, place, utterance, or, in the last instance, individual from consideration. We have the phrase "sent to Coventry," or Banishment, which may begin to convey—in nature, never in extent or virulence—this excommunication which constituted the essential aspect of their spiritual practice.

I have witnessed such behavior in the Naval Wardroom. Here Officers are reduced in their intercourse to their own society, its members few, and those few mired exclusively with each other for months or years. The *social* commerce of these few (as opposed to the Professional) is further restricted to the Wardroom, or Gun Room, which is both their shared habitation and their Club.

Here, good humor, or, better, circumspection is the iron rule; for the least slight, real or perceived, once cherished, may mature into immutable hatred, and, indeed, to homicide.

My observation of Island Taboo led me to meditate upon its practice in the wider world. This is a great benefit of travel, for those mechanisms found among the Aborigines may well be discovered, differing only in form, in polite society—how otherwise, for human nature must be everywhere the same. The forms of observance will change, as they have developed, each, in response to the particularities of local stimulus—the Islanders' understanding of sex, for example, being shaped, of necessity, by that virtual nakedness demanded by the climate; their particular fatalism a product of their helplessness before the Tsunami (their Tidal Wave), volcano, or typhoon.

In later years, I met a man who, as a young officer, had been upon the island of Kumaii during the Great Tsunami.

He and a small crew had come ashore in his ship's launch. In the afternoon, the Sea receded in a freak tide, leaving their boat beached up some hundred yards. The new-uncovered shingle was carpeted not only with dying marine life, but with the detritus of ages. Flotsam and jetsam, long submerged, now lay open to the eye. And some of it sparkled.

The boat's crew, at liberty, began combing the beach, attracted by those Treasures which would prove but the old nail, fastening, or ship's fitting. None-theless, having been granted by the Watch this temporary respite, their time was their own, and the Officer looked upon their antics with indulgence. This holiday, though indeed harmless, was not without cost, for they lost their lives thereby.

How was their Officer saved? Through curiosity. He alone, standing, as he must, aloof from their depredations, had the leisure to observe that the local inhabitants had, one and all, abandoned the beach, their occupations there-upon, and their homes, and were hurrying, en masse, toward the Island's high point, whither he accompanied them out of curiosity, and where he found himself when the tidal wave struck.

The rapid or freak ebb of the Sea was not unknown to the mariners who stayed behind. Those who had not experienced it had heard of it. Though exceptional, it was no occasion for alarm. I have seen it myself. How, then, I asked the survivor, or by what portent had the Islanders known to flee?

This question having, to him, more than a theoretical interest, he had posed it, at length, to his fellow survivors. But his knowledge of "South Sea," the lingua franca, though practical, was insufficient to probe the mystery, discussion of which, he explained, partook of the Taboo. These matters were treated by misdirection, their very presence being suggested, at first, only by the ritual avoidance which attended the possibility of their discussion.

A child, for example, might call an elder's attention to a rapid ebb of the tide, and find, on the elder's face, a stolid inattention.

This, the Island child learned, signalized a proximity to Taboo. Of what special purpose this elaborate misdirection? I believe I know. A child is impelled, by his own helplessness, to acquire knowledge of the world. Speech serves the purpose but badly; and, indeed, the infant must find sustenance prior to acquiring the faculty of speech. His main tool is observation.

For the adults to link discussion of an occurrence with shame is to excite in the child, not the need, but the *necessity* of investigation. He must, in order to avoid shame, plumb the limits of the Taboo. (I note that to further ensure the education, the child becomes not only pupil but instructor—the withdrawal of his Elders' interest forcing upon him the necessity of his self-instruction.) He will not forget this lesson; and its primacy having been seared upon his mind by his parents, it will be retained and practiced by him, in later life, as a prime responsibility of parenthood.*

How the two races are alike—that which we call civilized and that savage— bred by our cultures to elaborate, unconscious repetitions of forms; some, like the Taboo, essential, some adventitious, as my own rejection (for I, in age, see that such it was) of my own son. Each are the transmission through performance of an unconsciously acquired idea, than which idea there is none more powerful. For such lie, thus beyond reason, as beyond our knowledge of their existence.

The Islanders, as far as the Officer could learn, were motivated in their

---

* I believe my absences are the cause of much that has befallen my own son, and I may perhaps explain though I cannot excuse my dereliction by reference to my own lack, as a child, of a present father.

retreat from the beach by the intersection of at least two and probably more occurrences, of which the recession of the surf, the most obvious, was, to them, not the most important. *That* signal was the silence, during the dark of the previous Moon, of the Island's birds, which, though insufficient in itself to prompt their exodus, was, when coupled with the sign from the Sea, an ancient herald of the need to pray.

Observe the subtlety of the human mind: the long-transmitted mechanism for survival was linked, in observance, not with safety, but with sanctity; for that Altar, otherwise unused, to which, upon the intersection of the signs, the Village must repair, was on the Island's height of land.

One might describe the characterization of the warning as a "call to prayer" as a useful conceit, or as a savage paganism, but this, I believe, begs the question—for whatever entity or power instituted in Man the ability to frame duties for self-protection in just that way as to ensure their transmission over millennia—could not this power be called "God"?

Devoid of formal Religion and ignorant of the goals, insights, and limits such might bestow, I came to these ruminations too late, I fear, to be of service to my son. I hope, should he come upon this book, that he may accept my confession such that, if not forgiveness, perhaps understanding may somewhat ease those burdens which I have entailed on him.

·　　·　　·

I believe each has his destiny. In some its pull is strong, in some of little consequence, but for each I believe it is written. Some struggle; some submit; the great, perhaps, exult.

Who does not know the kind girl who never seems to marry, or the talented, hardworking soul, forever just balked of success? I differentiate between these phenomena and lack of character. There, the lack of success may be ascribed to a want of resolve or courage. But there is another thing, independent of effort or worth, which force may be called destiny.

I have written of those, in the Navy, whose appearance always signaled some change for the better—a welcome change in the wind, or a moderation of enemy motion. I am aware such observation might be but unwarranted correlation of two observable facts: Fell has come to the bridge, and the Enemy has missed Stays—unconnected but through prejudice of the observer.

But time and again, we see the like: this or that man first to find in the hunt, first to sight game; to have, time after time, divined or guessed correctly on Exchange. And one peculiarity of this "Lucky" man is the lack of rancor or envy which greets his success. For his contemporaries credit it not to any personal trait, the presence of which in him would throw into relief its absence in themselves, but to the operations of the gods, under whose sway we all reside.

The fortunate man, here, is perhaps not unlike that fictional Rich Man of our grandfathers' time, the display of whose excesses was said to delight the Poor.

Some of us are blessed with a profound destiny; and some, so blessed, have declined the honor. Some are Called yet destined to fail, to grieve, to work in vain. Our Religion suggests to those patience, courage, and faith. These, with us, have replaced the sacrifices of the flesh. Perhaps this is progress.

·   ·   ·

The tale of Jonah has, of course, a special resonance for sailors. Our lives are preserved but by a two-inch plank, and the indulgence of God. And the constant reminder of the first enforces a conviction of the second. There are those whose destiny is to destroy. This they seem to do without will or evil intent, and despite their own efforts and benevolence, dogged by bad luck, and linked to catastrophe. Biblical sailors, we are told, cast the so afflicted from their midst, and the Sea was Stilled.

I have alluded to a similar occurrence earlier in this work. It is that incident, depicted in *The Raven* as the cause of the conflagration which brought the ship to grief.

The novel sets the scene upon the quarterdeck. Here Hodges, impressed as arbiter in a discussion of the relative merits of two hunters, leaves his pipe on the taffrail. He comes forward. A lee-lurch sends the pipe into the midst of coiled-down line. Hodges, on leaving his two friends, returns to his pipe and, finding it gone, concludes he must have left it below in his cabin. He goes below, the pipe ignites the rope, the ship burns.

In full truth, the pipe belonged to ———, our second. He was a "hard-horse" much addicted to flogging; and, as is not uncommon, that further, frequently allied exploitation of Power which I shall not here name.

He was, all independent of his character, a Jonah. Given the deck, a turnbuckle would fail, a pin shear, the signal to the Flag be mis-sent, or any of a myriad misfortunes befall, none of which could logically be attributed to his miscredit. But attributed they were. And after each accident or misfortune, the crew, thinking themselves unobserved, would exchange a look communicative of the deepest philosophy.

None of these serial misfortunes could, by the laws of cause-and-effect, be set against him. And yet they were—the justice of such verdict, though never enunciated, shared by all aboard.

The afternoon before the fire, he'd had a man seized up. His crime was "disobedience," particularly "silent insolence," which may be defined as the suspicion, in an Officer, of a foremast hand's insufficient concealment of a disaffected opinion. An accusation of this crime, often the last resort of a bad, exasperated officer, was understood as a display of rage at one's exasperated impotence.

The man was flogged. He was cut down and led away. The day began to wane. The Second Lieutenant had the quarterdeck. And as he strolled, he lighted his pipe. This the crew understood as arrogance. For though the regulations did not absolutely bar the Officer of the Watch from smoking on deck, it was uncustomary. His strolling with the pipe, therefore, was understood to've been done neither absently, nor with a real satisfaction, but to convey, to the crew, a certain nonchalance.

But this portrayal hardened in them the conviction not only that he had done wrong, *but that he knew it*. The verdict against him, then, was raised from incompetence and viciousness, each of which can and will be borne in the name, if not of Duty, then of necessity, to willful evil.

He lighted his pipe and strolled the deck. Darkness fell, and brought with it that apparition familiar to all sailors. This is variously called St. Elmo's Fire, a "Holliman," or a "corpusant." It is an electric fluid, playing, like a localized lightning, around the rigging or masts. It is sometimes congealed into a ball, and landsmen liken it to "ball lightning." In this rather than its more dispersed form, it is called "corpusant," or "Holliman," each indicating attribution to it of a personality or power.*

In its physical effects, it is benign. But its appearance is always both noted

---

* "Corpusant," from "corpus sanctus"; and "Holliman," "Holy Man."

and respected. For the sailor connects with this phenomenon much power of prognostication, and unearthly influence. And, perhaps in gratitude for its general harmlessness, it is accorded this respect aboard ship: it is *never* alluded to.

Here the Lieutenant added sin to crime. For, in his assumption of the form of nonchalance, he apostrophized the fire, speaking not only of but *to* it, as a witness, and suggesting it had come to comfort him in his frosty exclusion from the happy wishes of the crew.

In the boat, after the fire, Fell and I endeavored to reconstruct the story's end. We knew the man had put the pipe down and come forward upon some errand. The next notice of him came, some time later, from the helmsman, who called a request, to which there was no response. A search was instituted, in the midst of which we heard the cry of "Fire." The mystery of his absence was subsumed in the ensuing emergency.

A reconstruction of the ship's Log, upon which task I, as a surviving officer, participated, upon our eventual return, contained no mention of the Officer's disappearance. He was listed as Lost in the Fire.

How did I come to know the story of the pipe?

From whispered fragments, half-heard, at night, in our various captivities—the identity of these unseen gossips impossible to ascertain with any certainty.

$$\cdot \qquad \cdot \qquad \cdot$$

What was the meaning of the Holliman? For in this, sailors are like the Sages of the Bible: If an event has no person associated with it, and elsewhere a person is named but connected with no particular event, the Sages will conjoin the two.

Similarly, sailors, facing an occurrence of note, will either link it with a previously unexplained event, or, failing that, will count it as a prognostication, and wait for their clairvoyance to be proved.

It was evident to the crew that the Holliman was a sign. But they did not, even in their rage at ——— and his unwarranted floggings, take it as a sentence of death upon a malefactor; rather, I gleaned, they understood it as a warning of those calamities which *would* ensue *were* the man (and, thus, his sin) not removed. Thus, I believe, they excused themselves from their crime. For the Holliman was understood to mean "How long will I be mocked?" The

Jonah's end, then, was an act not of revenge, but of contrition, and he, it may be said, the guiltless but unlucky sacrifice.

So it may have been in Biblical days, of which in reading we may find clues not only as to the actions of *those* men, but of their forebears in primordial times, the legends of which persisted eons in the Mind of Man, before their eventual Biblical transcription.

I instance the tales not alone of our Savior, but of the patriarch Abraham. Abraham was instructed and took his child Isaac to the Mountain, to slay him, as instructed, as a sacrifice to God.

Our Lord improved upon this tale of the Jews, taking upon *himself* the burden of His Own sacrifice, and, in so doing, the Sins of Man. Isaac was guiltless, but Christ godlike. Both, however, and it is this which recommends their juxtaposition to the writer's eye, were saved, for the hand of the Angel stopped the Patriarch's knife, and Jesus, sacrificed, rose from the Dead.

A tale, though true, may possess mythologic import, such resonance elevating rather than detracting from "the facts of the case"—and raising it from the status of a report (however awe-inspiring) to that of Poetry.

We may find meaning, also, in the most banal, and instruction in the most superficially unconnected of circumstances. How much more so, then, in the report of Sublime Acts? The Sacrifice of Isaac, and the Crucifixion, thus, I suggest, not alone in themselves, but in the care which has been taken in their transcription and preservation, suggest the age-old, ineradicable survival of the trauma of human sacrifice.

I saw such memory played out in the aftermath of the Holliman. The act itself I put down as another shipboard crime, of which there are many. The ship is a town, men are close-cramped, there are no women, there is no escape, there is no privacy, and the practice of enforced civility—as of any other human exercise—is finite.

The occurrence partook, as does many another aboard ship, of the supernatural. Life aboard ship is mainly habit; habit blends, over time, into sentiment—we like the things and ways we know—and sentiment into belief—our beloved things and ways considered not only right but ordained. Objects and natural phenomena are anthropomorphized, and any slight deviation from the normal is likely to be greeted as a portent, miracle, warning, or sign.

The ultimate quiddity to me was the complacency which greeted ———'s absence. It was neither smug nor triumphal. It was not surprise. It was the acceptance of a new state. And, after ——— was gone, and order restored, why would one dwell upon it?

Afore and abaft, the mood was mutual, though we Officers, of course, presented a show of assiduous inquiry (though we knew where the man was), and concern (though we were glad of it).

Such must have been the mood of the community in the times of pagan sacrifice: such and such has occurred, now it is done, the gods have been paid, now we are done.

But the gods, here, had not been satisfied, and presented their new demand in the form of the fire, which broke out during the morning watch.

.   .   .

A burn is the most exquisite pain. The smell of burnt flesh assaults all and assails the unafflicted with the greatest horror. It invested our clothing, our selves, our stores, the sail, and the very strakes of the jolly boat in which we took refuge. Washing in the Sea would not eradicate it. Neither sweat nor wind nor sun would eradicate it. It was our companion during our time in the boat, and for that time, long afterward, when no physical particle could have remained. This persistence I was forced, at length, to locate in the Mind. This I lay to its connection with the fact of our cannibalism.

(I have suggested this connection to Carstairs, but he neither shared the experience nor endorsed my perception.)

One says, "I will never forget such a wave, such a freak wave, such a sunrise; the way a woman, rising from the bed, ran her hand down the back of her thigh." But these are recollected, if at all, as the experience not of the phenomenon, but of the attendant emotion.

.   .   .

There is this of the Sea: it is the great teacher. All is constantly in a state of change. Adventure, gain, and tragedy hidden just beyond the horizon are understood, in fact, to be casting their prodromal influences upon us *now*, and would be comprehended, were we but sufficiently sensitive. The sea breeds philosophers. A man with whom I served in the Navy found a doubloon upon the sand at St. ———. We were strolling together, indolently, speaking, as I thought, to no particular end, our voices being merely, if I may, a pleasant counterpoint to the sound of the surf. But, at a change in his tone, I stopped, and turned to him. For I then understood his desultory conversation as a space for introduction of a theme or point. This intrigued me, for we'd served together several years, and he had never been other than open and candid and forthright. I saw him prepare to declare that subject which, forming the (I now saw) ulterior purpose of our walk, revealed in him a previously unsuspected capacity for duplicity.

We stopped, I say; he cleared his throat. He began to speak, and, in his diffidence, looked down. His eye caught something on the sand. I looked, and there, just washed up by the tide, was a worn gold doubloon.

He looked up. "What shall we do with it?" he said.

The question puzzled me, until I divined his meaning. He meant that as the two of us had, together, come upon the coin, it, in equity belonged to us both. Our choices, thus, were to divide it, (actually, or, upon sale, in value,) or otherwise adjudicate its disposition.

"You keep it," I said. "Put it in your waistcoat as a good-luck charm." He was delighted at my donation of that which he felt bound to suggest as my portion. And after (I must say,) rather rudimentary and scant disclaimer, displayed his happy ownership, preening himself now upon the coin's bright integrity, now upon its curious defects.

"See," he said, "it has lain in the Sea for perhaps a century, yet it is not scoured clean." He smiled at the portrait of Juan Carlos, and smiled again, now fingering the cleft in the edge, made by a knife, perhaps, which scar increased his pleasure, provoking a fantasy of its obviously romantic cause. At length he slipped the coin into his waistcoat pocket, whence, upon our many meetings over the years, he would offer it to our joint appreciation.

This I always understood as a gesture of both thanks and apology. For I believe he felt that in my quick renunciation of a share in the coin, he had taken advantage of me. I understood. For, on seeing the doubloon in the surf, he was overcome with a great covetousness, which he, to his credit, mastered in his immediate offer of its disposition. But the memory of his lapse, I saw, shamed him. A better man, I saw he thought, would have made the offer wholeheartedly. A better man would not have rejoiced when it was declined. Poor fellow, his openness spoke well of him. He was an excellent man and a good Officer;

of an honesty so transparent that the merest hint of deviousness shone on his face.

I found him charming, if predictable; this last not a bad quality in a fellow Officer; and so was surprised to find the actual matter of our walk was his invitation to me to join that Secret Service of which, for years, he had been an important part.

The essence of war is deception. War is not a trial of strength, but of duplicity and resolution. On Service my friend put aside his native forthrightness, retaining only its appearance, which shielded him, in foreign wars, through many adventures of great profit to his native land.

(The doubloon was discovered, by my operatives, not among my friend's possessions, but upon the person of his murderer, shot dead, while fleeing the scene of the assault. Both sets of effects were returned to me, and I considered, for a time, including the doubloon with those possessions which were, eventually, returned to my friend's Widow. But I thought better to return it to the Sea.)

.   .   .

What is "belief"? It may mean "assurance," as "I believe that a barking dog will never bite"; it may mean the conviction of the improvable, as "I believe God exists." Or it may mean the acceptance of that which, though probable, is better not put to the test. "I believe," one may say, "that my partner is honest," or "that my wife is faithful."

A subset of this last is the conditional acceptance of a tale, rejection of which, though almost certainly false, would, if expressed, redound to the discomfiture of the speaker, and acceptance, if withheld, to the enjoyment of the recipient. I instance particularly the Sea Story.

Here, one, though withholding judgment upon the plausibility of the narrative, possesses a belief in its *form*. This is more than mere casuistry, for the form succeeds, as do all modes of entertainment, as it is consonant with a basic human need. The reductionist might dismiss this as the "mere need for entertainment," but this is tautology. The Sea Story pleases as it gratifies our primal desire for mystery, such desire to be acceptably slaked in a form not challenging to our profound (if deluded) love of our own reason.

One may say many interesting things in the Club, or Wardroom, without endangering one's credibility. These, falling between the assertion of fact and the offer of amusement, are judged, like the utterances of politicians, more for their rhythm and sound than by reference to either experience or probability.

In a traditional prolegomenon, one asserts that his tale is true. But this is not an invitation either to consider or substantiate its plausibility. To the contrary, it is an announcement that such consideration should be withheld. Through use we come to forget that a "true story" is not a coupled, but a simple noun, the application of whose modifier can do no better than confirm the noun's essential connotation of falsity.

The Log of *The Redwing* and the contemporary journals of the castaways both were lost. Had they survived, they would have confirmed the fact of many of these occurrences I published as fiction. That such would vindicate me from accusations of solecism in the matter of the Whale was, for a long while, the theme of my wounded ruminations. A better (or more cunning) author would have left the section out. I did possess, however, the wit to delete that portion of the encounter which, though true, would have certainly trans-formed the critics' scorn to outraged sensibility. For the assistance rendered us by the Whale did not end with his direction of us to Fell.

The whale swam slowly, and we pulled after him, and discovered the long-presumed-lost Fell. Fell was hoisted into the boat, dead-and-alive. We bent our energies to his resuscitation, which, at last being effected, we raised our heads, surprised to discover the whale was still with us. He lay a half-cable off, his head toward the Northwest. And we sat quietly, looking at him, until, after some time, he sounded. We then, by unspoken consent, set our sail, and changed course from that which we had followed those three weeks. It was on this new course of Northwest, upon which there was no charted land for seven thousand miles, that we, at daybreak, discovered the Island.

.   .   .

Each is the Hero of his own tale. Some dream of glory, some of revenge, some of release. This last is the amorphous, virtually subjectless reverie of the cap-tive. It is mirrored in that deep, precious solitude known to the man in a tragic marriage.

Farrier was such a man. He unburdened himself in the cell in Africa, but I did not understand his tale until I had undergone its like.

My notion of Love was based not upon the Romance, but upon my experience of the South Seas. I was not the first to've been unsettled by his enjoyment of the variations of a foreign culture. Some fall to the opiates, some to drink, some to the shedding of blood, many to lust.

As the boat is swamped by too large and rapid corrections, so is Man overturned by sudden, violent reactions. And just as the fallen ascetic may become the sybarite, we have observed the violently reformed degenerate become the prude.

In the African cell, I dreamt of that woman whom, upon my return I would in fact marry. But at the time of our marriage I had no love for her.

Over the course of my voyages I had changed and she had changed, passing through her first young-womanhood, through a, to her mind, ever-diminishing span of nubility. Our union, leached in the contemplation by anxiety, distance, and time, was finally removed from her anticipation by the announcement of my death. And I am sure she brooded that her constancy had squandered what she considered her marriageable years to no end whatever, such brooding leading to a resentment which, understandably, persisted upon my return, when she discovered she was no longer in love. For what, then, had she waited? But we married.

I was reinstated and acknowledged in the Naval Lists, in that seniority which I deserved. My restoration, however, could not supply my absent years, and I discovered the want of those constant and growing interactions with those of my Class which are always the key to advancement. I was, in effect, passed over.

This, eventually borne in upon me through protestations to the contrary by my superiors, prompted my resignation of my commission and the acceptance of the invitation to join what was, ostensibly, the Foreign Service—in that capacity which I have earlier described.

It was suggested to me by my then wife that the alacrity with which I embraced a life of perpetual absence told of my lack of ardor for her company. This was, upon its face, unjust, for my continuation in the Navy would have had the same effect. But it was in its essence true. For we, though the engagement had hung fire for several years, had married in haste, and now enjoyed the sequel.

The blame is mine. A better man would have correctly interpreted her demurs upon my return not as a maidenly request for reassurance, but as a plea for release. My persistence in bringing the engagement to its fruition, I described to myself as "doing the right thing." It was, to the contrary, arrogance. Had I, as I claimed to do, consulted her needs rather than mine, I would have called off the affair. Equally, had I had the strength to place her needs before my own, it is not impossible that the wedding might have had as a result a happy union.

In any case, we married and spent those two years each in a hidden and protracted agony. Our eventual separation, though affording each superficial relief, only bequeathed our despair to our union's issue.

·   ·   ·

For years I had fantasized a return to the Islands. The constellations of the Southern Heavens, to one raised in the North, are a lesson in reversion. In the observation of this new sky, one may become anew like the child, or the Primitive—touched with gratitude and awe. "Yes, that is the Cross; and Musca and Centaurus will always hold their positions relative to it, and one may steer by them."

These new Stars are a second language, which, when mastered, gives one, if not "a second soul," then some insight, perhaps, into the nature of the first.

In a natural state we live to learn. The child and the savage exist in a state of wonder born of fear. This state is lost to the civilized world through that accident called "progress"—but progress toward *what* but a complete separation from knowledge of the nature of the World?

Intimacy with the Southern sky was an acquired treasure, for which I was always grateful; and I am surely not the first sailor who, upon returning from the South, found the Northern Heavens strange, and this feeling inescapable. Memory of Southern adventure, danger, love, and youth were, of course, bound in his feeling. But they were not its totality.

·   ·   ·

I dreamt a house upon one of the Southern cliffs at Maro, its prospect to the South and East, overlooking the Bay, set back into the rock, low, in deference to the Hurricane.

I had seen a likely spot from the beach. And although I had never ventured there, I knew that behind the jutting ledge I would find a small plateau which would accept my house. I was certain of it, in that same way in which a man is aware of a woman's unstated acquiescence.

In the periods of my captivity, I fashioned my house in my imagination. It had the one room, the coconut logs notched into a low rectangle, broadside to the sea, the roof of split logs, fitted and lashed with sennit, of a single pitch, the low side toward the water, overhanging the door.

It is a matter of course that the sailor, the prisoner, the castaway, discover in and around themselves those crafts necessary to their survival and entertainment. The carvings, the braidings, the lashings and workings of the foremast hand are the product of scant resources save time, imagination, and necessity. My observation of them helped me in my dream-construction, in which I enjoyed the exercise of these primitive skills, noting that the artisan as well as the dreamer both begin by an act of fantasy—envisioning their operations in exactly the same way.

The dreamer, of course, is denied their implementation. But the house and its construction became, to me, real. That it was a fiction did not debar me from its contemplation and, so, enjoyment of that which would have no referent in the natural world.

A philosopher might ask what, then, are anticipation and reflection—might it not be argued that they, too, are fantasy, and nothing but the exercise of imagination under a more stately name?

A man may plan a marriage proposal, a venture, a voyage, and delight in the contemplation of that which, in fact, may prove to have no real component—his suit rejected, his venture debarred, his voyage misdirected, canceled, failed, or delayed. Whereof it is written by the Bard, "I would that such men had their object everywhere and their destination nowhere."

In any case, call it diversion or delusion, I, in my imagination, built the house, of which, lest it offend the scholiasts to say "it became real," I will say my love was real.

The laurel is Achievement's Crown as _____ pursued the goddess (Demeter?). He, upon capturing her, was changed into a Laurel Tree. And yet one seeks the crown.

I never returned to the Islands. For years I cherished the desire. It was a sobering moment when I perceived that the desire had, in truth, long ago died, leaving only a sort of promise, which, like many another infidelity, was made acceptable through collusion. This is an old man's book.

·   ·   ·

I do not know that time is continuous. I do not think it is.

I am unclear as to the difference between a habit and a superstition; in fact, I believe I have generally been confused about the notion of cause and effect.

I recall splitting wood, when, in the final days of our African captivity, we were given a small stone hand-maul for the purpose. Our captors had, we inferred from this gesture, been in negotiations with our Embassy for our release. Our food improved somewhat; we were issued coarse, indeed, abrasive blankets for which we were immeasurably grateful; we were supplied with wood, and were given the use of the maul.

This last was particularly cherished as a sign of impending release, for, although dull upon its edge, plied as a mace or hammer it would have made a formidable weapon. But the first thing a sailor learns is that the intelligent way is the easy way. The easiest task upon ship is to haul on a rope, and the first piece of information the bluejacket learns is his ignorance of how to go about it. For, left unguided, he would pull upon the rope, bootlessly exhausting the strength in his arms. His first tutelage is the command "Walk *away* with it," the pendant but unspoken addendum, "you fool."

Given token of a probable release, the easy way in prison was to enjoy small benefits, rather than attempt escape. Which we did. And as various physical strictures lessened—we were given the freedom, first for one half-hour, then for an hour, and then by degrees, without limit, to walk the ramparts; we were allowed free conversation; and, near the end, the very doors of our cells were left open at night—so did our sense of oppression at the limitations which remained.

·   ·   ·

It was my job to split the wood. And I enjoyed it.

Here is the trick of splitting wood.

There is, in each piece to be split, a *check* or *crack*, occasioned by separations of the fibers or grain. If the maul is brought down into this crack, the wood will generally split "of itself." The ignorant apply their muscles to the task, the educated their eyes.

It is, thus, a rewarding pastime, grateful to the sensibilities, to see one's perception triumph, as it were, over the piece of wood—to gain one's object through the application of as little force as possible.

When so involved, from time to time, it seems, *and may well be*, that the piece splits before the maul comes down on it. It is split, that is, by the *intention* of the worker. Is this possible? I only know that it appears to be the case. Can this feeling (or phenomenon) be brought about by will? No; it seems to appear only in moments of complete involvement with the task.

It can no more be bidden than that universal experience of the observed turning his eyes to determine his observer. Here, some primordial animal instinct has become involved. Reason cannot duplicate it. Neither can reason explain it; yet we all know the phenomenon exists.

And I have experienced a disjunction of time. I have known it adventitiously, as when I remarked upon watch one night, offhandedly, that on the morrow we would speak *The Dolphin*.

Unaware that I had said anything remarkable, I was surprised to see in my companion's face a look compounded of confusion and consternation. "Why did you speak of that Ship?" he said. For both he and I knew that *The Dolphin* was reported lost, having gone down with all hands in the recent gale. I had spoken offhandedly, I explained, hardly knowing why I spoke, or, indeed *that* I spoke. And I was as concerned and perhaps more concerned than he when, on the morrow, we descried, a half-league off, *The Dolphin*, which the storm had only blown off-course.

· · ·

A philosopher told me that Madness is the attempt to preserve the illusion of autonomy. Here, the mind, he explained, rather than confront the horror of its own dissolution, assigns the horror to the world outside. I thought his explanation false and told him so. We have, in the world, scant autonomy. "Madness," I said, "is the surrender of the illusion of autonomy."

Madness is a recursion to that terror of the infant: helplessness. The infant cries; if help comes, it is sated. If not, it dies. As the infant grows, it learns to equate its cries with the satisfaction of its needs. The world, then, is understood but as an adjunct of its desires. Later, the infant having obtained some measure of self-individuation, its cry not being met occasions rage. This rage is the birth of his true understanding of the separation of his world and his self. The healthy man learns either to mask his desires or to study to still or to fulfill them. For his world, which he once thought his servant, is now correctly understood as a conjunction of forces either uninterested in or inimical to his survival.

It is not only the weak but the strong man who shatters under psychic hardship; the weak, as is his nature in all things, and the strong, as the horrible fact of his own helplessness is borne in upon him.

In captivity many found refuge in that fantasy which was, after a time, indistinguishable from Madness. These, as the philosopher suggested, did, in fact, default, taking refuge, first suppositionally and then in fact, in a better world.

Some simply devolved into a depression often relieved by suicide; some embraced suicide, of a sane mind, as the most sane alternative.

Some, in the Galleys, and in Prison, seemed able to *suspend* that life- or mind-force the constant exercise of which, the body fettered, depleted the reason. These engaged in a sort of mental hibernation. I believe I was one of these.

We are told some Hindu Mystics have the ability to still the heart to beat but once an hour, once a day, their bodies becoming near-immune to time. I know the mind has a similar capacity.

To me, the remarkable aspect of the feat of the Yogi, is not that these processes can be suppressed, but that such suppression may be reversed.

War abounds in instances of the miraculous. The onetime combatant, even in the most ancient old age, does not tire of relating the incidents of impossible escapes and the freak occurrences of death in the midst of supposed safety. There is a well-known capriciousness, for example, associated with explosives, whose detonation may destroy all within a wide circumference, sparing only that person nearest to the blast.

How may this be explained? It cannot. The warrior does not name this "accident," but the operation of some deeper, unnamable force.

I count my physical redemption from bondage less remarkable than my—eventual—return to a sort of sanity, and both as inexplicable freaks of war.

The success of my stories I attribute to the general if not universal experience of the descent to nature's tragic states, and, if not the fact, the *hope* of their reversal.

It is said Man cannot live without hope. This is untrue. To the contrary, its extinguishment may be sometimes necessary for self-preservation. But Man cannot long live in despair—the stasis lying between these two conditions (as in my case) might be described as a sort of Acceptance.

A minister of my acquaintance suggested that this was Faith. I said it was not Faith. And I thought him not only wrong but foolish; but I was wrong.

·   ·   ·

My grandfather walked his land with me and so instilled in me a great respect for topography.

I found this useful in later life, in assessing land, when Margaret and I searched for a farm; as a sailor; and in my Government career, as an aid to my sense of direction. For the essence of the farmer's wisdom is that the output of the land must depend upon the soil's essential nature, and that such may be determined from superficialities.

It is obvious, of course, that a field shielded from the cold north wind may be more suitable to the raising of fruit trees than one which is not; such is clear even to the city dweller. The farmer's deeper understanding sees a line of trees, declining increasingly in height over the course of its run. He knows that they decline not only in response to the prevailing wind, but in response to a decrease in depth of topsoil, and he may, at a glance, thus assume the intersection with a run of ledge.

My grandfather taught me to observe the land thus, as an interplay of forces, and the superficial as an expression of an underlying structure. It is no great reach to elaborate this observation to the behavior both of men and of Man.

Most human beings are taken in by appearances. We respond, fairly predictably, to the *signals* our fellows display: I am Rich, I am Strong, I am Unapproachable, Nubile, Important, Powerless. Experience is hard-pressed to teach us that these signals, though both inevitable in and necessary for human intercourse, are like false colors thrown out at sea, a matter of stratagem, rather than either a confession of substance or a proclamation of intent.

The Man and the Man-of-War, that is, do not *advertise* either what they are or what they want, but in order to lull, attract, or distract so that they may *take* what they want.

Is this a harsh view of life? I know only that it is a view which has, as a sailor, saved, and as a writer, supported my existence. I do not consider this an indictment of human beings, of whom, in any case, I have no very high opinion.

I ask little of my fellows and am grateful to have generally received it. I ask to be left alone, and success has allowed me privacy. I am grateful that my books have provided me both insulation and comfort; but, absent this success, I believe I must have sought a different sort of solitude, which, if less comfortable, would not have been less necessary to my happiness.

"The Wild Man," we cry. But the true wild man would neither return nor philosophize, which perhaps is a form of envy. He would not be as the riven stump, but whole, and lost to the world, which would, as per his fondest wish, forget him. It is the half-grown, weak, meditative sorts who fantasize the dual life—conscious of civilization but preferring, at least in thought, the practices of savage lands. These are at best visitors, in body or mind, in climes they lack the courage actually to inhabit. They are disaffected with the land of their birth, but in no wise better than tourists in the world they mythologize, incapable of the happy exercise in the first, or of abandonment in the other world of their perquisites: weak, doleful, pitiable creatures. I am one of these.

It was given me, had I availed myself of it, to live perpetually in the other world, with the love of the Island girl—to both live and die free of that coruscating conscious life to which I, in my weakness, returned.

What drew me back? I have offered to myself and have had suggested to me that it was a sense of Duty. But Duty was merely the convenient hook upon which I hung my decision, which I cannot even say was made from Habit. It was dread of the unknown.

This, mixed with prejudice, motivated my return to the ship. What prejudice? you ask. And I will name the fell apprehension that the darker races, however we may delight in their differing sense of license or their simple wisdom, are our inferiors, and that to dwell with them is to open oneself to some sort of contagion of inferiority—those abandoning reserve being most in need of fearing the disease.

It was for this vile superstition, which I had not the strength to counteract, that I rejected a life of bliss.

After the wreck I had but to retain my place among the Villagers one extra day, and the crew, searching for survivors, would have marked me "discharged-dead," and so I would have remained. But I rose, sought them out, and announced myself returned, and so I was.

Like goes to Like. Just as the attraction of woman to man cannot be denied, so the need of one's own kind is near insuperable. A better man would have stayed, and a better man would have overcome the Western urge to chronicle his thoughts; for there, in truth, lay much of the impetus of return—for of what worth would be such a chronicle to the Islanders, who could not appreciate my subtlety, and from whom the act of individuation must separate me?

A better man would have let it go. He would now, in my fantasy, be old and valued in his Tribe, the great-grandsire of many, revered as a Sage, content, replete, unassailed by remorse for a life he had surrendered. Or so, at least, runs my fantasy.

I enjoy the play of human nature. I have reached that time of life when both wounds and rewards at its hands are less probable, and I am grateful.

To extend the conceit of the Farmer, I can assess the land, its latency and nature, impassively. I need not factor in to my assessments my needs, nor, thus, my potential for self-delusion.

We are blinded by lust. We are blinded by ambition, envy, and greed. The truer nature of the world becomes clearer to us as these die. It is a tragic exchange, and a mercy of God that it comes near the end.

English differs from South Seas in every particular but this: each is the attempt to communicate.

Land navigation, similarly, served me in my time at sea, mainly in having supplied me, if I may, with a belief in grammar. But the sea is more mysterious than the land. For it changes not only in nature, but in composition, and this continually. It must be studied, it cannot be mastered, thus, it is held, by the serious man, in awe.

My grandfather taught me astronomy. And these lessons served me well at sea. The sailor loves the Stars, for they alone, of all his world, do not change.

One may take against the water and the wind, controlled in his blasphemies according to his understanding of these elements' resourcefulness. One may also blaspheme the Sun, which, being the One Great Fact, is understood to be above the wish for revenge; one may rail, similarly, against the Moon, whose lack of light, against the shore, or presence of light, against the Enemy, may imperil the ship. But the Stars are uninvolved, blessing the Earth with their most beautiful, impassive, and useful predictability.

No wonder that we, Primitive Man, assign to or intuit in that predictability a message of predestination.

The most-quoted passage in *The Raven, or The African Captive* was that of the Astrologer. Her speech to Captain Marrion was interpreted, in the book's first release, as an indictment of Religion.

It is difficult for those born after that time to understand the heat these religious and quasi-religious controversies generated, offering to every man, the brevet rank and avocation of Protector of the Faith. It was my good fortune to have my work come to the Public View just as the contagion (or fashion) had come to its peak and was beginning to wane. Had the book appeared but some few years previously, it is likely that it would have been suppressed, or, perhaps, that no publisher would have dared attempt its release, which is, of course, the same thing.

I was stunned, in the event, by the reaction of outraged sanctimony. I later learned that the good noun "indignation" is never without its inseparable adjective "righteous," which righteousness is ever an entertainment to those too indolent to draw their own conclusions.

I'd thought, before the publication of the book, that there were chapters, particularly those dealing with the celebratory practices of the South Seas, which might wake sleeping sanctity to vigilance. But that such Sanctity might anathematize that, to me, innocent and unobjectionable passage which indeed awakened wrath was a surprise and an education.

Some wag said that the critics of that sanctimonious time could suss out the taint of atheism in a pie plate. In my case, I believe they came quite near.

Captain Marrion, my readers may recall, encounters the Hag upon his return with the Raven's crew. Rescued from captivity, he is at liberty in Mahon, and just at nightfall, he is proceeding up the Pigtail Steps, late for an appointment. He puts his hand to his waistcoat pocket to consult that watch which, he now recalls, is long gone. He smiles at this oft-repeated error. His face, then, clouds, as he recalls the circumstances of its loss. He then looks to the sky, to gauge the hour, and is about to continue his progress up the Steps, when he becomes aware of the Old Woman's gaze.

We learn that "there was that in her countenance ..." and so on, which draws him to her. They stand by the side of the Steps, where she narrates to him the whole of his adventure, of which, as he is just returned, she must necessarily be ignorant. He asks, but half-jokingly, if she is a Witch. She replies that she is merely observant. Further, she says, the errand upon which he climbs the stairs will come to no happy end.

He asks how she knows. "I know," she says, "because *you* know. You are late," she says, "but only mime a sense of urgency. Your errand, then, you find either objectionable or unimportant. And you are willing to be detained, meaning you, yourself, foresee a disagreeable outcome. How can such an errand have a happy end?

"It is right, then," she continues, in the passage which occasioned such comment, "that you look to the Stars. For they control all things."

"I was raised to believe," the Captain says, "that God controls all things."

"No," she says, "you were raised to *assert* that God ruled all things, but to *observe* that that power lay with the Devil."

They stand for a moment, the Captain considering her speech. He then remembers himself, and reaches again, into his pocket, this time for a coin, with which to pay, and, so, conclude his interview. He finds no coin, shakes his head, remembering, again, his state as a returned captive, without possessions.

A group of sailors mounts the Steps. The group contains Blane. The Captain calls out, "Blane, give me a coin." Blane does so. The Captain turns back, the coin in his hand, and finds the Old Woman gone.*

·   ·   ·

When we left Portsmouth, on the cruise, which would result in our capture and imprisonment, the Fort made the signal Ps. 107.23, a well-known sign for parting, which is beloved as the Mariners' Prayer: "They that go down to the Sea in Ships, and do their work in Many Waters, have seen the Deeds of God, and his Wonders in the Watery Deep."

---

* This incident concludes the adventure of *The African Captive*. It is the final image in the book, and the point of departure for the second novel in the series.

The same port, upon our return, and ignorant of our presence on board, made Ps. 107.6: "Then they cried out to God, in their Distress, and, for their woes, he rescued them." And 107.16, "For he smashed copper gates and cut asunder bolts."

At my first opportunity, I visited the Fort and inquired the identity of the signal Midshipman of the day of our return, and I found him.

I asked if, though I could not have imagined how, he somehow knew of the carriage on board the returning ship, of us who had become known as the African Captives.

He replied that he had not, but that I was not the first to've asked him how he chose those verses.

He looked around, and, seeing we were alone, asked if I could, in good conscience, give my word not to reveal his secret.

"Why?" I asked, since he had, it seems, already unburdened himself to the Press.

"Yes," he said, "but to them I lied."

"What did you tell them?" I asked; and he said that, after Church, the preceding Sabbath, he had lain down, and been visited in a dream, and in the dream were the numbers of which he made the signal, that night, on his accession to the Watch.

"Very good," I said. "Now, between two men in Blue, is there a greater, or perhaps *different* story?"

He smiled, and confessed that he, to while away the dead watch, was amusing himself throwing dice. Psalms 107, 16, and 6 being conjured out of the throw: one, six, and six.

"Very good," I said, "but how did you chance upon Psalms?"

"I leafed through the Bible," he said, "eyes closed, and stabbed my finger down at the page."

I do not know that this, more than the tale of the dream, adequately explains the extraordinary encapsulation of my journey by the two sections from Psalms. I believe it falls under the heading of Coincidence.

We know, of course, that the extraordinary thing about Coincidences is how many of them do *not* occur, how our reasoning about them includes the logical fallacy post hoc ergo propter hoc. Which is to say, we find ourselves thinking of X, and, that afternoon he appears. Well and good, but we forget, when we first thought of him, we did not suggest to ourselves, "That means I will see him later today." Nor do we recollect, on seeing him, how many others we have thought of that day yet not seen.

I have to date refrained from revealing the story of the Midshipman's choice of Scripture, as such would have been to indict him of both inattention to duty, and blasphemy.

But not only those who might punish him, but the boy himself, are long dead, and the only memory of the event will be these pages.

"Do you believe in the Bible?" I asked him, and he looked at me blankly, for those were, if not Puritan, then, at least, as pertains to Religion, Conventional times, which is to say that the matter of Religion, as Religion itself, was tempered by reason, the essence of which was the reasonable asseveration of the Orthodox.

Belief can finally be nothing more than the sentiment of its object having been put beyond investigation. Our sentiment of our wife's affection, a matter more of habit than of ongoing fervor, such sentiment, in fact, only brought to the conscious mind by suggestions to the contrary—and, then, easily shaken.

It is reasonable, therefore, to accept the *habit* of the sentiment of belief for that more stringent certainty or zeal toward the existence of which the Fervent might strive.

Secondly, it is reasonable to adopt belief's appearance, or approve the same in others whom we cannot think on the whole more religious or less hypocritical than ourselves. For such mutual endorsement, far from being blameworthy, is necessary to the function both of the community and of the State.

Do we upon maturity discover in our parents a less-than-perfect observation of those precepts of whose worth they have striven to convince us? We must. But who indicts them, save the ingrate and the adolescent? For we understand not only their attempts to inculcate in us those virtues which would ease our lot, but that their methods and perhaps their motives were less than perfect—that they, finally, were human, as we are, but that this tragic, shared state, no less than another, neither exempts us from responsibility nor excuses us from effort.

The Naval regulations of that day held that the possession of gambling apparatus was liable to reduction in rank and forfeiture of pay and privileges. This, though seldom enforced against Officers (indeed, the Wardroom and the Gun Room were, as respects this and many another rule, long-exempted by custom). But the Penalty for sleeping on watch—understood, by extension, to include absorption in any task which would entail inattention—was Death.

At the time of my meeting with the Signal Midshipman, we were still technically in a State of War.

I visited the Battlement but in the capacity of Curious Observer. Had I, however, been Captain of the Watch, or, in fact, had I come on the scene in any *operational* capacity (including my passage, on Duty, from one part of the Fort to the next), my discovery of the Midshipman's inattention might have resulted in his indictment and court-martial. Further, had I felt *enmity* for him (and love of prerogative, and Martinet Stringency, are rife in this as in any other hierarchy), my testimony as to the gambling apparatus might have gone far to sway an undecided Court to the accused's sorrow.

Consider. Such a Court-Martial, its members having perforce themselves risen from the inexperience, youth, wandering mind, and high spirits of the accused, would understand that the Watch was long, the day was calm, and the possibility of Strife—though the State of War technically still remained—remote.

This Court, however, also would be charged to account for the accusing Officer's indictment, and if not, indeed, crediting his discretion in the double-charge, at least forced to consider its fact.

For had a Court, in light of the sworn testimony of a superior Officer, and in the absence of testimony to the contrary by the accused, *dismissed* the charge, it would have stood as a violent censure to the accusing Officer, a rejection of his sworn statement, and thus, of his Honor, which he had put at risk by coming forward.

I realized years later, it was I who may have erred; not only in ignoring but in licensing the Midshipman's inattention (by my conversation); and vitiating, by my smile, that residual instruction which would have been conveyed by a stern demeanor.

For the Enemy will always attack at the time he feels most propitious, which is to say, when diplomacy, weather, darkness, decoy, or deceit have rendered the defenses lax. Better for me to have upbraided the boy. Better for him.

Well, in Command, as in the rearing of children, we are always and ever misunderstanding opportunities for endorsement as those requiring rebuke. The opposite is equally true.

The Midshipman died, some three years later; falling, with Honor, at the head of a file of Marines at Puerto Viscaya. My son knew him there.

.   .   .

I spent a portion of a sea-voyage (as passenger) frustrated of reading matter save the Bible. I profited enormously thereby; a part of my investigations were that perusal of the Psalms, in attempts to find, as I said, concordance with my personal trials.

"He gathered them from the Land, the West, the North, and the Sea"; "They Cried Out in their Distress," as, indeed we did. After the shipwreck of *The Raven*, "He led them to an Uninhabited City," that is, to the Island. "He sated their souls, and filled the hungry soul with good," our treatment by the Islanders, and mine, by Taya.

But because they defied the Words of God (of which more later) and the Counsel of the Supreme One they scorned, so "He humbled their hearts with Hard Labor." When we were taken by the Corsairs, "They Cried out to God to Break Open their Shackles," as we did in the Galleys, though our prayer was of a coarser kind.

In the Galleys, our suffering, deep as it was, was deepened by the impossibility of communication.

This, however, we overcame by a sort of speech, a re-creation of the first Speech of Man, which must have been a prayer. Here is the manner and matter of ours.

Chained to the oars, we all, of course, faced aft. The rearmost in the boat, at Daybreak, would incline his head toward the Zenith, and then cast a backward look at us, holding each, our gaze for one half-instant, in which both would nod, in the silent, and shared, acknowledgment that we had survived another day, and that all which befell or might befall us, happened under the Watchful Eye of God.

Was this litany, you may ask, communicable silently and on the instant? I assure you it was. And more. As when the Leader would, as part of our prayer, incline his head, to the starboard or port, indicating, we all understood, not only some occurrence of the day before, but the light in which we might, under God, understand it. (The appearance of the Whale, the ship to leeward, and various other events familiar to the readers of the novel.)

"He smashed the gates and cut asunder Iron Bolts, and we were taken from the Galleys and sold into slavery in Egypt. Our soul abhorred all food and we reached the Portals of Death," as we did, during outbreak, in prison, of Fever.

I will not further belabor the concordance of the Word, and our ordeal. I am not the first to have found, in Scripture, a connection between my fate and divine Ordination. And I am neither so naïve nor self-involved to be ignorant of the solecism of the same.

But I will endorse with every atom of my being the Holy Wisdom of that signal which began, and with which I conclude, my experiences of my voyage: "They that go down to the Sea in Ships, and do their work in Many Waters, have seen the Deeds of God, and his Wonders in the Watery Deep." Praise God.

NOTES ON PLAINS WARFARE

The two questions, they say, one gentleman should never ask another are "Do you know the time?" and "May I borrow your knife?"

The Army wanted to standardize revolver caliber, so that one man, having shot himself dry, could turn to his fellow and ask for a loan of powder or ball. But just as each man should have his own knife and watch, each should be entitled to the ammunition which he carried, and upon which, in a firefight, his life might depend. So held the Lieutenant, in opposition to the dictum of the War Department. The charitable attributed his stance to his affection for the .36 Colt's he wore. His father had carried it from Bull Run to the Wilderness, where he had fallen.

The piece had been retrieved and returned to the family along with the man's general effects. His widow, on her son's graduation from West Point, had returned it to Colt's, who refurbished it, converted it to cartridge, and engraved it copiously and well. It was a beautiful gun, and the Lieutenant shot it well, but I held against his theory. Here is why.

At the commencement of a Campaign, newspapers might prognosticate a loss of, for example, ten percent of effectives. The soldier reading this thinks, invariably, "Those poor, luckless unfortunates." He is incapable of imagining himself among that number. Indeed, if he were, what could induce him to fight? Or if to fight, to fight with that abandoned courage which is, sadly, the possession, mainly, of the neophyte?

He must assume the other man will fall. No, he knows there will be casualties, they being the essential difference between warfare and other structured antagonism, but conceives of them and their misfortune as a result of some fault or lack he does not own: they must be inattentive, lazy, lacking in martial spirit or ability, or merely *luckless*, meaning, finally, intended by God to fall. If they did not fall, the nature of war and the probity of the newspaper would both be called in question. The necessary loss is sad, and war, to the philosophic novice, is tragedy. To the veteran, it is a horror.

The Lieutenant could conceive a situation where the luckless or incompetent soldier, having expended his ammunition, begged his more prudent comrade for a share of his store; but he, being unblooded, could not imagine a time wherein he, through either fault or circumstance, had expended his own rounds, and would need to turn to his comrades. In this he was thinking as a bad, or selfish, private soldier. His error was the greater, however, in that he was an officer, the essential duty of whom is to consider, first, the state of his troops and of their mission. As a bad officer, he could not imagine a situation in which the sharing of ammunition was essential to the lives of a *group*; for example, the platoon of which he was in command and which found itself surrounded by Hostiles, and attacked at irregular periods, and on all sides of the farmhouse and barn into which we had been driven.

It is difficult to keep the mind focused upon potential danger over long intervals. Part of the skill of a raiding leader is the ability to gauge or anticipate a period, in the defenders, of this lessened attention. It is taught, I believe, in our Military Academy, to attack at times when your opponents are likely to be less attentive. Night, and its attendant association with sleep, is the prime example, but the fatigue at the end of a day is mimicked and many times surpassed by that engendered by a long period of physical exertion. Less well-recognized by the academic, but understood by the combatant, is that such fatigue can be the greater as the result of exertions mental and spiritual—for example, a long, anxious watch, by day or night. Such a watch is so wearing that it need not be accompanied by attack to induce fatigue and may, in fact, be employed by the attackers for rest.

It was the suggested plan of Sergeant Murray, therefore, to utilize this period of the attackers' rest, and set upon them. This we all thought good Napoleonic thinking, who had written, truly, that the logical end of defensive warfare was surrender. But the Lieutenant refused us permission to form a raiding party.

What would we have lost? We risked the lives of that party, certainly, but we risked them equally in merely defensive posture, for neither water nor ammunition would hold out indefinitely. And by counter-raiding we would inculcate in the enemy that need for watchfulness the corrosive elements of which he was happy to employ against us.

It is not for nothing that the savage screams when attacking. For the scream, primordially, has the ability to shock the nervous system into momentary inanition. Those unused to combat may attribute this immobility to fear. And the neophyte attributing his lack of movement not to physiology, but to cowardice, his mistaken understanding of himself as a coward breaks his will and weakens his ability to fight, the savage, thus, achieving his result. But note that, to the more experienced, the scream is but a sound, and has about it nothing magical; for it is not less horrible to be set upon by horsemen intent upon your death, than by horsemen intent upon your death and screaming.

The essence of combat is husbanding and concentration of energy. The blooded trooper, knowing this, is perfectly content to let the savage scream, and expend energy in screaming.

The Lieutenant, in his maiden firefight, had expended most of his revolver ammunition firing at the first charge. I believe he considered it beneath him, at the opening of the attack, to have recourse to the rifle, the badge of the mere trooper. We did not fault him for his actions, which had about them, perhaps, the air of a performance. For he was in his first battle, and he, further, must have felt upon him the burden of example, without being entirely sure in what such example might consist.

And now his revolver cartridges had been expended, and the piece was a mere deadweight not only on his hip, but, if I may, on his mind. For, as the second night fell, he sat apart brooding. And as he brooded, he fingered the stud on the flap of the holster which covered his now useless revolver.

I saw that Sergeant Murray had seen it, too, and we exchanged a look across the barn, the meaning of which may have been unintelligible to observers, but which conveyed, between us, as would have a sad shaking of the head, the knowledge that the fool, with his useless sidearm, now brooded on the impossibility of suicide.

All newcomers to Plains warfare are frightened by the old hand's adage "Save the last bullet for yourself." This chaffing has been part of all combat, and is a licensed amusement and right of the veteran. Much military information is conveyed by adage and jest, and that passing as mere badinage may and often does contain at least a bit of instruction and truth.

For we veterans had, each of us, seen the results of capture; each speculating, then, on his ability to withstand the same manfully, and reaching the inevitable and frightening conclusion: In what would such steadfastness consist, and to what end?

For there was the triumph, in the mind, of savage warfare: that the captured man, destined for mutilation as amusement to his conquerors, would be denied even the prospect of a stoical resistance, which, to the savage, would be as one with a prolonged womanly screaming.

The Indian held as nothing our Christian forms and traditions. Doubtless, he had his own, and his own God, and was schooled in that God's worship. But that worship and its laws did not include mercy to enemies, and he, indeed, would have found such a suggestion not only incomprehensible, but sacrilegious.

Christ, our Savior, himself cried out while under torture, and He was assured of life everlasting. What, then, of the mere mortal, trooper, or officer, facing, for all of his protestations of belief, the end of his life in extended and systematic horror? Might the mind go first? And, if not, at what point did the martial Code of Honor cease? Would a prolonged stoicism decay into madness or death before the onset of a cowardly pleading or weeping?

These questions are, of course, moot, for who can answer them with certainty save those undergoing the trials themselves, at which point they will be occupied in agony?

The answer to this campfire chat, then, was, and could only be, practical advice (the word "therefore," being understood): "Save the last cartridge for yourself."

Here, then, was certainty, free will, and a form of both courage and honor—one reserving to himself the right to prefer that which must be called integrity, over vile dissolution.

What point in prolonging life a mere few hours, and those hours of torture? Did one perhaps owe it to one's God to disobey the "strictures against self-slaughter" in such circumstances?

I have heard alienists say, and once, in fact, attended a lecture at my College's medical school upon the subject of suicide, wherein the theory was propounded that the act is an attempt to preserve integrity—that all human acts *must* so be. The lecturer adduced the case of the mother animal sacrificing herself for her young. Here, clearly, the sacrifice is altruism, but this merely puts the question at one remove; for as altruism may be described as the sacrifices of the individual, made for the benefit of another, his group, or the Whole, the question remains: Why should the individual think these sacrifices worthwhile?

Honor, for example, is altruism. It is the sacrifice of personal advantage in service of a higher code. Its practice, lauded, inculcated, and even observed, in our military, brings great satisfaction as it allows the individual *autonomy*: he, in its practice, finds himself superior to that mere "circumstance" dreaded by those less honorable. He may forfeit one goal, and thereby gain a higher.

The game bird, similarly, feigning an injured wing, as she lures the fox from her young, is spending her life to protect lives more important than her own, and she does so without question. Her actions are instinctual; those of the soldier are ingrained, through precept, drill, and formal and less formal presentations and experiences of the central idea: that his life is less important than that of his group.*

This is the central notion of an organized military. It is this which distinguishes it, in ethos and in practice, from the mere raids of the savage.

For these, whether by the Plainsmen of our country, or the Mountain warriors of the Indian Northwest Frontier, fight as individuals, and in a display of that philosophy known as "anarchism."

This creed, as I understand it, holds not that government should not exist, but that it should and will emerge spontaneously, ad hoc, amongst the members of that group engaged, by happenstance, in some particular struggle; and that the nature of that struggle coupled with an individual self-interest will, spontaneously, give rise to those rules pertinent to and in force only during the particular task at hand.

The "anarchist," thus, models his philosophy upon that organization of children at the beginning of a new game. Here the rules of the game will be related, the more practiced instructing the newcomers, and modified, all

---

* Put somewhat differently, that the purpose of his life is to serve the group, and in that service lies his importance.

(practiced or not) having a say in the game's structure, limitations, and scoring. For the game, among these children, could not proceed until all are agreed as to the rules. And at the game's conclusion (such, as with the rest of the rules, having been determined by mutual assent at the beginning of the enterprise), the group is dissolved, and any powers the individual has ceded to it, thus, revoked.

The wars of the savage, of the light horsemen of the Plains or of the Mountains, then, partake of the nature of a children's game. These horsemen, though they may attack in force, value individual achievement, as the goal of their endeavor, and any alliances or coalitions they have formed for the purpose of the one attack, relate to that attack only, and in no wise constitute a precedent or express an understanding of the individual as subordinate, in any ongoing sense, to the group.

The savages, it is well-known, will, for example, likely disperse after suffering a percentage of loss which, to the Cavalry, would seem negligible; for their definition of honor differs from ours, and does not include the submersion of individual interest, nor does it include the acceptance of an authority superior (whether overt or implied) to the actual combatant on the scene, who is free to define for himself courage, honor, and accomplishment.

The British Laureate wrote of the ineffable, ineffaceable glory of the Light Cavalry at Balaclava, who, upon receipt of orders which they knew to be mistranscribed, nonetheless obeyed them with alacrity, at the cost of their lives.

This is a pretty story, beloved of those in the West who have never engaged in combat. For the experienced soldier understands that, in the tale, something is missing—that it could not have been uniquely a sense of honor which impelled the Light Brigade into a pointless death, but that sense with, or, indeed, overridden by, a fear not only of disgrace, but of death; for be assured, as any soldier will assure you, that though there were certainly those in command who, knowing the orders flawed, exhorted their troops in the name of honor, there were others, officers and noncommissioned men, who shot and sabered, and most certainly turned, and probably discharged, cannon upon the recalcitrant and unconvinced private soldier.

The Western soldier fights for Purpose, and he fights, though he may admit it solely to those of his ilk, from fear. He fights from fear of discovering insufficient manhood, from fear of censure, from fear of betraying his comrades, from fear, in short, of weakness, the conquest of which is known as courage. It may not be the love, but it is certainly the *ethos* of his Country which aids him to choose to face the fear of combat rather than the shame of cowardice.

But the savage is raised differently. To him there is no shame in a withdrawal in the face of inequality of arms, or upon the suffering of casualties. He is raised to combat as the central fact of life. The male natives of the Plains know no other life or occupation than hunting or war. They do not fear their courage; they do not fear combat—it would be, to them, incomprehensible as a financier fearing those transactions which are, day to day, his occupation, his joy—and, indeed, his addiction. Further, this financier is like the Indian in that withdrawal from a false position is accounted not cowardice but simple common sense. To both, to attack when the odds are favorable, and to retreat the moment they shift is the essential fact of strategy, any deviation from which would be literally inconceivable.

Thus, neither the savage, nor his simulacrum in our world, the financier, contains, in his philosophy, the notion of suicide.*

---

* In re: the financier, I speak of "suicide," meaning not the taking of one's own life, but the spontaneous destruction of that possessed essence of his endeavor, his capital. The financier, it has been observed in the late Panic, may, upon reversal, take his life, but not while there remained to him that which was the *essence* of his life, his money.

Here I will note a curious exception. I shall leave it to the reader to decide whether it falls within the scope of the concept "suicide." I will aver only that this curiosity, to my mind, partakes of something of our Western concept of martial honor. It is that of the "Sash Warrior."

He it is, among the savages, who has taken a vow, in a particular attack, to fix himself upon a spot, and to stand fixed, until victory has come to his side, or death come to him. He wears a long sash fixed over one shoulder, and carries with him a stake, which we would recognize as a tent-peg. In the attack, he dismounts, fixes the stake to the ground and the sash to the stake, and from this position fights until one of the two alternatives mentioned above shall have come to him.

We see how this partakes both of the anarchism of the children's game, and of the Western code of obeisance (for example, of the popular understanding of the Cavalry at Balaclava).

The casuistical among us may, therefore, conflate that Charge and a children's game; and, indeed, there may be something in the supposition. But we are "as birds in an evil net," and each man is subject to the ethos of his time and place, and may transgress it only at his peril. The Radical endeavors to dissect his culture, choosing from among its features those he finds salutary. But however he asserts his Epicureanism, one may deduce from his actions in opposition that code which guides him, however he may assert its absence.

There exist, of course, those individuals, called Saints or Martyrs, who opposed the ethos of their times and politics, and, in so doing, brought to the world a New Truth. Many were good and great, and One was Perfect. But the iconoclast, the radical, self-proclaimed or not, self-understood or not, does tend to arrogate to himself this comparison, excusing, indeed, lauding, his particular lack of compliance as an example of his superiority. See the decision by the Lieutenant to proclaim his individuality by retention of the superseded revolver.

A civilization, its institutions, and, in particular, its military, is a working out of many decisions by many men, over a great deal of time, and in response both to those threats the civilization has undergone, and to those understood as potential to its own unique imagination.

The savage understood the threat as the small contingent, detached to find and confine or kill him. To this threat he was and will always be superior, for his ethos allows him to attack and disband at will, harrying those who, by their martial philosophy, are unsuited to the small, abrupt encounter. But the savage, of course, ultimately lost.* He was incapable of imagining the threat both of astronomically superior force (of combatants, and also of settlers who, in their wake, will hold the new land as an impromptu implacable militia), and of the ability of that Western force to adapt—both the weapons of war (the Gatling Gun, inter alia), and its strategy (see General Sheridan).

That evolution which rendered the Plains Indian superior to the Whites— their horsemanship, and their derivative ability at ad hoc tactical maneuver, their license to disband, retire, and regroup in the face of unfortunate odds— eventually ensured their destruction by a culture which was *in its totality* more adaptable.

In his decision to carry the outmoded revolver, the Lieutenant, like the savage, devoted to a code no longer practicable, increased the chances of his own demise.

He chose romance over reason. There was, to him, nothing romantic about

* Even Quanah Parker, greatest of the latter Comanche war chiefs, prevailed, as a leader and an individual, only through the process of accommodation.

the interchangeability of firearms or ammunition; and his limited intelligence and experience combined to lead to his own death.

Some, the more philosophical (or superstitious), opined he was doomed when he shot the Sash Warrior.

The murder of the much-wounded Sash Warrior, paralyzed, it was apparent, and rescued by a valiant brave, at the close of the conflict, was held in obloquy by all. It was part of a code, unwritten but nonetheless clear, that to shoot the rescuer was fair within the rules of our Plains warfare, but to shoot the dying object of his dash was an obscene violation. So it was felt by all, on our side as among our opponents; and, so, it came as no shock, to other than the neophytes, that the savages, beaten and retiring, at the close of the day, attacked again that evening, having mustered additional recruits sufficient to overwhelm our small troop, to kill those of our mounts—the majority—abandoned in the melee, and to force our retreat to the ruined barn, where we then found ourselves, without food or water, and desperately short of ammunition.

.   .   .

"I would like to know you better," he said. "And I would like you to know me."

"If I did," she said, "what should I find?"

"A ratification of what I hope are your first impressions," he said.

"Which are?"

"A fairly good man, I think, who, through having seen some rough service, has developed certain strengths, and, perhaps, philosophies."

He remembered being shocked when she, at the close of that party, had come up to him. She was accompanied by her father, who, at the moment of her speech, turned back to his host, in a continuation of that conversation begun at the dinner table, and touching the party's mutual interests in the upcoming elections.

He had attended as the friend of a cousin of the host, and had, during dinner, spoken once or twice in response to various questions bearing upon, as the hostess put it, our possessions in the West. She had addressed him as "Colonel." He had put her aright, and the conversation had swung, for the brief moment, to brevet versus permanent rank in the Army. This, he understood, was in compliment to him, and his service and decorations in the late war.

At dinner, he had felt the eyes of the young woman, again upon him. He saw that she appreciated his courtesy in responding, at the riverside, with grace to questions, which, he saw she saw, must have been asked him innumerable times, so as to become, for him, quite literally, his "party piece." For was he not of course that Colonel Herbert whose actions were described and whose image depicted on the cover of Harper's Magazine? *Yes. He was the same. And why reduced in rank? And so on.*

During his recitation, he turned to her gaze. She did not look away, but there was nothing of boldness in her glance.

When they spoke of it in later years, he said he felt it was surprise he saw there.

Yes, she said, perhaps surprise, as if discovering an old friend in an impossibly remote foreign spot.

When he first took notice of her, across the dinner table, he thought, "That is the loveliest young woman I have ever seen." Eight years of marriage had not changed his opinion.

The light was falling, and as the Sergeant bent over him, his shadow cut the light from his eyes.

"We're going to have to push the arrow through," the Sergeant said.

He nodded; of course, they were going to have to push it through, though she had taught him, and he had always meant to write a paper on it, of the Spoon of Diocletian.

"What virtues do you not possess," he'd said, "cook, clean, act as an ornament, and hold forth on the martial accoutrements of antiquity?" To which she'd responded that the fault was not hers, but her father's, who, finding his daughter, as he'd said, insufficiently attractive to secure a mate, had overeducated her for the life of a bluestocking.

"Yes," he'd said, "a coterie of women with moustaches, smelling of camphor, in stout walking shoes, and bearing pamphlets explaining various Causes of Worth."

"Yes," she'd said, "and how would I have conversed with them, being ignorant of the wisdom of the ancients?"

"You would not," he'd said. "You would have been reduced to sitting in the window, with your work, and stitching 'Gallia est in partes tres divisa,' or however it is."

"Very good," she'd said. "Your mastery of the classics grows each day."

"There is much to be said for proximity," he'd said.

He should have written, he thought, the paper for the War Department, on the operation. For here he was now, shot through the shoulder, the shoulder blade, surely broken, and the arrowhead lodged, point probably turned-in-bone, and the barbs caught such that they "could not come out the same hole."

But the Spoon of Diocletian, that implement known of yore, a thin bronze shaft, spatulate and turned back at the end, pushed into the wound, along the arrow shaft, and past the point, then pulled back, the curved, spooned "sheath" allowing the missile's withdrawal, easily fashioned, could have been included in each outfit of the Surgical Corps, for all deployed against the savages. So he saw the legend run, upon the brown-paper wrapping of the implement, the legend taken from the conclusion of his note to the War Department, a note which he'd never written, the Spoon never produced, and, so, unavailable to him, and here he was with the arrow in him.

Well, if he lived, it would make a nice scar and a nice story, if one omitted the pain of the arrow, and the inevitably greater pain of its removal, and of the sure to ensue fever. He smiled and continued, to himself, "and the pain of the scalping," for the Indians, having withdrawn after the last attack, were, as the sun set, howling their intention to attack again.

It was in their last attack that he had taken his arrow. A savage, flanking the barn, through minuscule movement, over many hours, rose from the ground on which he'd lain invisible, his bow drawn. Captain Herbert caught the movement, turned, and took the arrow in the chest which was intended for his back. The Indian was nocking his second arrow, which he'd carried, crosswise, in his mouth, during the crawl. Its progress to the bowstring seemed, to Herbert, infinitely slow, as did his own in traversing his revolver, and in bringing it to bear. His first shot went wide, and his second caught the savage in the chest, his arrow at full draw, shot harmless in the dirt.

The arrow wound had felt, to him, like a sharp blow from a blunt instrument. As if he'd been struck, smartly, but with no real malicious intent, with a single-stick, in the left chest, just below the collarbone. As if an instructor were demonstrating the correct placement of a blow. Who would that be? he wondered. A Cavalry Sergeant, perhaps, at the Academy, pointing out a correct target for the lance?

Or a doctor, he thought, demonstrating—but he could not think what the doctor would be demonstrating, and he was overcome by pain, and he knew he had been struck badly, on bone, that the point had severed nerves, and that, should it be capable of extraction, it would sever more. It's likely, he thought, that, should I live, I will lose the use of that arm, or the arm itself.

He wondered what Mary would think of that, as the Sergeant spoke again, his face, this time, much nearer Herbert's own. Herbert saw that the Sergeant was making a great effort to cut through what he saw as the victim's stupor.

But I understand you perfectly well, Herbert thought; you needn't speak as if to a child.

"Captain," the Sergeant said, "we're going to have to push it through." He saw the Sergeant raise his head to the sound of firing. The troopers were firing at the new charge. For God's sake, hold your fire, he thought, and then the screaming was closer, and the Sergeant was gone.

He woke from a dream in which he had been suffocating. In the dream the skiff, in which he had sailed many afternoons with Mary, on the bay, had capsized. And she was not with him in the boat.

He searched for her in the water, and found himself caught up in the cordage and sail. As he tried to fight his way through, they wrapped themselves around him, and he panicked. The harder he fought, the closer the waterlogged sail and lines held him. He was roused by the pain, which was different from that of suffocating. It was localized in his left shoulder, and brought him awake instantly, but sufficiently confused to attribute it to torture by the savages. But it was the attempt to remove the arrow which he felt.

The arrowhead was fashioned, as were the bulk of the war arrows in the war's late years, of tin, the tin cut from the provision cans supplied to the Plains Cavalry. The point, then, sharp, thin and, on pressure, flexible, would, upon striking bone, "set," which is to say clench, making its withdrawal difficult. His comrades had wrenched the point out, and dragged it down across the shoulder blade. He screamed, and found something between his teeth. It was the Sergeant's doubled belt; and he felt two very strong hands pressing down on his shoulders. He heard the Sergeant saying, "Don't stop, you're right at the bottom. Don't stop. Now."

His body was moved roughly so that he rested on his right side, and the exquisite pain of the arrow point scraping on bone was replaced by an almost grateful change, as the point dropped below the shoulder blade. He felt a tentative push, and then the Sergeant's order, "Don't fuck with it."

He felt the Sergeant remove one of his hands, and then the arrow was pushed by a sharp blow through his skin out the front of his chest. The arrowhead was free. The Sergeant said, "Gimme the goddamn tongs."

Then he felt the shaft cut, and pulled free front and back, and the thing was over.

"We're going to wash you up now, sir," the Sergeant said. "It ain't going to bleed much, and it don't look as if there's much cloth caught in the wound."

He meant to say, "Don't waste the water on me," but found he could not speak. When he awoke again, it was night.

He smelled the mesquite, and the residue of the black powder, and of the cold fire. He smelled the night, and understood the story. They had lived through another day. No one had fired in some time; neither had they cooked, which meant the fuel was gone. He felt the rough, stiff bandage which could only have been torn from a canvas shirt; the shirt was stiff with sweat and blood, not only around the wound, but at the hem, far from the wound, which meant it had come from the dead.

.   .   .

The fellow who taught me to play Poker had been a gambler during the late War. This is not to say merely that, as a soldier, he gambled, or, even, that he loved to gamble. No, he had, in fact, enlisted *in order* to gamble. And had devoted his energies, under the martial discipline, to distancing himself from those areas where conflict might debar him from the exercise of his profession.

He had a job as an assistant to the Quartermaster-Clerk of my Company. And he was always to be found in the rear; where, I must say, he did his job well. The job was not demanding, and, in contradistinction to the rigors of actual line-soldiering, its hours were fairly regular, as, therefore, were those of the games in which he participated.

The line had shifted, and we were "not engaged" for some two weeks.

I utilized the time, personally, in rest, and correspondence, and, professionally, in reprovisioning my Company. In this latter, the gambler was most helpful.

During the day, he was to be found at the railhead, dealing with the stores. He discovered and shepherded those earmarked for our Company with determination, thus discouraging that pilferage and subvention which is the insuperable difficulty of all martial supply; and, when found short of those items of which the Company was in need, he was not above resorting to those stratagems decried above. In short, he was an excellent Company Clerk, than whom one could desire no better. The days found him at work, the nights in the sheds surrounding the railhead, or under canvas, in the Cook or Quartermaster tent of some adjacent Company, and playing cards.

I came across him, one noontime, in a lean-to out beyond the farrier's shed. I'd gone in to collect a set of buckles for a martingale. The blacksmith was out, and the forge was cold. I turned to go, and heard a sound I recognized as the shuffling of cards.

The playing of cards in this spot and at this time of day was contrary not only to Army order, but, more importantly, to that unwritten code of actual operation by which an organization differentiates between permitted lassitude and sin. So I approached, in my official capacity, to scold and threaten with punishment the malefactors.

I peered over the low wall of a stall, and saw this man, the Clerk, seated, alone, on a keg and dealing, onto the keg before him, now this and now that stunning set of hands of cards.

He would deal out a full house or flush, gather in the cards, shuffle them thoroughly, and deal, again, the same two hands; or he would shuffle and then deal out four queens, four aces.

I watched, amazed, and so intent was my gaze, that he felt it and turned.

He pocketed the cards and rose, and said, "Beg pardon, Captain."

I asked what he was doing, and he said he was "just practicing."

"Corporal," I said, "are you a *thief*?"

He denied it.

"But I have just seen," I said, "you manipulate the cards. To which great skill I must attribute your near-universal success."

He laughed. I asked him why, and he responded that he would not cheat, as it was, first, immoral, and, more importantly, unnecessary.

My request for an explanation led him to teach me to play poker.

"Poker," he said, "has nothing to do with cards."

His opening lecture likened it to dueling in the dark.

It will be remembered by the aged that in that period previous to the war, the gentility, and those who wished to ape them, in the South engaged in

dueling. It may also be remembered that much of this dueling took place neither with the pistol nor the sword, but with that short-sword known as the
"Bowie knife." This knife, closer to the Roman short-sword than the "hunting
knife," was a frontiersman's all-purpose weapon and tool. It had a straight
blade of ten to fourteen inches, and a guard (those of the Secessionists in the
late war bore a "D"-guard, which is to say, a closed half-circle protecting the
fingers, fastened to the top of the hilt, and joining the crossguard at the hilt's
bottom).

It was useful as a small or camp-axe, and in any of the myriad chores for
which a knife or axe may be employed. It was also a formidable weapon of war.

New Orleans, among many Southern cities, sported, in the antebellum
years, schools of dueling with the Bowie knife. Such schools were conducted,
in the main, by Frenchmen, who had adapted their skill with saber and épée
to the new, indigenous weapon.

The Code Duello, as of old, allowed to the insulted choice of weapons, and,
to his challenger, the choice of ground. Further rules were adjudicated mutually by the two appointed seconds.

The Bowie knife being chosen, the rules for the encounter admitted of no
restriction save the limits of the seconds' imagination. A common duel required the two combatants each to have his left arm tied to that of the other;
or for both to hold ends of the same handkerchief in their teeth. It is also re-
corded that men fought across a table, with their breeches nailed, each, to his
bench; or facing, straddling a floating log, and likewise affixed.

But the metaphor which began the Corporal's instruction in the skill of
cards was that of the darkened room.

Here, at night, a room was emptied, and all doors and windows treated to
allow the admission of no adventitious street- or moonlight. Each antagonist,
armed then with the Bowie knife, and blindfolded, led into the room, by
his and his opponent's second, and placed, by the light of the lamp, in one of
the room's opposing corners. The light was extinguished; the seconds left, and
closed and barred the door, which was not opened until one (or, as often occurred, both) of the duelists was dead.

This, the corporal taught, is the situation in which one finds himself at the
card table.

The information shared by all (as in Stud, where there are open cards) may be discarded as an aid to victory—how otherwise, for it may be exploited by all? The only advantage one may gain in Poker, he said, lies in the ability to determine or prognosticate that information which is hidden, which skill is the near-totality of skill at cards. I asked what was the rest. The rest, he said, lay in concealing and misrepresenting the nature of one's *own* strength. Learn to do these, he said, and the identity of the cards you hold is essentially moot. He then taught me to play cards.

How did he do so? He took some packing cardboard and cut it into fifty-two shapes, approximating the full deck; he then, and when our moments of leisure coincided, gave me lessons.

In these lessons he would deal the (featureless) cards in five or seven hands. And he would deal me five cards from an actual deck. He would then "play" the blank hands, one hand following the other, and ask me to analyze, from my "opponents'" bets, from their position at the table, and from their response to *my* bets, (a) what cards *they must hold*, and (b) how to convince them that my hand was superior, or inferior, to theirs, as it became, hand-by-hand, in my interests to induce them to fold, to call or raise..

He taught that one holds, in cards, an inestimable advantage over the two "blind" fighters in the dark room: one may retire. When the cards or this position is worthless, or when, through analysis, one determines he is beaten, throw in the hand, and save the chips.

And so, I learned the game. First Draw, in which all cards are hidden; and then Stud, in which three, or four cards are visible. As I improved I began to see that the information in Draw (the "blind" game) was not less than that in the hand of Stud. As, in Draw, all opponents suffered, or played, under the same ostensible handicap: they did not know what *I* had; and so, their various, essential "bids" (or "bets") endeavoring to erase their ignorance, *must* reveal, to the knowledgeable, the nature of their weaknesses and strengths.

It will not take much cogitation to perceive that I mean to widen this history into a conceit about the Art of War; which is exactly what I wish to do. For the gambler-clerk inspired me to the study of small-unit tactics; which study I will not say "led me to success," but, certainly, at least on occasion, saved my life, in the Rebellion; and a misapplication of which had brought me and my Company into the ambush at which I received my arrow.

The greatest mistake in any conflict is an underestimation of one's opponent; and, of mistakes, it is most common. It is to induce this misestimation that tactics first evolved from the set-piece battle, in which all was known.

For to create the illusion of strength is only a means to the end of creating the illusion of weakness. For battle cannot be won by defense. No, the appearance of strength can serve only to divert enemy forces to that position which they, mistakenly, have adjudged a point of weakness.

Napoleon wrote that, war being, essentially, the inexact attempt to execute a set of evolutions based upon faulty knowledge, when one's plan is proceeding perfectly, one has just walked into an ambush.

This was, of course, the fate of General Custer, whose education in martial philosophy was capped by his scalping and torture—to his admirers a tragedy, and to those not so disposed a coda worthy of the Master Hand, whose work, of course, it was.

All soldiers are philosophers. I will add Plato and Socrates to that list headed by Napoleon; and I will add to the list the great Hiram Grant. For what is strategy but philosophy—addending to the intellectual work a wager on its objective provability, said wager being one's life and liberty?

. As was Sherman a philosopher, his strategy in the East a reduction of war from the consideration of the material to that of the spiritual: his inspiration and the bedrock of his faith that when the enemy's hope is exhausted, the battle is done. For it has been written, by many a fine and bloodthirsty, otherwise Christian journalist of our Northeast, that the purpose of that late war was to instill in the Good, which is to say the Nationals, the will to kill the evil men of the South. But how is any conflict won? A duello, when one of the parties is dead, but in a National or, Heaven forbid, an International war, when the *will* of one of the opponents is gone. Sherman understood this; commentators, both North and South did not—those in the North objecting that he was paid not to destroy property but to destroy men; those of Secession complaining, to the contrary, that this strategy was inhuman and savage—more (curiously) than the mere licensed taking of life.

Sheridan, of course, understood this, too. He conducted his reduction of the Plains savages with that rigor he had learned from his superiors in the Rebellion. And, as a great general, he learned from them the same lessons which the British had learned from the woodsmen of the Revolution—those lessons which they had assimilated, sufficiently, to then employ to good effect under Wellington in the Peninsula.

But, as we are taught, "old men forget," and the notion of the set-piece battle, it seems, dies hard in the mind of the Hero-warrior. Who is he? He it is that has been corrupted by tales of Romance, by *Le Morte d'Arthur*, and the Waverly novels, who aims for a clean victory, its glory assured by an irrefrangible, irrefutable equality of force between the opponents—such balance broken only by a secret, simultaneous superiority on the part of the dreamer. (The cost of this criminal arrogance will eventually be paid in blood, and that blood usually of those who have sworn, to the criminal, allegiance.)

There may be said of Custer's folly this: that he paid the ultimate price. But he did not, unless one believes in eternal damnation. It is impossible that his torture by the savages was sufficiently prolonged. He murdered many of my friends.

Custer was, of course, a fool, than which no greater proof could be adduced than his insistence on retention, among his cronies and his sycophants, of the brevet rank he had achieved in the Rebellion.

There is a military custom by which one may indicate, to a superior, not necessarily insolence, but most certainly distance.

This is employed by a subordinate, of the enlisted or noncommissioned rank, in most instances of first acquaintance with an officer. It consists in the use, at all points at which, on a matured acquaintance, the address would be "sir," of the officer's rank.

Thus, the newly acquainted Sergeant will preface his remarks with "Captain," or "Major," as the case may be, who, with a more assured familiarity, will later simply say "sir."

This use of rank is the inferior's right, and, again, indicates not direct opposition, but distance, or, on later acquaintance, withdrawal of familiarity.

George Custer let it be known, however, the knowledge transmitted by that instant, molecular process incapable of analysis but recognized by all who have served, that he, to the contrary, *preferred* to be constantly addressed by his rank, and, further, by a rank to which he was no longer entitled.

I am told the question of brevet rank, has given some puzzlement to the general public. But to the military mind, its application and its theory are quite simple, viz.: *rank* indicates not merely status, but distinct responsibility. The

Lieutenant is, ideally, in charge of a Platoon, the Captain of a Company, and so on. The *Brigadier* has the responsibility of a Brigade (which is to say, a unit of the strength of several Regiments, each commanded by a Colonel).

Casualties in battle cause vacancies in the chain of command. The vacancies must be filled, and filled upon the instant. This chain of progression is clear. The most senior of the subordinates to the Brigadier (the most senior Colonel, or, in his absence, as in Custer's case, Major, and so on), will, on the Brigadier's incapacitation, as a matter of course, take charge of the Brigade. At the conclusion of immediate strife, the raised Major may be instructed to hold his position as Brigadier, and may be assigned the temporary (brevet) rank appropriate to his duties. Such rank is held as temporary until either *confirmed* (by Congress and the War Department), withdrawn, or allowed to lapse by cessations of those duties which gave rise to its award.

This brevet rank may, again, be confirmed by an act of the War Department in any case as a mark of favor. If not, upon removal of the officer from the post, he reverts, absent this action, to his previous, or *substantive*, rank.

This reversion need not be interpreted as a demotion; it may simply be a necessary realignment of the Army's Table of Operations—a response to a differing or decreased requirement for the services the rank required, as on the cessation of hostilities, this being the case with Custer.

On the termination of the Rebellion, as at the conclusion of all wars, the size of the Army was reduced. The enlisted soldier was released, and returned to his workbench or the plough. His absence, of necessity, lowered, in correspondence, the requirement for officers. Many returned happily to that civilian world and the professions which they had foresworn. But what of the professional soldier, whose life, whose career, and whose home was the Army?

War had inflated not only the number but the rank of officers, and both must now be reduced.

Almost all officers promoted by war reverted immediately to their permanent (substantive) rank. But the demotion did not end there, and many a Colonel or Major was offered the choice of a Lieutenant's billet or the street. Some were not offered even this, and remained in blue adorned only by Sergeant's stripes. And there were those to whom even this recourse was closed, and were free to pursue the benefits of Army life but as an enlisted man. (Among this last were found men, professional soldiers, sworn defenders of the Constitution, who had subsequently renounced their oaths, and accepted commission as Confederate officers and taken up arms against the Nation. What can one say of these? The war is long over, the case tried in the most conclusive of Courts.)

It was an ex–Confederate Captain who, as a noncommissioned officer of the United States Army, tended me at the time of my arrow wound.

Sergeant Murray was a most expedient soldier. Prior to the war, he had been a saddler. He enlisted as a Private in the Army of Virginia at the outbreak of hostilities, and rose to rank through his own excellences and exertions. He had never served in the National Army, and, so, never broken that oath of allegiance. So I, at the beginning of our relationship, reflected, staving off judgment until use and propinquity—philosophy's ablest squires—banished from my mind the last vestige of rancor, and he was left to me, per se, as that most valuable human being: a good soldier.

What does this mean? One who may be relied upon; who values, if it must be put plainly, his honor more than his life. In what does this honor consist? His oath to his Country. In what, to him, does his Country consist? The soldiers with whom he serves.

Some men are fortunate, and some are not. This superadded quality of worth may not be explained, but can be and has been observed by any employed, over time, in a communal enterprise. There are men whose advent seems to bring with them good fortune, good weather, an advantageous arrival of supplies, or of error on the part of the enemy. They are known to all. Such a man was Sergeant Murray.

I was not such a man. I fear I was an awkward soldier. I'd received a wound at Milk Creek from, I fear, an accidental discharge of my own revolver, at the successful conclusion of a skirmish; I had been thrown by horses easily ridden by and docile beneath the hand of tyro riders, and so on.

Sergeant Murray perceived this quality in me. And he sought—thinking his efforts unobserved—to protect me. This, I must say, I found a mark of especial favor.

This compliment of gracious courtesy extended by the ranks to those in command cannot be overstated. It can neither be extorted nor propitiated. The soldier cannot be forced nor fooled. He sees not "too much," but, indeed, *everything* of his commanders. And his endorsement is made not in ignorance of their (necessary) faults, but in their despite—having weighed a man and found him *on balance* worthy. This finding is, equal to the unreserved award of a lover's hand, the closest we may know on earth of a Divine forgiveness.

Sergeant Murray is long dead. He gave his life, long after my retirement from service, in the last excursions against the Hostiles. My wife and my son are gone. My comrades of the Great War are gone. Some, the most of them, fell in Virginia and Pennsylvania. Some few, having retired to civilian life, perished from age.

Of these last, I did not, in any case, preserve much correspondence after the Surrender. One goes to one reunion and finds not only that one mourns the dead, but that one envies them. The dead are together, and the survivor is apart, and feels himself, if the truth be told, if not disgraced, then certainly lessened by the fact of his own continued existence. This is a shame which can be banished only by complete love; and ah, that such shriving is to be found, in its perfection, only—or so it seems—in battle.

The most indelible of memories is war.

Mr. Lincoln, the greatest prophet of Christianity since Christ, was born into a log cabin, which held, above the door, as did they all, the long Kentucky rifle. As a young man, he marched as citizen Infantry against the Indians, and presided over us in the Rebellion, a conflict which, in scope and savagery, would have been, to all previous ages, unimaginable.

The new father sees, everywhere, about his infant son, the fatal object. When the child is young, he is forever moving, removing, or barring the possibility of mortal danger. Then he, as the child grows, turns from apprehension of the physical to the moral threat, and comes to lecture and scold until he is the prototype of irascibility. He has grown so from fear.

This paternal anxiety has as a close congruency that of the commander in battle. The lives of the troops are, literally, in his keeping. God forbid, then, that he has deployed them wrongly, inefficiently, thoughtlessly, or pointlessly.

The commander, in his choices, may be wrong; he, in any extended career, *must*, in fact, err. For war is essentially the progress of choices made, each, with insufficient information. War is error. But God help him who would commit men thoughtlessly or brazenly.

Arrogance on the part of the commander is but infrequently paid with his own life; indeed, but infrequently with his own inconvenience. Its cost is the lives of those of whom he is in charge.

The commander stands, in his responsibilities, like a father, with this difference. The father's mission is unitary: to raise, protect, and prepare his child. But the commander has *two* charges: his troops, and their mission. These two charges he must have before him always: the accomplishment of his objective, and the health and happiness and welfare of the men in his command. Both must be fulfilled equally, up to that point in which they are in opposition, at which point the mission must predominate—else what is the purpose of an Army?

The commander's task, here, is to *choose*. This is the burden of command. It is in recognition, if not in recompense, of this burden that the Officer is awarded status.

He who does not accept the challenge of the necessity of choice (upon which choice depends the lives of his troops), indeed, of choice made with insufficient knowledge, will never be a good commander. He will, in actual fact, not be a commander at all.

The worst of these delay and call it prudence. But such procrastination in a commander cannot be prudential, as it merely cedes initiative to the enemy. This can never lessen the jeopardy of his troops. It may only increase the likelihood of their demise in defense rather than attack.

All information in war is limited. That is the nature of war. If cards were displayed faceup, in what would the contest consist?

Delay by, or in anticipation of, a "Council of War" is, as Napoleon wrote, simply "taking counsel of one's fears." This we saw, in the Rebellion, in the absolute dereliction of McClelland, whose refusal to act, on the edge of absolute success, at the James River, prolonged the War by three years.

Who does not know the indecisive man, he who casts about now for this, now for that advice, until he comes to an adviser whose instructions he finds pleasant?

The Roman Catholics long ago understood this human frailty, and addressed it thus: he who has a moral problem may take it to any Priest of his choice. But he must, then, accept the chosen Priest's direction or decision as binding.

This relationship, of the worried and his Priests, is not unlike that of a married man, who has chosen, also, here in advance and once and for all, her to whom and for whose advice he will address the insoluble problem. Her position, here, is replicated, in the Army, in that of the Troop Sergeant, or Troop Sergeant Major.

It is to this wise veteran that the troubled commander may, and the wise commander will, refer. The Troop or Company Sergeant Major is known, colloquially, as the "first Soldier." That is, he is *of* the Troops, but, of them, most close to command.

His position, thus, is essentially maternal, he being not only adviser to him in charge of decision, but intercessor for those most affected by the same. He, if efficient, is again like the good mother, for, though most concerned for his charges' state, he cannot and must not be fooled. He must know the difference not only between malingering and illness, but between exhaustion and near-exhaustion. Upon this knowledge will depend, time after time, his charges' lives.

The commander, without sacrifice either of status or distance, may refer these most difficult questions to his Sergeant Major, who may, in turn, respond bluntly. This, again recapitulates the actions of a good marriage, where the opinion of the inferior may be more freely expressed, as it is opinion only— the final choice ostensibly being in the hands of another.

Sergeant Murray was a Roman Catholic. He had been, as I have stated, of the Rebel cause. He was a most excellent soldier, and came, as did the best of them, of the South, from those Western hills settled exclusively by the Irish and Scots.

These men make superb fighters, as they should, having been bred and raised for generations in those two locales famous for the growth of warriors: the Mountains, and the Borders.

Those groups are historically imbued not only with the endurance and martial valor called forth by their terrain, but with that of brave peoples subjugated—in the case of both, by the English. The late Rebellion, in fact, may be understood, inter alia, as a continuation of the strife between those lands settled by the English, the American North, and by the Celts, our South.

The question of slavery becomes here, secondary. Few in the South owned slaves, and fewer among its warriors. For the Celts, who were the greatest portion of the Rebel Army, were of the Mountains, where slavery was impracticable. And their parents or grandparents had in many cases themselves *been* slaves, or virtual slaves, to the English rule.*

I believe the war may not only be seen, but be primarily seen—from the battlefield—as a conflict between Briton and Celt, here played out as part of the endless strife between the Mountains and the Plain, between the country and the town, the sown and the wild; its current iteration, between man and machine. For the Southern soldier, the Mountaineer, the Borderer, was, perhaps, as a fighter, the better man; but, in the New World as in the Old, doomed to defeat, as weaker in tradition and material.

How could it be otherwise? The British North—the Protestant North, if I may—was dedicated to thrift, which thrift produced that surplus of capital sufficient for invention, experimentation, and mechanization; thus, for Victory.

The South, the Celts, oppressed for centuries by the English, possessed, neither in the Old World nor in the New, a tradition of thrift. They were and are notoriously profligate. Why should they have been otherwise—for the yield of their farms was not their own, and any supposed freehold of land, granted by the English, could be and regularly was revoked by them? Those people settled our South.

The Irish, in the main, were Trinitarian, and the Scots, mainly of the Protestant Church. But even in this last we must recall that Protestantism was, at first, entailed upon the Scots at the time the Catholic, Stuart—and, to them, rightful Queen, and heir to the British throne—was slain. This rancor persists to this day, among the now-Protestant Scots, in their love of a grievance.

These Celtic races were sifted yet again in the American South—between the Highland and the Low. The purebred British and the pro-British Scots were, as first comers in the Chesapeake, possessors of the finest land. The later arrivals—the irredentist Scottish, and the Irish, this latter in especial numbers

---

* Many English travelers wrote of the condition of the Irish in their native land, comparing it unfavorably with that of the black chattel slave in the American South.

after their Famine of 1845, migrated to the poorer lands of the Mountains in the West.

These men, as we saw in the late war, were the hill fighters par excellence. They were of that same mold discovered by the British, in India, on their Northwest Frontier—the descendants of the Mongols of Genghis Kahn.* Those Pashtuns, like the Celts of the South, are marginally subsistence farmers, more generally hunters, and bred-from-birth rebels against the Lowlanders, who, to their minds, have, variously, expropriated the good lands, the Throne, and the operations of the Courts, and from whom come only demands for taxes, conscription, or abandonment of their ancestral practices or homes.

I would rather have these Celt hill fighters under my command than any other men. For all that I fought against them, I was blessed to fight in their command.

The ferocity of the Scots' Protestantism, in their home, and in our South, has about it, of course, the flavor of resistance to religious oppression. This in them has remained and persists even through their acceptance of the Protestant Creed. Their very renunciation of Catholicism bears about it not only the dedication but the *preference* to fight for principle.

All armies and all generals have valued, or proclaimed that they valued, surprise; but it was left to General Sherman, and to General Sheridan, to codify the theory of surprise-by-*method*. Their practice was based upon the observation that deviation from warfare's accepted *norms* itself constituted a surprise, which might, on a strategic as well as a tactical level, break the enemy's will.

"They won't stand and let us strike at them," for example, is not an observation, nor, indeed, even a complaint, but an admission of surrender.

If the Comanche, like the Afghans, strike and retreat; if when retreating scatter, effectively thwarting Cavalry doctrine and productive pursuit, then it is our *doctrine* which must be changed—as must the commanders reluctant to accept such doctrine. To complain about irregular tactics in the enemy is

---

* Among the various maps in our Staff College, there hung one depicting the distribution of forces in the twelfth century, of the Mongol Genghis Khan. His Dominion was in blue, and stretched from the Dnieper River East, through India, and encompassing all lands in between. The one break in the blue was a small oval in red, showing the last unconquered people, those of the Afghan Mountains.

to suppose the presence of some adjudicating entity—one may scream, "They are not playing fair," but to whom?

Sheridan's genius was in recognizing that Plains warfare was, to oversimplify, not unlike Draw Poker. For the uninitiated, in Draw Poker each player is dealt his cards facedown. All his cards are hidden from his opponents. Nonetheless, no one can make a move (bet, call, raise, fold) without that move indicating his strength and strategy.

Every action of the Comanche, likewise, was, to Sheridan, a page in the book not only of their tactics, but of their psychology, to study which was to determine those patterns which would allow the wise commander to engineer their defeat.

They would not mass for a decisive battle, so complained the Solons of the Staff College, in command in the West. These wished, in effect, for that superbellum agency to establish a community with the savage *first*; to lay down mutually acceptable rules, and *then* proceed to war. But if such a community could be established, could it not as easily lead to peace? Would it not, in effect, *be* peace?

But such peace was not to be. Many have blamed its absence on our government's inability to keep its various treaties with the Tribes; or on the venality of settlers, Sooners; or upon the greed of Indian agents, or the ineptitude or corruption of the Indian Bureau itself; on the discovery of gold in the Black Hills, and so on. But the issue was larger than any of these, granted, contributory causi bellum. The issue was control of the Western Lands.

Could an influx not of millions but of tens of millions of Europeans not displace the native and his ways? It must, and it has. Could it have been accomplished with more honesty, more forethought, equity, and humane behavior? Of course. But by whom?

"Politicians," you may say. But who has ever met a politician who was other than shortsighted, self-interested, prevaricating, and, if not actually dishonest, then, at the very least, given to deceit and misstatement in favor of his purse, his creditors, and his ambitions?

To wish, again, for a superpower, superior to the Struggle, to envision a potential referee in the melee of politics, differs not much from the same wish applied to war. Both are ugly businesses, yes. In politics, we observe, we have a Constitution, and note in the same instant that, in the memory of many, we fought, over its interpretation, the bloodiest conflict ever known to Man.

Yes. The savage has gone to the wall, and has gone driven by unnecessary cruelty and in unfortunate, inhumane squalor. The Comanche takes with him this: that he never surrendered. Sheridan learned from the Comanche. And his lessons were communicated to his troops, and cherished by them. They knew that he would never commit them to a strategy which did not, if possible, allow them a superiority of force and of tactics—that is, that he would never involve them in a maneuver not best calculated to ensure both their survival and their victory.

If, to the Comanche, there was no surrender either offered or accepted; if this (as it did) struck terror into a Western Mind capable of envisioning death or the wound, but unseated by the thought of torture, then, Sheridan reasoned, the Comanche possessed a tactical advantage which we must render moot. To do so, we must similarly unseat his mind.

Noncombatants may believe in the power of rage as a martial tool, but rage will always be proved inferior to resolve, and its inferiority displayed in every contest. Rage clouds the mind and weakens the body. The inculcation of rage in the Enemy is the great, unappreciated tool of war.

This was Sheridan's intent—born in the war of the Rebellion, and matured in the Northwest—to strike at the *will to persist*. When this will is broken, the battle is done, however much strength in manpower and material remains on the enemy side.

He did not endorse, neither condone, torture and rape, but advocated all methods up to that point, such to include the burning of villages, the dissolutions not only of Tribes but of families, the destruction of crops and livestock. The eradication of the Tribe, and its concentration, upon the Reservation, alongside its ancestral foes, was a tool similarly effective at breaking the enemy will.

The reader may call such behavior heartless. It is. It is the essence of generalship: to break the opponent's heart. It may be called cold. Of course it is cold: What martial strategy could be effective which, in planning and execution, was not?

Did it progress to extremes? What does not? And were there instances of rapine and torture, of outrage, in short, perpetrated by our own troops? Yes.

As were perpetrated upon *us*. But remember this, you who are removed from both the threat and the memory of battle: *each man risks his life*. And, in that ultimate stake, all are equal. Each may or may not abide by his particular code, or the code of his Tribe, but note that the same occurs in the Civilian World: an army will contain the same number of the weak, the unbalanced, the "sadistic," and the cowardly as will be found in any civilian aggregation of men. You may say that the soldier is sworn to a code, and this is true. He is also exposed to the greatest stress known to man.

All land is won and maintained only through martial strife. And it may someday, may that day be far removed, eventuate that this Union and its peoples will be overcome and conquered, its land repeopled by an alien invader. It is inconceivable, but how, sub specie aeternitatis, could it be otherwise?

From whence could this invader come?* How, and by what means, and by the operation of what mechanical superiority dominate our men and culture? It is unthinkable; it is as unimaginable as would have been a half-century ago, such decimation to the Indians of the Plains.

.   .   .

He looked down at his journal, and wondered how, after the passage of so many years, one might relate with accuracy either the events or the emotions associated with battle. "Time," as each year he taught his students, "is one with distance, in this: that perceived over distance is understood but imperfectly, proximity increasing, as a matter of course, understanding. Congruently, in the realm of thought, time for reflection will increase clarity, as we come, though only metaphorically, 'closer' to the essence of our problems."

For it is in the details, he would always think, as he came to this part of the lecture. The details. And we may parse an argument in logic, separating it into thesis, dependent theses, antitheses; and our own arguments into reasoning by

---

* The soldier, like the farmer, trusts in nothing. That all things fail which might fail is but the bedrock of this distrust—its superstratum is the certainty that miscarriage and disaster, not only from an unknown quarter, but of an unimaginable kind, await only their own leisure to visit him.

Such was the nature of the chain of circumstances which, for example, deposited us at the Burnt Farm.

deduction, induction, analogy, and reference; but that distant object which may portend danger, or death, we must judge upon the instant—not only that most basic distinction between the animate and inanimate, between the shadow of a rock and that of a man, but between men, friendly and hostile, and, further, between the meanings of occurrences of nature: Why has the one crow flown in the distant field; why has a fault in the wind raised the horse's ears; has it, in fact, in ruffling the grass at the next rise, left immobile that one spot sufficient to conceal a man, or was that merely one's imagination?

He saw the blank faces of the students, and realized he'd spoken his thought out loud.

Now, the year later, he smiled at the memory, and the memory was this: that he had felt no embarrassment—that he realized that he had, indeed, some time ago, incontrovertibly grown old, and there was no shame in it.

The Indian, he wrote, had explained it to him, some time ago. Two days' ride from Fort Kearny, as he remembered it. In a reconnaissance, in bivouac, with the half-Company. At night. The relieved picket brought the Indian in, an ancient man, and quite the carte-de-visite of a Plains Sage, which was what he was.

They fed him. The interpreter tried to extract from him, in passing, some intelligence of the movements of the Tribes, of Crazy Horse, and of the Ghost Dance. But the old man demurred, feigning neither ignorance nor outrage, but dismissing the request as simply inappropriate between men of goodwill. They offered him tobacco, and they smoked. The Moon rose, and the old man began to speak to the Captain, man-to-man, about the future.

Much of his speech was in Cheyenne, which the Captain could follow but poorly. But it was accompanied by commentary or amplification in Sign, which he perfectly understood.

The Indian spoke of events which would transpire some thirty or forty years on, when the last of the Buffalo would be gone, when the Tribes would be gone, when the cities, of which he had heard, would cover the Plains.

"There was," the Captain wrote, "in this nothing miraculous, for, 'westward the Course of Empire' was, finally, less an exhortation than a simple, inescapable fact. That he alluded, or, in my memory, seemed to allude to specific developments, in Mechanics, in Science, in Industry, need not be attributed to the supernatural—for memory is both weak and selective, and it is the technique of the Sage to speak in generalities—one not only recalls those predictions which have

come to pass, and forgets those which have not, but misremembers the predictions themselves, in order to avail oneself of the thrill of an encounter with the supernal.

"Further," he wrote, "there is a misunderstood or, indeed, overlooked bond between prediction and inspiration. Did not Jules Verne write, before the war, of submarines, and airships? How could these have, as they have, come to pass had they not, previously, existed in Man's mind as fantasies?

"Is this to say that the musings of a savage, on the Plains, could have influenced or inspired inventors, with whom it was impossible that he have contact? No. But, rather, that the same fantasies which ran through their mind ran through his.

"We note that no sooner had Marconi come forth with his invention, than several, and more than several, men around the world produced machines, upon which they had been working, simultaneously with, but in ignorance of, each other's efforts.

"And was not the same true of Edison and the Electric Light; of Bell and the Telephone, which case was tried in the courts for twenty years; and of Morse and the Telegraph; and so on?

"There is no such thing as the 'unthinkable.' We said, in response to this or that outrage, in the Rebellion, and on the Plains, and alleged or proved of either side, that it was 'unthinkable.' But, of course, it was not, as someone had done it, and, previous to the act, had imagined it.

"Nothing is unthinkable. In this, the massacre at Wounded Knee, and the torture of the Nationals at Andersonville, are united with the Electric Light and the Automobile: all rose from the common consciousness of Man, and found their expression in action.

"Jules Verne envisioned a ship which could travel against wind and tide, beneath the sea. Some ten years later, such a 'submersible' was employed (in Charleston Harbor) by the Secessionists."

The Sage observed, suggested, envisioned the course of the future; this, to him, was nothing remarkable.

"And why not?" the Captain wrote. "The grandfather can see, in the infant, the course of the being's life. It is written in his disposition, in his intellect, in his corporality and general health, in his relations to the world and its inhabitants. Barring accident, what surprise remains?

.   .   .

There was a man on the Police Force of a neighboring town. We learned in the newspapers that he was but recently retired after a long career as a patrolman walking his beat. That career was preceded by his service in the Army. He'd been a Trooper in the 7th Cavalry, and had rid with Custer, to the Little Bighorn. He was dispatched, we read, before dawn, on the morning of the fight, from Custer, with a note for Benteen, and so escaped, and was the only man in Custer's troop to escape annihilation on that day.

The newspaper interviewed him on his retirement, as it had, I believe, on every five- or ten-year anniversary of the massacre in the thirty years intervening since his retirement from the Army. Over these years, he was quoted speaking of his luck, of his Faith in God, and questioned, in every interview, in a perfect example of journalistic invention, on the similarities between Plains warfare and walking a beat in a suburb of Boston.

He was periodically asked about his feelings upon learning of his Troop's destruction. He would then catalogue, as would you or I, sorrow, surprise, shock, and, of course to his credit, a certain shamefaced relief that he was not among the slain—this tempered by an ill-expressed, but nonetheless powerful for that, sense of his particular unfittedness for his deliverance.

But the man never mentioned that which must have been his first, overriding, and most persistent thought upon receipt of the massacre's news: "Thank God I received a written order."

Has not General Lew Wallace spent his life, since the War, bootlessly, frantically, endeavoring to expunge from his name the accusation of cowardice, in his command at the Battle of Shiloh?

I read, and will suppose we all have read, his book, *A Tale of the Christ.* I—perhaps "searched" is too strong a word—but, as I read, I was alert for any hint, in the fictional tale, of exculpation for his actions at Pittsburgh Landing. I cannot say I discovered such; but might not one indict a fiction, any fiction, toute entiere, as a beatification of its author (What else could it be?) by his transubstantiation into the person of his Hero? Under this theory—with apologies to Professors of Literature, who, no doubt, will know more than I—or will, at the least, possess theories and doctrines, if not more cogent, then more interestingly opaque—might we not identify Lew Wallace in the character of his creation, Ben Hur, who, though absolutely blameless, is cast into obloquy so sufficiently severe as to be redeemable only through the Intercession of Christ?

As Christians, the same must, of course, be said of us all; and Wallace, without injuring his claim of absolute innocence, may ask us, sinners all, to identify with him under the theory of Original Sin, which can be cleansed only through the Grace of the Savior. But in Wallace's case, the Savior was Grant, who, throughout his life, adamantly refused that absolution which, in his book, Wallace has Christ grant Ben Hur.

Let us observe Ben Hur, who, as his creator protests of himself, was innocent of all charges against him. Both suffered agonies, and both sought their end through complete submission to the higher power.

But, however Wallace may have been guiltless, Grant was not Christ.

Imagine Wallace, world-famous and wealthy, revered and lionized for his book, pleading, near Grant's deathbed, with Grant's relatives and attendants, for the one last interview, in which to be allowed to make his case to the dying man; to attempt to win, by reason, or, indeed, through pity, from Grant, that one word of absolution, without which the remainder of his life must be as dust.

But Grant believed him guilty.

What would I have done in Wallace's place? What, if I knew, or felt myself blameless of, that greatest sin of which the soldier may stand accused? I do not know. It is too horrible to contemplate. But I do know, that the Policeman—Trooper, to the end of his life—thanked his God that Custer had given him a written order to Benteen.

Cutting for sign I always found a joy. And tracking.

I would go out with my grandfather, in Maine, when a big buck was two hundred eighty pounds, and not only the Black, but the Brown Bear was in abundance, and the Catamount as common as them both.

We would Still Hunt, according to the ways he'd learned there, as a boy. And he had learned them, of course, from the Indians.

To hunt into the wind, or crosswind, is a matter of course; to follow the feeding and mating cycles of the deer, the bear, the moose, to examine their scat and rubbings, to determine their favored areas of use, and to predict their movements by the phase of the Moon, and of the weather; these and their like are the lessons open to the novice. They are both logical and clear.

Additionally, there exist those precepts of hunting which, I believe, as they approach the ethereal, can only be learned and appreciated in viewing their efficacy, under the silent tutelage of a master.

I instance adherence to that which I must call "the rhythm of the day": the strength and the direction of the wind and its shifts, of the soughing of the trees, and the run of the stream, of the passage of the clouds and of their shadows. This rhythm or character of the day exists. It may be felt and must be obeyed, and action made in reference to it. It can no more be analyzed, finally, than those movements a man makes in his approach to a woman, which, if they be anything more than a mere seduction, will be in response to that rhythm set and changed by her at will.

There is a rhythm in the woods to which the animals, hunters, and prey must accommodate themselves—each for the purpose of that concealment of presence or intent upon which ability depends its life.

A cloud passes, and a shadow passes. One may move at the speed of the shadow, in the shadow, and stop in the shadow's rhythm, against a tree, to break the human outline. Cutting for sign, one may hunt with the sun at one's back so that a print's depression will be accentuated by the shadow falling into it.

I was taught to scan right-to-left, as we read left-to-right, and have the habit of beginning any perusal at the left. Of a sign, a meadow, a rise, a book, if we, thus inclined, begin our survey at the right, we will find that our natural tendency drags our gaze to the left, and we must, once and more than once, force ourselves to begin again at the right. We will, thus, have forced ourselves to scan the vista twice and more than twice. This trick was taught to me by my grandfather, in Maine, before the war—he carrying the Kentucky rifle which was his at the Battle of New Orleans.

On the Plains we saw the half-stock Hawken and the Sharps, relics of the Buffalo Trade, and the much prized Spencer-Henry repeating rifle. In the arsenal at Harpers Ferry, our frugal government still housed the Brown-Bess muskets of the Revolution, perhaps against the day that conflict might break out again.

But it is never the old, but the new conflict, which is to say, conflict erupting from the unforeseen quarter, which arises to plague us. For if the quarter were foreseen, and the danger evident, why would we not have fought to extinguish the threat in its infant stage? If it were foreseen, would not the forces of diplomacy, the threat of intervention, and subvention have dealt with it?

The two great capacities of a commander: first, the ability to move slowly, and then to move quickly (or its inversion), second, the discernment to determine (which is always a guess) which of the two must apply.

But the hunting of the forest taught rules much different from those pertaining to that of the Plains. Here, the Comanche and Cheyenne depended for their lives upon the run of the Buffalo, the skill of *driving* which superseded that of stalking—this last more useful as a tool of the raider than of the hunter.

To divert from the herd a sufficient number of beasts, to drive them into a defile or a box canyon, over a deadfall, or, indeed, into a corral, was the most efficient of the savage's methods. These served him well, in his early dealings with the United States Army.

For we, like they, had trackers and scouts, and could prognosticate as well as our opponents, our enemy's probable movements and evolutions; but we failed, as they did not, in elaborating both this information and conjecture into cogent strategy.

A man can run down a deer. The deer is swift to, perhaps, one or two hundred yards. He then must stop. But a man, should he persist, can, over the course of one day, or at the most two, run the heart out of the deer's body—as he did, indeed, in the days before projectile weapons and the horse. But a man cannot run down the larger beast, and the Buffalo, to be taken in any great number, required concerted strategic action.

I learned my hunting lessons from my grandfather in Maine and took much game. But Phil Sheridan, learning his in Georgia and Virginia, gave to the world Modern War.

The penny-dreadfuls and dime novels of the postwar era featured the Brave Indian Scout, or his simulacrum: Kit Carson, John Frémont, and so on, capable of glancing at a hoofprint, moccasin print, broken branch, or long-burnt stick, and from the glance extrapolate not only identity of the pursued, but his state, including his age, his diet, the contents of his horse's pack, and, by extension, his intent.

These magical Indians and semi-Indians were, originally, found in the works of James Fenimore Cooper, and reached their apogee, perhaps, in the less vaunted, but vastly more readable, "Wild West" tales of "Ned Buntline," et al. Here the great frontier skills were abstracted as a whole from the Indian and assigned to the Cow-Boy, Desperado, Gun-Fighter or Peace-Officer, who, though representing the New Thing (the Advent of the European), held his position in our communal fantasy as an incarnation of the Old and Savage. (Thus, for example, the Prussian glories in a militarism he claims as his traditional own, but which is essentially an appropriation of the Nordic myths of Odin and Valhalla; the Spanish Grandee in the fainéant nobility which is a heritage not of His Most Catholic Majesty's dynasty but of his predecessor, the Desert Moor.)

War is savagery. The set-battles of the Age of Chivalry are presented as fact; but this must be, to anyone acquainted with combat, sham. How do I know? Their persistence, to this day, as "Parade" attests not only to our willingness, but to the *necessity* of our belief in a war with rules.

If such were, or ever had been, a fact of life, why the insistence on the confected ceremony? It commemorates, and perpetuates, not a tradition, but that which, perhaps, underlies all tradition, which is a wish, predated sufficiently to forestall its verification as fact.

Sherman's observation was that the more savage side must prevail, and that violence must be done not only to our opponents but to their notion of propriety.*

.   .   .

At night, and as often, perhaps, as once a month, he refought the fight at the Burnt Barn. He smelled the burning flesh in his own back, as Sergeant Murray probed for and removed the Apache arrow, and he heard the Lieutenant screaming—to his God, or perhaps to the attacking savages—to embrace the lessons of

---

* We note that it is less destructive to life to burn crops than to massacre men; but Sherman's name will be, in the South, forever anathema, though he killed a mere fraction of the men killed by Grant.

that Savior which, propounded, in his own belief, to all mankind, had, it seemed, been overlooked by the Apache. He saw, or he heard, or he imagined Sergeant Murray, rising from his ministrations, to one knee, to use one precious cartridge from his Spencer, to blow the back out of the Lieutenant, who, though mortally shot by the Indians, was still advancing toward them, his arms spread, in an apparent attempt to preach the Gospel.

Did this in fact occur? It certainly occurred as a repeated, almost standard feature of the Dream.

When he recovered from his fever he returned to Fort Kearney. There he learned from the newspapers that the Lieutenant had fallen in a brave and hopeless charge against the savages; the Lieutenant earned a commendation for it, and a ribbon, which was sent to his wife.

Never by the slightest word or expression did the Sergeant indicate that the Lieutenant's death or his behavior throughout the action had been anything other than deserving of praise. And the Sergeant had been offered now this and now that inducement to comment on the Lieutenant and the manner of his passing. He had not done so, either feigning or possessing ignorance of the hints and inducements both officials and journalists placed in his way.

In his dream, our Captain saw the beautiful Colt's Revolver, in its now-useless .36 caliber, its pointlessness displayed beyond cavil, as the Lieutenant raised it to his temples, and thumbed back and pulled the trigger now once, now again, and again, as if some cartridge could, by the force of his will, be conjured out of the empty cylinder.

On awaking, he sometimes wondered, "Where is that revolver now?" For, certainly, the savages must have taken it from the dead on the field of battle, on the morning after the retreat. And where was the knife with which Sergeant Murray had extracted the arrowhead? That knife he'd heated in the fire, which knife was the badge of the Secessionist, latterly joined into the Union Army?

Vanished with the Sergeant, at the Three Forks, where he fell, and, again, gone to the Comanche. But they used their tools hard, as they used their ponies, 'til the one broke and the other died.

"They said," he'd told his class one day, "that any fool can make a bow, but it takes a genius to fashion an arrow." But the arrows were meant, and only meant, *to be expended, while the Lieutenant cherished his useless Colt's Revolver, which he was incapable, at the end, of employing even for suicide.*

The Confederate Bowie, again, was the badge, on the Frontier, of the ex-officer. It was identifiable immediately by its D-guard, which enveloped the knuckles of the gripping hand. In this, it resembled the saber, which it originally was, and from which it had been ground down into the foot-long knife.

It was worn as a badge of honor-in-defeat, or of refusal to admit defeat, or some such thing or combination of the two.

"All wars of the future," Grant wrote, "may have their ends fairly accurately predicted: they will be won by the side capable of producing the greater amount of steel."

It certainly was true of the Rebellion, which was a lost cause from the first. One saw it in the appearance, on the battlefield, of the D-guard, or "Confederate," Bowie knife. For these had, universally, first been swords, or sabers of the Cavalry, or of the officer caste. These swords, broken, had been reground into long knives. An indication, on the Confederate part, of their lack of steel.

After the Secessionist defeat, many of the officers, still bearing their swords intact, broke them, and wore them on their belts as knives—a symbol of allegiance past and present—past to the Confederate States, and present, to their memory, and to the memory of fallen comrades.

Many of the actual Bowie knives, that short sword, which were worn on the Frontier, in the Gold Fields, in the Rebellion, and afterward, upon the Plains, were made in Sheffield, England, by the great cutlery concerns. And many were sold, in the East, to those embarking on, or wishing to possess the accoutrements of those embarking on, some Western Adventure. To this end, and to attract this market, the knives were, variously, factory-inscribed, or engraved, "Frontiersman's Knife," "California or Bust," "Hunter's Companion"; and during the Rebellion, "Death to Slavery," or, indeed, "Death to Abolition," and "Never draw me without reason, nor sheath me without Honor."

But the D-guard knife, ex-saber, of the onetime Secessionist, required no inscription on its blade, for the intent behind its display was clear. The inscription regarding honor could be read in its mere appearance, and, if I may, in the eyes of its possessors. Badinage, or, indeed, mere discussion of the late Rebellion, was, in the presence of those carrying this knife, undertaken, on the National side, then, in the face of a clear warning.

He smelled the burnt flesh and the hot metal in his dreams, and the all-pervading scent of the black powder, and the copper smell of blood, and the smell of the terrified horses.

Well, the dream was now an old, painful acquaintance, with which one learns to live. As such, it was like his useless left arm—his wound and disability—his own badge, like the Confederate Bowie, prompting the observant to silence.

He had been walking through the Yard. "What was it like in the War, sir?" the student had asked, at which the Captain had stopped, and thought, and finally, after how much time he did not know, looked down, back at the student, staring at him, caught between concern and something perhaps closer to fear.

Oh, the Captain thought, he wonders if I am insane, or perhaps senile, or ... And he recognized he had seen that look with some frequency of late. Well, he thought, I am getting old. Indeed, I am old. What could one expect?

.   .   .

The Ghost Dance phenomenon was an example of that eschatology which overcomes, in whole and part, all cultures menaced by oblivion.

By the end of the Eighties, the Plains warriors had been defeated in battle and co-opted or subdued in Council. Their subsistence, and thus their culture, which had, for millennia, depended upon their interaction with and understanding of Nature, now lay in the hands of the Bureau of Indian Affairs.

Its bureaucrats, as with any large Governmental organization, were, by turns or generally, overworked, corrupt, or misguided. They were inclined either to punish those acts they deemed as transgressive of their authority, or to reward an ostensible docility with gifts scarcely less destructive than their corrections. The Indians had been convinced, badgered, or exhausted into the acceptance of Government promise of privacy and subsistence in the various Reservations whose sanctity and inviolability Washington had pledged.

These pledges were, sequentially, proved empty, unenforceable, or provisional; and, even where they were none of these, were found, by the savages, to have been the ultimate of Devil's Bargains, acceptance of which meant the absolute end, if not of their lives, then of their way of life; this being, to most, the same thing.

Imagine the young, among the Tribes, those just come into manhood, and, politically more important, those of proven prowess, and on the cusp of matriculation into positions of leadership. This latter group was deprived, by the Capitulation, not only of that life of battle essential to the Indian young, but of those positions coveted and earned by the years of service of the now matured warriors. Their culture was in the process of destruction, their status, thus, not only eroded but demolished, and, with it, their hope for any future other than as wards of the State which had subdued them. Superadded to this was the absolute conviction of the rectitude of their cause, which was the integrity and longevity of their People. (The parallels between their position and that of the Rebel officer caste after the Surrender are apparent.)

In the last years of the late Century, Lakota in the Territory of Nevada reported an apocalyptic vision. These, particularly, their Medicine Man, Wovoka, recounted the appearance during a vision quest, of a White Buffalo, attended by various signs and manifestations, which, in their totality, indicated to him the designs and desires of his God: that the Sioux were to propitiate their dead, who would return from the Spirit World, and lead them in a war against, and which would result in the vanquishment of, the Whites.

These celebrations, in their entirety, were known as the Ghost Dance. As its nature became understood (conclaves away from the various Reservations, and celebration followed by attack upon the Whites), its suppression was entrusted to the Army, successful prosecution of which brief effectively marked the last phase of that War upon the Plains in which I had participated earlier.

Victorio, war chief of the Apaches, had attacked a party of settlers near what is now Chloride, New Mexico, and a punitive expedition was dispatched, including one-half of my Company of the 6th Cavalry.

We followed Victorio's band for three days, and, on the morning of the third, our outriders came upon the scene of an apparent attack in progress upon a small ranch or farm.

This farm consisted of the farmhouse, a barn, several outbuildings, and a large corral. Our scouts reported that these sat upon a small plateau, of perhaps one hundred acres, that the savages had encircled the compound, their arrows having fired the barn, and that the White inhabitants, some eight or nine, women and men, had taken cover and were firing on the attackers, who, absent our immediate appearance, would soon overrun the defense.

We formed and galloped to the site, some two miles distant. There we found the situation as described. Now both the barn and the house were burning; the Whites still were firing, their success marked by the bodies of ten or twelve savages fallen near the farm's perimeter. Access to this was to be gained by a cutback, or incline rising from the level of the ground, to the height of the eight or ten feet of the natural mesa upon which the farm was situated.

We galloped, firing, up this incline, and into the area of the farm. There we found the supposed White defenders were, in fact, Hostiles, their number increased by some twenty or more braves secreted behind the burning barn, by those supposed fallen, who had been busy shamming dead, and by a force of some, at that time unknown number, hidden behind the back and the sides of the small butte.

Our momentum carried the forward element into the compound, and, thus, into the trap, which was closed behind us by the above-named elements of the Hostiles. The remainder of our half-Company, numbering some thirty men, found itself still some half-mile back when the trap was sprung. We later learned that they, on seeing our situation, and in riding to our support, had been attacked by the reserves of Victorio's band, and waged their own battle in the wash of Cuchillo Negro Creek. (It was a galloper of this group dispatched to Major Meeker, who brought down those Companies whose arrival eventuated in the salvation of that small number in the Farm, of which number I was one.)

But we, myself as the senior officer, and so I must say "we," through my fault, had ridden thoughtlessly into an ambush only made more perfect by its elaboration of theme into a destruction not only of the first group, come to save the settlers, but of the second, come to save the first.

This was a principle of conflict at which the Indigenes excelled, and of which we Whites were what cannot even be called inept, but rather of which we must be characterized as ignorant: the exploitation of Psychology.

Note that this trap was founded upon two interrelated understandings: the first, and simpler, that rescuers would come to the aid of the beleaguered, and the second, more sophisticated, that such rescuers, faced with the apparent spectacle of women and children under fire, would suspend their natural and professional estimations of the possibility of a staged trap.

For surely a less emotionally involved commander (in this case myself), if not consciously descrying the anomalies of dress and behavior in the supposedly beleaguered Whites, might have received some feeling or "intuition" prompting a reserve before debouchment into an area which, in common with all man-made or natural defenses offering protection from attack, held also the concomitant danger of isolation and, thus, eradication of its occupants.

It was Sergeant Murray who first scented the ambush. I had looked around, finding him not at his accustomed place at my side during the charge, and saw him, hesitating, at the top of the rise or ramp leading to the mesa. He saw me, turned in my saddle, and spurred forward just as the trap was sprung, and we found ourselves fighting through the "settlers," and the first bands issuing from their hiding place behind the burning barn.

My horse was shot out from under me in the first moments of the charge. I found myself rolled up on the ground, and helped to my feet by Murray, who was already shouting orders.

I directed him to take charge of the 2nd Platoon, and push back toward the North, or side of our ingress, and fan outward. I took the 1st, formed them en bataille, and commenced firing toward the South. The two ranks gave a good account of themselves during the first few volleys, and I, seeing the Hostiles' momentum broken, ordered the men to fix bayonets, and to charge, which we did, driving them back and down over the far sides of the ravine.

It was here that the squads issued the new repeating carbines told.

At the end of some half-hour, Sergeant Murray's Platoon and my own found ourselves in possession, not of the entire mesa, but of a defensible perimeter formed by the three natural defiles of the ridge sides, or ravine, and that cover offered by the remains, on the South, of the farm's buildings, and the stone foundation of the well.

We drew the wounded and the dead inside our lines, the difference between them not being immediately apparent in the haste of their retrieval under fire.

Those capable of continued defense we supplied with weapons and ammunition, giving them cover against the stone foundations of the house, the remnants of the barn, and our mounts, slain in the ambush, or by our own hands in the aftermath.

These carried in their saddlebags ammunition sufficient, when added to that each man held in the bandoliers, to amount to some one hundred twenty rounds per man.

We found ourselves, then, in the same position as that of the settlers whose presence had attracted the original attack. The difference lay in this: they numbered twelve, five of them women and children. We were, at this point, a troop of thirty-five well-armed soldiers, supplied with both weapons and ammunition, holding the high ground, and lacking only the one thing, which thing was water. For the Hostiles had, we quickly learned, denied us the well, using the expedient of throwing into it the naked and mutilated bodies of the settlers.

Two expeditions were attempted to retrieve water from the creek. It lay but some twenty yards to the East from the bottom of the ravine, its position clearly marked by the inevitable cottonwoods. We attempted to divert our opponents by the feint of a breakout back down the Southern ramp, in which feint four troopers died, as eventually did those next four who, laden with canteens, and making a dash for the creek, found, on their arrival, their opponents, behind the cottonwoods, holding their fire, and waiting to execute another ambush.

These four men, as night fell, we saw crucified and tortured, for our amusement, just out of rifle range. (Though Dixon, with the Sharps Buffalo gun, did slay the one torturer, as described earlier, at the distance, afterward measured, of over one mile. After this shot, the Hostiles dispersed, leaving the four men dead, half-dead, or screaming, in another invitation, to us, to suspend good judgment, and be provoked into a senseless attempt at rescue.

We may decry but we cannot demean this battle strategy—that of the Guerrillo, which we Americans ourselves practiced in the Revolution, and which was adopted by the Rifle Corps of Wellington in the Peninsula, and by the Moros in our war with Spain. All these, essentially partisans, fought from cover, attacked when conditions bade well to guarantee success, refrained when not, dispersed when followed, and utilized not only terrain but Psychology to defeat those forces numerically superior and better-armed.

This was the strategy of the Plains warrior—not to *fight*, neither to measure strength against strength, but to prevail.*

What debarred them, the better fighters, the better strategists, from ultimate victory in our century-long struggle? Lack of cohesion, and the inaccessibility of modern weaponry. These brought about a defeat which the mere numerical inferiority would not have guaranteed. That their defeat was inevitable and that they knew it is established by their recourse to the supernatural (the Ghost Dance). That these brilliant fighters, who owed their tactical successes to will, daring, proficiency, and understanding, trusted their strategy to the metaphysical represents the surrender of both intelligence and will which are the precedent for the demise of any power, be it a squad, an army, or a Nation.

To trust to the gods rather than to Luck may be the more supportable to the religious—but it is not more rational; indeed, it may even be seen as an act of impiety. I do not indict the Indians' gods, who served them well for millennia; neither do I invoke the God of All, who has in his care both the Red and the White races, whose Destinies are known only to Him. We know that He helps those who help themselves, but a truer casting of the proverb might be that he does not help those who do not help themselves; and he is free to choose among the conflicting claims of those who do.

For certainly both the Red and the White implored supernatural aid in extremity. I know I did. It was forthcoming in the arrival of C Company, dispatched, as it turned out, not in response to our plea for help, but as part of a routine random sweep conducted under the program of General Miles.

I had, and my children mocked me for it, been a devotee of both the dime novel and the Wild West show.

Caro, when young, had written what she thought was a sonnet "to her Father, on watching a reenactment of an Attack on the Overland Stage by Indians":

"Showing neither that which might be called
Nostalgia for the thing itself nor

---

* That it is, to this day, taught in our war colleges, as mere history, rather than as doctrine, is criminal folly.

Excitement at its simulacrum
But a quizzical, removed, and vigilant mien ..."

I was touched by her affection, as always.

She and my wife took my reading habits more to task, chaffing and chiding me for *The Warriors of the Black Hills*, *The Broken Stirrup—A Tale of the Pony Express*, and so on.

How may I explain my taste? For those written homages to or explanations of that era were in all respects false, as to names, dates, procedures, philosophy, and practices, vide: "He imitated the call of the owl, to lull the Savages in to the false security of the notion that the threat, whatever it had been, was passed. And the Hillside, and all its inhabitants, slept as before."

It was not even that I enjoyed, as many do, when reading fictional depictions of their own profession, the writers' solecisms, greeting them with laughter or enjoyable contempt.

It was more than that "they brought me back," not by their content, for, save their titles, there was nothing in them to spark the memory or nostalgia, neither of which were, as with any soldier, ever far from me in any case, but, perhaps, by their titles and gentle vacuity. I don't know. But they, like the pipe or the cigar, allowed my mind to run on memory or dreams.

The memories of Army life are in the main compounded of loss and love.

In this they are like those of the survivor of a long and joyful marriage, on the passing of his spouse.

In the Army, the loss is felt not only on the conclusion of a career, but throughout it. It is occasioned not only by the terrible excision from one's command and from one's life, of one's comrades—indeed, grief at their falling is most usually incathectable at the time, one's energies being devoted to salvation of oneself, one's command, or one's mission—but throughout one's career, intermingled with the sharpest love, in that recurrent and overwhelming sensation known to those who have served, of wonder at and gratitude for the very experience.

Who does not recall with a pang that recurrent moment, in solitude, at dawn or dusk, perhaps—coming off watch, onto the parade ground, rising from the tent, or waking, on the ground, in moonlight, to review the watch—to walk to the cook fire for the tin cup of coffee, and exchange two words, in the night-voice, with the fellow there?

It is like a marriage also in this: sometimes the closeness is almost unbearable, and one thinks one may die—the unlucky from terror at, the fortunate from gratitude for, the intimacy.

When it is gone, as, for the soldier, it one day must be gone, and as with the love of the surviving spouse, its loss is made more bearable by the love one always bore it. For one always knew that one day it must end.

Those who loved warfare—and I was not one—adored it, as Shakespeare wrote, "going to their graves like beds." By this the soldier understands that they went to *battle* as to their beds, and those the marriage beds.

The soldier understands this simile to concern not *death*, but *lust*; that is, lust such that one, were he told that the end of his final conquest of some woman would be death, would not only proceed in any case, but find the warning fatuous.

Perhaps the word is misapplied, those in love with battle being better called, not "war lovers," but "fey." There were few of these, but each company had at least one.

It has been said that proximity to such a man was dangerous. I did not find it so (but neither was it salutary, or an "encouragement to the Troops." I never found them to require encouragement).

No, this lover of battle, often (though it is a cliché) the Scots-Irishman, made one part of that phenomenon of random distribution every soldier, down through time, has discovered in his Company. There he will find the philosopher; the scout gifted to find the enemy, and him who is gifted to find women and wine; the prognosticator or sage who could foretell the weather and the movement of troops; the artisan; the Cassandra; the Giant; and so on—a distribution of talents and proclivities which must have influenced the ancients in their construction of the Pantheon. (How otherwise? Where could they have seen it, but upon the Earth?)

I have instanced also the Lucky Man, and his doppelganger, the Jonah—the second often remarked, but the first also invariably present—allusion to his presence circumscribed by that most ancient of superstitions.

It was not that the Celt was bloodthirsty. He was not bloodthirsty, which, to the soldier, curiously, is a most weighty opprobrium; he loved to *fight*. And neither was he reckless, an inclination worthy of the utmost derogation; for, first and last, a soldier must be careful. But he rejoiced in battle. And why not? What is there more exhilarating?

These Celts proceeded, not toward death, but, again, as into the arms of their beloved wives. Did they embrace death? I deny it.

They were found, in the Rebellion, most predominantly, on the Southern side, for that is where the tide of immigration had deposited their ancestors—the English, in the main, having settled the North. They were instructive and honorable opponents in that war, and invaluable comrades in the following—and the remove of time might reveal that, as much as the war was fought over the issues of States' Rights, the Union, and slavery, it was, additionally, a continuation of the British Border Wars and the second trial of Culloden.

The Lucky Man could be of any race or heritage. He was not, to the best of my recollections, usually found among the Celts. Indeed, and on consideration, he may have come, to the contrary, from the Northern, or English, stock—his dispensation, perhaps, granted originally to the Danes. He, in the English, certainly derived from the Saxon, rather than the Norman strain—whose luck seems to exist very rarely, visited but on the person of a Napoleon or a Joan, there to exhaust itself until the next incarnation.

The Lucky Man came from the stock, in our late times, of the artisan, small farmer, mechanic, and was often found also among the Negro troops, or "Buffalo soldiers."

He was the man upon whose advent, the sky cleared, or, should it be necessary, clouded. Whose presence on the limber ensured that the shattered shaft would hold 'til we reached safety. There was no rancor in his presence. And a different time might have known him as a Holy Man. We counted him as other than this, as, to our mind, such a designation would have been both sacrilegious and insufficient.

The Indians saw God in everything and in every action. If I understand them aright, and to the extent that I understand them, I believe one may say, better, not that they "saw" God in these things, but that these things, to them, *were* God. That everything was God.

I am sure they would have a name for this Lucky Man, and a place accorded to him in their Tribe such as he as possessed in ours.

For, in his presence, we were aware that all things are connected. Such, on his appearance, was, to us, not a revelation or enlightenment, but a recollection.

The Wild West shows I always found a delight. The yearly announcement of Buffalo Bill and his Congress of Rough Riders filled me with anticipation like that of a ten-year-old boy.

Mary and Caro so enjoyed their shared appreciation of Father's idiosyncrasy; and I, of course, "Father," as in any happy family, enjoyed my part in the participation (even, as is traditional, as subject) of the Family Joke.

For years I deluded myself that I did not hold with "souvenirs." This was, on examination, a statement not of anathema, but of aesthetic sensibility. It was coincidentally and demonstrably untrue.

For though our mantelpiece lacked the embellishment of my Cavalry saber, and my study, the display of quilled quiver and arrows of the Sioux; though those ribbons it had amused various commissions and politicians to award me rested not in the glass case in the hall, but at the back of some drawer, I, to confess, of course took, if not pride, then, at least, enjoyment, in their absence. This a more truthful man might call a sort of ostentation.

However, the paperweight within my rolltop desk, was (and is) my Colt's Patterson pistol, and I cut my cigars, and open my mail, and trim the string on the packages I send to Caro and hers, with the small clasp knife which, in the war, belonged to a friend.

I love the dust and the smell of horses and of harness in the Wild West shows at the Coliseum. It is more like the smell of the Plains than that of the tack-room, and of peaceable stables.

One knows the state of the harness from the smell, compounded of age, and sweat, and insufficiently frequent care. And one could generally deduce, by the smell, the state of the horse from that of the tack.

One sees in the eyes of the performers, some of them, both the White and the Red, the unmistakable gaze of the fighter.

The various trick-shot artists are diverting. One sees the revolver shot, by a rider standing on the saddle, perforating a playing card, held in the hand of some dignitary, brought down onto the tanbark. Good shooting, yes; but the playing card, if of a stock size (and I suspect it is somewhat larger), is 2½ by 3½ inches; and the ball (or bullet, I should now say), at .45 caliber, is almost half an inch across—thus, as I explained to Caro, any hit, within a 3½ by 4½ area, will prove the performer's skill.

This, curiously, is the effective area of the head- or heart-shot—that necessary, in a fight, to drop the opponent instantly, with no risk of retaliation. I will note also that the trick shot is accomplished while the performer is advanced to a spot some twenty feet from the target, that he shoots at a known and predetermined range, and that no one is shooting back at him.

Ah, one might say, but he shoots *while moving*. But reflection will reveal that, in an actual fight, even were he still, his *opponent* would be in violent motion. So his accomplishment, though laudable as entertainment, is not actually extraordinary.

These Wild West shows, latterly, included also the rifle artist, capable of breaking any number of glass balls, thrown into the air. The record, for I enquired, is, to date, some sixty thousand continual hits, occupying the shooter for the most of eighteen hours.

(I sent my enquiry to the manager of the theatre, and he returned the information to me, along with one of the glass target balls, which rests upon the top of my desk, waiting only for the next or the following visit of Caro's boys.)

But what of the shot from the barn? This, I know, has been celebrated in various dime fiction, and even, I am told, in a stage-play, *The One-Mile Measured Shot*.

General Sedgewick of the Nationals was, of course, famously, killed by a Secessionist sniper at the distance of a mile, at Spotsylvania Courthouse. His aide-de-camp reported that he looked with concern at the Confederate line and urged the General to take cover, to which the General replied, "They couldn't hit an elephant at this distance." His last words. Or so the report runs.

Perhaps. But who paced off the mile? To which I will add the further vitiation of the feat, that it was accomplished with the aid of a telescopic sight (the sniper's weapon being retired, in glory, by his command, tagged, commemorating the feat, and recovered after Appomattox by the Nationals).

But Dixon shot with a Sharps rifle, over iron sights, at the Hostile, on the

East Ridge, during the fight at the barn. And it was Sergeant Murray, who, after the fight, paced the distance off, and reported it at one mile and thirty yards.

I had divagated (appropriately), during a lecture, on a detour and frolic into a discussion of Natural Right. A student, thinking to curry favor, or, perhaps, simply by way of compliment, produced the old saw that God created Man, but Colonel Colt made them equal.

Well. I had come across the tag before. Not in the precincts where one might have assumed it to have had currency, but in one of my dime novels.

In this book, whose title I've forgotten, was also a passage wherein the Hero Cow-Boy reflects on his suspicions regarding a drifter who has joined their campfire, and who, indeed, later is proved to have nefarious intent.

The Hero confesses to a friend that he cannot excise his suspicions of the new-come stranger. "It nags me," he says, "like an uncleaned gun."

Colonel Colt, then, might make men equal; and a feeling might nag one like an uncleaned gun. What, I wonder, would the student have felt had I topped his tag with mine?

And what of Natural Law, existing, as it does, but in the abstract—that Ideal which one must strive first to understand and then to employ in this imperfectly ordered world?

Upon the Frontier, it devolved, of course, to the ultima ratio regis, as interpreted by Colonel Colt, who was, to J. S. Mill, as Coke upon Littleton. The young fellow was quite right.

Is this by way of an endorsement of, or to excuse, the Jacobin, the Radical, Anarchist, or thief? Decidedly not. It is an acknowledgment of their existence, and a suggestion of the means of their improvement.

There was a series of books popular in the University on my return. These dealt with Occupation Marks. That is to say, on the distortions and callosities on the hands occasioned by their constant use in specific trades.

The hardened striations of the sailor's rope-burned palms comes to mind, as does the large callus, high on the right hand's web, which, together with the thickened and discolored forearm, identifies the blacksmith.

Of note, also, at the time, were the spatulate fingers of the ironworker, fingerprints virtually eradicated by the chemical reaction of their constant contact with the iron.

(This last instance was much cherished, at the time, as the fingerprinting of criminals had just begun to replace the Bertillon system as the surer method of identification.)

These books were popular, in the Psychology and Philosophy departments, as a practical (or vulgar, if you will) endorsement of some current theories regarding the mind.

The argument, if I remember, went generally thus: that just as any constant physical application must re-form the physical body, and such re-formation, in turn, must re-form the mind or consciousness, so any constant application (or, indeed, concern) of the mind must work upon its somatic partner, mental choices being enregistered by the actual electric or molecular pathways thus cut into the brain. (The prime proponent of this theory, Professor James, cherished the notion of habit changing the mind, and the mind, in turn, changing the brain.)*

The sailor, he reasoned, debarred from fine, manual work by the habituated musculature of his hands and their attendant stiffening, cannot *imagine* various occupations and remedies apparent to one with a less moderate dexterity—his body has, in a complementary operation, taught his brain, which has taught his mind. He further mused, though did not write (for I heard many of his lectures), that Phrenology, though largely by that time discredited, perhaps held certain truths—that though the process of the brain and mind re-forming each other did not eventuate in a revelation of that history in the shape of the skull, perhaps a future science could discern those "Occupation Marks" upon the brain itself, at some molecular level, observation of which was currently beyond our means.

I followed his lectures not as part either of my continued studies, nor of my duties as novice instructor, but out of interest in his philosophy, which,

---

* This, he explained was, inter alia, a refutation of the anthropologists' law that culture is not biologically inheritable. This notion he dismissed as "quaint," adducing that if habit could change the physical brain, those possessing the more adaptive habits would, necessarily, have more opportunities to interbreed, as would, in turn, their offspring, man, thus evolving toward perfection.

as I understood it, was the attempt to discover truth, beginning with as few preconceptions as possible.

Such, historically, is known as heresy. This label he escaped not only through his demeanor and wit, but actually, surprisingly, through his wisdom, which I may describe as a most evident humility before the various and conjoined mysteries of life.

The Occupation Marks, many of them, have vanished (the transverse callus on the hands of the wheelwright—his spokes have largely been consigned to the museum; the perfectly round ridge in the palm, caused by the leather "palm" of the sailmaker). Phrenology has been discredited, and Bertillon's "27 indices," once deemed infallible as an identifier of a single possessor, have been debunked, and supplanted, in the arsenal of the police, by fingerprinting.

What did they have in common? A desire to find the seat of individuality.

It was the multiple applications of this quest which fascinated Professor James. For, he taught, its questions, charmingly, were essentially transitive. That is, the enquiry was capable of being conducted either backward or forward, and of possible application deductively or addictively; therapeutically, to aid the individual, or teleologically, to determine his place in the cosmos. (To simplify, e.g., not only "how to cure suffering," as in the investigations of the Austrian "Psychoanalysts," but "What *is* suffering?" thus, "Why does it exist, and to what extent is it not only caused by, but *identical with* individuality?")

Considered individually, these various endeavors—Occupation Marks, Phrenology, Psychology, "Psychoanalysis," and Neurology—may be seen as scientific, quaint, provocative, or outmoded. Taken as a whole, they may reveal in the Western mind an animism which only our ethnocentric pride restrains us from identifying with that of the savage.

For how do they differ, the beliefs of the Spiritualists and those of the Ghost Dancers; the "talking cure" of the Psychoanalysts and the machinations of the Medicine Man? They can grow only from our universal human nature, and differ only in its expression, not in its essence.

The cosmogony of the Savage was attractive to me, as to all who possessed the leisure to appreciate it, in its fixity. This, to me, constituted its main structural difference from our European worldview. Their understanding, fixed in the

Stone Age, was never challenged by technology to adapt—thus, they warred over horses and land, and not over those doctrinal differences which were, during two thousand years of Western war, used to explain to the supposedly rational mind, wars over wealth and land.

The motorcar, the aeroplane, dirigible, steam engine, were to the savage mind, marvels, but they did not inspire awe—he had been raised and lived among marvels which did. These he called the progression of the seasons, childbirth, the return of the Buffalo, and so on. That God was capable of all things was not a confession of faith, but the essential fact of his life, participated in constantly. His philosophy was in contradistinction, if I may, to that of Shakespeare's Hamlet; for the Prince taught that there were more things in heaven and earth than were dreamt of in it. But the Savage's world, though it may have contained things not yet encountered between heaven and earth, did not contain more things dreamt of.

He would not and did not scoff at the Miracle of Christ Risen from the Dead; yet we laughed at the resurrection propitiated by his Ghost Dance.

Were we the same? Essentially. Though our cultures differed. We were the same, for we were men. And our great prophets taught us that all men are created equal. The lesson, of course, continues that we are, thus, endowed with certain inalienable rights, which rights, to life, liberty, and the pursuit of happiness, it was my profession, in those years, first to ensure in the Rebellion, and, then, to abrogate upon the Plains.

The war we took to the South was—whatever the inevitable revisionists may claim—to broaden the definition of those who were created equal; that which we fought in the West, to narrow it.

I fought in both, and have lived to that age sufficient to distance me from those passions, and thus, like the Savage, to wonder at it all.

The essence of Natural Law, I explained to my students, is the Right to Self-Defense—which, however contravened, sophisticated, or abridged by Man, all must acknowledge to exist—for what is any other right without the right to live? Following close and inevitably derived from such, we find the right to property, thus, the security from unreasonable searches and seizures, and, in short, and by extension, the whole of our Constitution.

But what, then, my student responded, of the Natural Rights of the Indians?

I am a soldier, and went where I was told, and did as ordered upon my arrival. Is this to excuse outrage or profiteering by the Whites? Not at all. Neither on the field nor in the sanctity of various treaty rooms in Washington.

But, given the nature of Man, of his desire for land and his lust for gain, what other than the misuse, the conquest, and the exploitation of the Indigenes could one expect?

For it was not only the Westward expansion of the Whites which was inevitable, but our subversion, serially, of any treaty which might interfere with the desires of any person with access to or immunity from law. And what else are politicians?

At the end of the seventeenth century, the native population of our Country was one inhabitant for each three hundred square miles.

What wise or kind body was, or could have been, capable of adjudicating between the, at least supportable, claims of these Stone Age civilizations and the World's first drive for "free land"?

Who was that man, or what that group, and how would they have gained and how possibly held power?

Further, the Plains Indians were, in the main, and to the Eastern mind, which had no contact with them, considered Aboriginals, which is to say subhuman.

These they were not. For, though differing in technology, their moral codes, their art, and their philosophy were not only as developed as our own, but, perhaps, more universally observed.

Who knew this who was not exposed to them? No one.*

There was a third apothegm upon the subject of the Indians, and this I found, as I did the "uncleaned gun," in popular fiction: "that if the Redskins had known the use of their rifles' rear sight, they would be in possession still."

In the late war, we have subdued or displaced the Moro population of the Philippines, and the Spanish in Cuba and Hispaniola. The former had machetes to

---

* Note that it was equally a mistake to impute to them, as some romantic and unconcerned philosophers have done, a greater moral power than that found among the Christian nations; for as surely as we, and as they, dealt harshly with each other, in our struggle for a Continent, they, Tribe-by-Tribe, dealt harshly and savagely, Red man to Red man, in taking and in holding this or that freehold or easement—doing so, as did we, by statecraft and subterfuge, bad faith, martial adventure, and savagery.

wield against our Cartridge arms; the latter held arms equal to our own; but, for all their vaunted glory, their Hidalgo officer class proved, upon the field, quite lacking.

Is Cuba and are the Philippines now "free"? They are under our sway. Is there an improvement in the lot of the common man in these locales? I do not know, and I suggest no one knows.

The Rebellion was, I believe, the signal case of that notion which, for some time to come, will cloud the minds of those charged with contemplating war as a tool of policy: it was, whatever the revisionists may say, a noble and a true Crusade. I speak as one who fought four years, and not only for myself, but for those alongside whom I fought. Our Grail was the eradication of chattel slavery and the preservation of the Union, which is to say, of Natural Law. Our cause was just.

But the enormities of precedent this war will establish will abide with us until the end of our American Experiment. It is as true of ideas as it is of men: none will escape unscathed.

A passion for drink is the lot and recreation of the soldier. I added to this an increased reliance, during the years of my convalescence, upon morphia—these were responsible, beyond doubt, for most of the troubles I and my family endured. Though the fault was mine, its price was not only shared, but bequeathed, until the time of my Resurrection through Christ, to my family.

I understood Religion first (though, at first, I did not call it such) in the campaign to eradicate the Ghost Dance.

We studied its observance to determine strategy, guessing the likely time and place of its next appearance as we would the movements of game.

We learned to take into consideration the phases of the Moon; the state of the weather, and its probable allowance for that travel necessary for a convocation of the widespread Tribes; the state of the game, and its sufficiency at that place and season for potential convening wanderers. We studied, also, and prognosticated the most likely celebrants, and, thus, the spot most central or accessible to these various constituencies, and so on.

But our studies, however we described them as a mechanical and military exercise, dedicated to eradication of that savage performance, led, as they required knowledge of the ceremony's outward forms, to a half-conscious, or unconscious occupation with the ceremony's meaning.

Why, we asked, was it invariably performed in the new Moon, why in a rounded depression of a certain circumference; why did it require the skulls and hides of the Buffalo killed within the previous fortnight (this last, of course, aiding our deliberations, for if and where fresh animals were not attendant, within the prescribed time, et cetera ...).

Those learned in the Bible could read, if inspired to do so, of those congruent observances in Scripture—of sacrifices requiring now this and now that animal or store, possessed of this or that quality, and prepared and offered at a specified time, place, and manner, by a priestly class, its very vestments and appearance specified.

In a long night watch, one might wonder at the universal distribution of the religious instinct; and question the previously accepted notion, if not that the Aborigines were savage, at least that their devotions differed little in essential intent, from our own.

That they engaged in mortification of the flesh is true. The Ghost Dance, like the Sun Dance, involved the devoted in various submissions which, though elective, nonetheless would be characterized, absent such consent, as torture.

But, one wondered, could not the same be said of the religious self-flagellant of the Christian sect—of the South American Catholic cults of Crucifixion; of the Hierophant and his hair shirt; or, though it may be blasphemy, of the Glorification of the Physical Death of Our Savior Himself on the Cross?

An examination of such practices per se reveals that consistency one must name Religion, which is, operationally, a self-contained and self-sufficient compendium of myths, and the practices deriving justification therefrom. These are expressed, in any Religion, under the various heads of laws, sanctions (Taboo), parable, and cultural stigma, the interdigitating quality of such (deriving sanction from the Foundation Myth) enforcing both group cohesion, and, thus effort.*

---

* A friend on Service in Peru saw and reported a long-standing native observation at Easter Tide. Here, the devoted caused himself to be nailed to a cross, and the cross erected in a public square. Here he stayed, in this condition, for a period of several hours to a day, being removed and revived, with, seemingly, little effort, and vowing, as he revived, to repeat the ceremony on the following year. I cite, also, the Iberian and Mexican ceremony of the bullfight, which is

To what end are these various ceremonies, many of which one might denominate as savage, directed? Toward a greater affinity with the Divine, and, thus, morally, toward increased capacity to understand and inclination to fulfill the Divine Will upon earth.

Were not such devotions (the Ghost Dance, the Sun Dance, et al.), tending, as they did, to increase the hostility to the Whites, misused by the Indigenes? They were used, to take their part, to increase the opposition to those practices (our own), which they found both offensive and threatening to their way of life; and as that way of life was Animistic, which is to say suffused with Spirit, to their God and his intentions. Is this absurd?

Do we not make the same claim?

Contemplation in this vein led me to the view that, while we were opponents, the Indian and I were not enemies. We were, each, contesting a parcel of land, through the various tools of warfare, stealth, and statecraft—the Indian and I, no less than he with other Tribes, or I, as a National officer, previously against my Southern brother. The essential nature of these struggles—as in the last named—was religious.

For, in what consists the philosophical distinction between the proposition that a country half-slave and half-free cannot survive, and the unalterable conviction of the sanctity of the Black Hills?

Both are a priori, which is to say religious, convictions—they rest upon an unalterable belief about the nature of the world. They may be accepted but cannot be proved. Men, nevertheless, die for them.

I, in my rebirth in Christ, came to a greater understanding of the Indigenes' intentions in their above-named ceremonies: they desired to die in order to be reborn.

What else is Baptism?

There were men who went raving mad. I saw such during the Rebellion several

---

most certainly derived from the ancient Greek and Roman worship of the animal gods, and the Suffragists' "hunger strike," which, though passing as a political tool, is *formally* a plea, through self-mortification, for divine intercession.

times. This was by no means always expressed as cowardice, sometimes taking the form of insane daring, sometimes of simple hebephrenia.

At times, of course, it was expressed as cowardice, and rightly derogated and treated as such. But that a man under infinitely prolonged stress may now refuse to move from a place of safety into mortal peril is not more astounding than that he previously agreed to do so.

I often wondered at the incidence, comparatively, among the Secessionists, of insanity, or of mental dissolution under fire.

I, of course, would not have seen it, for it would have taken place predominantly behind their lines.

Did the Rebels suffer less incidence of cowardice than we among the Nationals? I would suppose this was the case. Why?

There is a universal, if unconscious, understanding that, in a budding conflict, the side or person farthest from its own home is the more likely to withdraw—put differently, we never fight more forcefully than in defense of our own territory.

The Secession soldiers, of course, fought not in Defense of Slavery (few, and none among the enlisted ranks, owned slaves)—they fought as their home had been invaded. Such a man may possess not more *sanity*, per se, but more *certainty* than the intruder. And fear grows from uncertainty. Witness the soldier who, rather than face the Enemy, takes his own life. What, to him, could have been the difference? Why not fight, even in a forlorn hope, where there existed, however remote, at least the theoretic possibility of survival? But suicide eliminates, of course, not death, but doubt, and, so, intolerable fear.

The Northern trooper might, at times, question the abstract worth of his Cause—weighed against the worth of his own life; the Southerner saw his home and livelihood destroyed around him.

Any soldier, over time, may doubt the worth of his particular cause. How otherwise, as he finds it perennially mooted in the mouths of the weary, the disaffected, and the Corrupt—and, if not of his Cause, then the worth to its accomplishment of his own sacrifice?

Some may decide against the last. It is largely to deal with this phenomenon that all armies are divided into an enlisted and an officer caste, each schooled in the sanctions against cross-fraternization. For an officer may be called upon to kill a coward.

Why must he kill? As the disease of doubt and cowardice spreads, in panic, as an instantaneous contagion. It is the officer's duty to excise the cause upon the instant. It is not only he but the onlookers who will understand his act, which, while ending one life, has been performed to preserve the lives of many. They may thus be returned, to a sense, not of duty, but of self-preservation, recalling that in a fight one would be well to fight.

After the Little Big Horn, we learned that there were those in Custer's troop who took their own lives, and those who, in pairs, performed a suicide pact. This is, of course, a special case, as few would prefer the certainty of torture to the certainty of death. I would not. To what end?

More curious is the tale of the escaping Trooper. He broke free from the Indian Encirclement, and was outdistancing his last pursuer. He need only have continued to have effected his escape. He, then, turned in his saddle, and looked back. He saw the lone pursuer, and though an instant's contemplation would have informed him the pursuit was lagging, he drew his revolver and blew out his brains.

I heard this story, in the year afterward, from two separate Hostiles, at Camp Kearney, each certain to have been at the fight. I have also seen it memorialized in the painted hide of a teepee, confiscated after the forced migration of the Tribes, and displayed, at this writing, in the Smithsonian Institution. Upon the hide are drawn, here, the depictions of the death of Custer, there, the encirclement, and, in the lower right-hand corner, the blue-shirted, mounted Trooper, turned in his saddle, looking back, a revolver to his head. You may see it there still.

In the midst of my withdrawal from the drug, I wished not only to kill myself, but would, as the horror progressed, have killed to obtain it.

Can I conflate the operations of the mind and of the brain?

The brain, of course, is physical; the mind a chimera. One may control or strive to control the second through habit, doctrine, reason, coercion, threat, or inducement; one controls the first, a physical entity, through the application of these, and through those physical substances called variously medicines or drugs.

Witness the soldier on the eve of battle whom no amount of alcohol can intoxicate, or in its aftermath, when no amount will satiate, until he fall insensate.

The morphia was taken originally against pain.

Perhaps, then, I am indictable of courage insufficient to withstand the physical pain unaided. But who is to say? Such assertion on the part of others would be unseemly, in one's own behalf, sententious. I will note that I raved, pleaded, and wept, and would, until my release, have engaged in any behavior whatever to obtain my drug. Can this be other than shameful? I do not know. I know that my Preceptor counseled me, in my conversion, not to exchange an addiction to pointless self-doubt, for that to the drug.

His suggestion marked, for me, the first tenuous beginning of a rebirth, the possibility of which I had previously rejected as absurd.

All soldiers deal with guilt, some for their actions, some for their omissions. Many for their mere thoughts. This may mask, as current diagnostic doctrine holds, a deeper, that is, a *suppressed, unnamable* shame. I understand this as congruent with the confessions of an incurable debtor, whose accounts, however produced and attested to with tears as a complete confession, will be but a mere fraction of that total debt he cannot admit even to himself.

The Catholic Church knows this as the Sin of the Confessional.

And so it is with soldiers. We, among ourselves, relate this or that tale, in which we, per custom, *cannot* be seen other than as misguided, shy, wrongheaded, or at the best, miraculously lucky—this is, of course, an acknowledgment of a deeper self-doubt—its existence, as with the shame of the debtor, signalized by the formalized, inaccurate confession of sin.

Here is an unusual instance.

On the eve of Second Bull Run, I had, newly added to my Command, a subaltern fresh from his abbreviated career in the Military Academy.

He was in charge (vice, of course, his Sergeant) of a platoon on picket duty; and he, as he should, had taken it upon himself, to oversee each of the various watches of the night.

I was upon my rounds, and had progressed to that sector under this Sublieutenant's command.

Well back of the picket line, I saw the fellow's Sergeant, seated, legs out, lounging against a tree, and overseeing, unseen, the progress of his neophyte charge. I raised my eyebrow, slightly, in question. The Sergeant nodded his head, endorsing the young fellow (he was little more than a boy) in the performance of this, his first duty as an officer.

I found the Sublieutenant, further up, walking from one of his outposts to the next, which was the last upon that particular tour.

I suggested we repair to one of the picket-fires, and have a cup of tea. He demurred, respectfully, as he did not wish, he said, to chance his night-vision against the fire. I said I saw that he must have been a hunter. He told me this was true, and he had spent much of his youth, in Maine, in the woods. I told him this would serve him well in battle.

There is no one who is unconcerned before his first battle. It is the great unknown, congruent only, perhaps, with a woman's first childbirth. Those who have not experienced it cannot understand it, and any attempts to codify it, even by those who have undergone it, must be understood, if effective, only as art. Such exist as themselves, and bear no relationship to the thing supposedly described.

This Sublieutenant was, of course, filled with that anticipation which grows as the combat approaches, the individual endeavoring, with no success, to tease out the strands of excitement, devotion, self-doubt, and fear of which it is compounded.

We sat for a while, and the young man, begging my pardon, began to confess.

He confessed not, as I would have expected, his concern over his own upcoming performance, but his guilt over an incident in his past life.

He had borne the shame of this incident for some months, and did not wish to die with it upon his conscience. He recognized, he said, that I was unable to offer him forgiveness, and that he presumed upon me much—that even any conventional assurances of the commonplace nature of his sin, or of his ability to, perhaps, make it right, or to atone for it by unrelated good deeds, could, with him, count for little, and would only be a burden upon me. Thus, he said, he, if he might, would not trouble me for a response, but merely wished to have another human being hear his confession. I believe he meant that he did not wish to die without having, at least, paid the price of having another know his shame.

He made the confession at length, and in detail. I will not trouble the reader with its nature or particulars; he may, himself, supply them from those which come first to mind, and he will not be wrong.

In any case, the young man, having completed his tale, thanked me, and rose to resume his progress, once again, among the troops of which he was in charge.

He did, in fact, survive the battle, and continued in the Army, which was, after all, his career, beyond both the Rebellion and the Wars on the Plains, through Service overseas, and indeed, into the Spanish War, by which time he had achieved very high rank. It was he who, near the close of that war, personally brought me the news of the death of my son.

* * *

The soothsayer had told him, that first evening on his arrival at Camp Kearney, that he would die in battle.

Now, near the close of his life, in the most sedentary of professions, his commerce with the world otherwise limited to his short walk from the campus to his home, he wondered at it. For everything else predicted had in fact come to pass.

The fight in the barn had unfolded as the ancient Indian had said. It was not a trick of diminished and unreliable memory, for he'd written the predictions down, that night, alone and unable to sleep—his first night on the Plains: that he would be led, as a result of his underestimation of the Enemy, into an ambush; that he and those under his command would be driven into the marginal shelter of a ruined house, and a burnt barn, the remnants of an overrun farm. It was predicted, further, that his troop, cut off from water, would stage now this and now that expedition and attempt the various diversions whose object was to distract the Hostiles from the quest for the well, but that the Hostiles would not be deceived, neither dislodged, and that the American troops would, over the course of several days, be reduced from a Light Company to a Platoon, and then to a Squad. It was further predicted that he would receive one of their arrows, and the Indian pointed to the place, just inside the left scapula, where the arrow would lodge. He predicted that the Army forces would be reduced to drinking the horses' blood; that one would go insane and, raving, wave his once-white shirt as a flag of surrender, and have to be shot; that, finally, devoid of ammunition, and four days without water, his forces would prepare to meet the final Indian onslaught with their swords, which, along with pikes, fashioned from the palings of the corral, and Bowie knives strapped to them by their belts, were the only weapons remaining.

·   ·   ·

On my study desk are worn dictionaries in the three classical languages, Blackstone's Commentaries, a silhouette of my wife, and the heavy key and fob from the Hotel on Cape Ann where we spent the first night of our married life.

I first saw her in the first week prior to my taking up duties at the University. Dr. ———, whose wife had invited the incoming faculty, presented me to the young woman, tendering those bona fides establishing me as of proper Eastern derivation, for, I fear, I looked, to them, somewhat, still, the Vaquero. Or perhaps I merely strove to look as such, or deluded myself that I did.

Having taken no particular notice of myself for the period of the various wars and skirmishes at which I had been present, I, at their conclusion, ran an account of the various deformities and Occupation Marks I had accrued, and found myself wanting for admission into polite company.

I took some care with my tailor, haberdashery, and the acquisition and stowage, about my person, of those few artifacts betokening gentility—that is to say, I bought a watch, stickpin, and ring. I had, however, left my hair and moustache just that fraction longer than the accepted Metropolitan norm, as to indicate a history the nature of which could be further inferred by reference to the scar and burns about my face, and its, I thought, rather manly discoloration by years of the Western sun.

Perhaps, through it all, I was, in the main, diffident about my more serious wound, and the actual deformity and handicap occasioned thereby. In any case, I was returned to civilian life for the duration, and, like any soldier, was, in my own way and speed, working through the intricacies of that transition.

The Doctor's wife introduced me to a young woman, a Miss whose name I did not fully hear. She gestured us toward one of the party tables, this set down near the River.

My fund of polite conversation having been depleted by my years of Service—if, in fact, I ever possessed such—I found myself in discourse with the young woman upon that one topic with which I held myself current, that is, Army life. I told her a story of a conversation I had overheard, and which I prized.

We were in Garrison. I had come in to the Sutler's Lodge, and there, at the bar, were two silver-tipped old Sergeants, sitting and drinking. One said, "So, I, having just laid eyes upon her, stepped up, and the first words which she ever heard me speak was, 'What's it going to take to win you, Pretty?' 'Wedding ring,' she said. And I said, 'You wait here. ...'"

I'd always found that story amusing, and often told it, as an example of the alacrity of our breed, to other soldiers. They, in the main, appreciated the humor. But when I looked at the young Miss, however, I did not see her smile. Indeed, she was grave.

The sun was in her eyes, for I had, thoughtlessly, seated her so. And she was shielding her eyes from the glare, her hand underneath the bonnet. Looking hard at me. I returned her glance, which we held, for the longest time, at the conclusion of which, I see, in retrospect, that everything was settled, and would remain so for the many blessed years in which I had her for my wife.

Though I had offered her that chair which put her, her bonnet notwithstanding, in the glare of the sun, though I had done so, certainly, without chivalry, I understood, upon reflection, that I had not done so randomly. I had, that is, been perhaps boorish, but not thoughtless; having merely employed the habitual use of the hunter and soldier, in keeping, if possible, the sun in the eyes of any opponent or prey.

The sun at one's back will also, of course, aid the tracker, throwing a shadow forward into the depression of the track. This is especially useful in the tracking of horses.

The Hostiles, of old, seldom shod their ponies. They came, later, to adopt the practice, with their usual tactical ingenuity, as an aid to deception.

In a large raid, for example, one with the intent of bearing away treasure or captives, they would strike, first, upon their unshod ponies, changing themselves and their spoil, at some distance, onto heavier mounts, upon which the shoes had been turned, and thus continuing their flight, giving the lie, if one were taken in by the trick, to the direction of their travel.

Had I had, in my commands in my two wars, officers capable of such good thinking, how delighted I would have been. For I, myself, was utterly deficient in the improvisatory skills which made the Hostiles such difficult and interesting opponents.

Napoleon taught that war is, in the main, deception, and that to be unaware of this is to squander whatever superfluity of men, material, or time the gods may have, momentarily, vouchsafed you.

It is true that superiority in these things mitigates toward success, but to rely upon them solely is to invite catastrophe—for will not an intellectually superior enemy (and the Hostiles were certainly this—as were the bands of Mister Jeb Stuart) employ his skills, especially if numerically inferior, in leading his opponent to the misplacement and waste of these possessions?

Equally, to possess both numerical superiority and the tactical wisdom necessary to mime the lack of the same is to lure the enemy into the destruction of his resources at little risk to one's own, else war would be reducible to a simple comparison of each force's possessions, after which that side discovering itself inferior would admit defeat, and amend its ways. But war is not only a comparison of forces, but of wisdom and will; and any short conflict may, and a longer conflict certainly will, also attract the notice of the gods of chance, jealous of their prerogatives.

There was an intricate time of circularity and self-reference during my addiction. Morphia reduces the human consciousness to that, perhaps, of a newborn infant—incapable of reason, but driven by that faculty which will become reason to review and wonder at the phenomena of the world.

Such, to the addict, is a state the degree of whose pleasantness is surpassed only by that of the unmitigated horror occasioned by the drug's withdrawal.

The Zoroastrians indeed could have been inspired to their noted Dualism by the selfsame process of delight and absolute aversion. So, indeed, may have the Indians, who not only live in a world made spirit by their beliefs, but indulge in practices whose aim is to impress this worldview irrevocably, first upon the infant, then upon the young, and, then, in successive steps as the youth strives to matriculate. This process is not unique to the Aborigines, being practiced worldwide and in every time, and known as "Culture."

But I will refer specifically to that of the Plains. I have mentioned the Ghost and Sun Dance, which last was the Indians' form of a crucified mortification. I will add, as an indoctrinary practice, the Dream or Spirit Quest. Here the acolyte removes himself from the Tribe, and sits, unclothed and unfed, for a period of days, or weeks, upon a prominence, unmoving, without sustenance or sleep until visited by knowledge from the higher, or Indwelling, Spirit World.

This visitation may take the form of an inchoate perception, but it is more usually reported as the appearance of a Spirit Animal, or "familiar," presenting itself as both a messenger and a mentor.

The returned acolyte now has acquired a guide and companion, piloting him through that world whose essential nature, or Spirit, it will make, to him, apparent. The new state of wisdom is that the world is not only other-than-it-seems, but that sufficient application of this insight may lead the devoted closer to God. To him, now, the world is understood as essentially immaterial, and that Spirit, which may of course take any form, is the only and true reality.

It is to him but the spirits' momentary *forms* which may be perceived, their actual true nature remaining unapprehendable until the ultimate accession of Knowledge begun by the acolyte's reincarnation in the Vision Quest.

This savage Knowledge, of course, is here one with that of Plato, in his story of the Cave. It is also seen in the most current revelations of the science of Physics in its discussion of the Atom.

These views of worlds essentially immaterial, while, amongst the Indians, freeing their adherents, terrified my mind, in the return from the poisoned state of my hallucinations, and threatened to consign me, even after the Drug, and as the price of its withdrawal, to a place of desolation.

The Indians knew and administered similar drugs, capable of inducing hallucinations. These, to them, however, were not analgesics, whose delusions are a side-effect, but intoxicants, their attendant phantasms being the purpose of their administration. These drugs were employed by them in their various celebrations.

I note that both the Catholic and the Hebrew rite from which the first evolved contain as an essential feature the consumption of wine. May we not see, in these rituals, the survival of an older, perhaps violent or transformative intoxication and communion, the nature of such celebration, perhaps, an Ordeal?

The images which first visited and then assailed me in my poisoned state put me in mind of the story of manna.

We are told that manna fell from Heaven, and each who ate of it found in it his favorite food. So equally, in my delusion, the objects in the room, the noises of the street, the breeze from the garden, the quality of the bedclothes, offered, in the initial stage, an infinite interest and delight. Their nature in the sequelae I have referred to.

But I was visited by no Familiar in my Ordeal; and carried no wisdom nor assurance back with me to the world—unless it be said, as one Priest has said, that I had undergone my Calvary to reduce my soul to that state of subjugation sufficient to allow the entrance of Grace. Perhaps it is true. The events, in any case, were sequential.

Were the Soothsayer's prognostications born from a true commerce with the Spirit World? Does such a world exist? If not, whence came his Visions? And mine. For mine, whether of God or of the Devil, or of some more physiologic freak of the physical brain, revealed to me a differed vision of the world.

What can one say of, and how understand, a man to whom such visions are the only reality, who would reject them, in that time of their benignity, for the more mechanistic view of the world, were such impressed on him?

And yet there were the men with whom we contended for the Western Plains. Their world and ours intersected only in that contest, and in the intermittent Councils attendant upon that, the nature of which, must have been evident to the wise of both parties, as portending the end of Indian Life.

Our vision has triumphed. Now we have, as any Victors, ascribed our success to the Hand of God, or to a "Manifest Destiny," which is, of course, the same thing. In any case, we rest in possession of an Industrial and Merchant Power, a Continent, this Continent once peopled by a race of hunter-gatherers surviving to the end of the nineteenth century after Christ by means and practices adopted in the millennia prior to His Birth.

It is inevitable, similarly, that we shall someday be supplanted, our freehold disputed not by another polity, but by a new Civilization, its name and nature as unknowable to us now as would have been ours to the Continent's possessors of four hundred years past.

It is not the respective merit of our practices which will be then disputed, but the nature of the very phenomena of our two worlds.

One hundred years ago, Lord Melville, then First Lord of the British

Admiralty, assured a populace in fear of an intended invasion by the armies of Napoleon.

"I do not say he cannot come," he said, "I only say he cannot come by Sea." And now a man has flown the English Channel.

THE HANDLE
AND THE
HOLD

Nicky Greenstein slipped the small pistol in his waistband farther to the left, just forward of the hip bone still prominent from his two years in the European War.

The pistol was a souvenir of his last days in Holland. He had taken it from the passenger in a motorcycle sidecar, an officer in the Wehrmacht, having just shot both him and the driver from cover, at a bend in the road.

He'd kept it through his retirement from combat, later that week, and in spite of the efforts of the litter bearers, ambulance drivers, and medics and the general rapacity of those caring for casualties on their route home.

"You could've gotten rather laid in Paris with that pistol," Sam Black said.

"I needed no help getting laid in Paris," Nick said.

"And pee ess," Sam said, as he played to the Poker game, "what is a confirmed *Yid* doing with a piece, and on the *handles* of it, fuckin Nazi Eagle?"

"It's a trophy of war," Nick said. "And a reminder of the essential fragility of the Social Contract."

"...nevertheless ..." Sam said.

The deal continued into the Up card. "Trey, Jack, Deuce, *King*, Fiver, and a Four," the dealer said. "*King*."

"King bets the fifty," said the King. The rest of the players folded. The red deck was gathered up, and the blue was passed to the next dealer.

Sam Black pushed back from the table. "Deal me out," he said.

He walked toward Nicky, who had seated himself by the door, his sportcoat thrown back over one shoulder.

"Put the fuckin coat on," Sam said, "You look like the Springfield Armory." They nodded at the doorman, who nodded back, looked through the peephole, and admitted them out into the hall.

"What's new?" Sam said.

"They figured out the short count on the Hold," Nick said.

"Tell me," Sam said.

"*Dealer*, 'ey? Something of a mechanician. *Mills* out, get this, hollow cylinders, millimeter larger than the chips, you finish it."

"Cylinders half-mike larger than the chips. How high?"

"Ah, yeah, you got me," Nick said.

"How high?"

"High as a half-stack."

"High as a half-stack," Sam said. "No, you got me. ..."

"Put you out of your misery, *top* of the stack, struck like a ten-dollar chip."

"Okay ..."

"Sides of the cylinder milled, look like the half-stack, you getting old? The *dealer* palms the thing, lets it down on a half-stack of hundreds, pushes it across, the film shows nothing but a stack of tens, costs the house four hundred fifty bucks."

They walked down the stairs.

"I like it," Sam said.

"Like it. I *love* it," Nick said.

"What'd they do to the dealer?" Sam said.

"They gave him a real talking-to. *Huh*?"

They came to the bottom of the stairs, and walked out into the heat.

"How's the redhead?" Sam said.

Nicky shrugged.

"Nice girl," Nicky said.

"You got the address?" Sam said. Nicky nodded. They got into the car.

•   •   •

It was a small cinder-block apartment complex, built for the postwar market, unpainted, and already graying in the desert sun.

They entered through a breezeway lined with inset metal mailboxes. Several of them bore names torn out of business cards, or scribbled on a scrap of paper. They passed through a small courtyard, ringed on the second floor by a gallery, off which were the doors of the apartments. Nicky raised his eyes, Sam nodded, and followed him up the stairs.

On the second floor there was an ice machine and a cigarette machine. In the space between the two stood a young man, watching the staircase.

"I got a letter from the Old Guy," Nicky said, and started to reach into his jacket pocket. The young man shook his head.

"How the fuck am I going to show you the letter?" Nicky said. The man gestured him to open his sportcoat. Nicky opened his coat, and the man reached toward him and took the small automatic from his belt. Then he turned to Sam.

"Yeah, okay," Sam said. He hitched up his pant leg, revealing the belly gun in the ankle holster. The man pointed at Sam's left hand, and Sam reached down with his left hand and handed the man the revolver. The man looked at the barrel of the gun.

"'Property of the U.S. Army Air Force,'" he read.

"Not anymore," Sam said. The man laid the revolver next to the small automatic, on top of the cigarette machine.

"You want to see my letter?" Nicky said. The man motioned for them to carry on.

The first bodyguard in the room paid them no attention. He stood at the window, looking out through the sheer shade. He held a Schmeisser machine pistol. The second bodyguard stood in a far corner of the room.

The Old Man sat at a desk. The desk held a shiny new black briefcase, and a sheaf of papers. He took one. He crossed out a line with his fountain pen, and made a note in the margin, and turned to look at the two men.

"*Well ... ?*" he said.

"All right," Nicky said.

·　　·　　·

The redhead tore off her cocktail waitress outfit. She stepped out of her shoes, stripped her stockings off, and stepped, as she always did, immediately into the shower.

Nicky watched her through the shower door, shampooing the hairspray out of her beautiful hair, then scrubbing her makeup off as she transformed herself, as quickly and as thoroughly as possible, from a confected and knowing sexual cheat back into a twenty-year-old farm girl.

When she emerged Nick handed her two towels, and she smiled.

She bent double at the waist. Her thick hair hung down to the floor. She wrapped a towel into a turban and straightened to smile at him again.

"So innocent ..." he thought.

She tucked the other towel over her breasts, and walked into the galley kitchen. She opened the refrigerator, removed the pitcher, and poured herself a glass of cold water. She perched on a kitchen chair and took a sip. She looked him a question. The question was: How was your day?

"We figured out that discrepancy," Nick said.

"I know," she said. "The girls were talking about it."

He took the water glass from her and took a sip.

He put the glass carefully down on the kitchen table.

"I have to go away," he said.

.   .   .

Nicky came awake as the sun revolved into the windshield of the plane.

Sam reached behind the control console and handed him the thermos.

"Fuckin kid on the staircase," Sam said over the engine noise, "I could've killed him twenty-eight *times*."

Nick poured himself a cup of coffee. He nodded.

"Where the fuck *are* we?" he said.

"Half an hour out," Sam said. He wiggled his flat hand to indicate "more or less." "How he *know*," he said, "that I don't got *another* gun, small of my back?"

"*Did* you?" Nick said.

"*Matofact*," Sam said. "What the *fuck*, I'm goin around *naked*? I *showed* him, he would have had the brains that God gave *geese*, was my *backup* gun. Fuckin *kids* ..." Sam shook his head.

Nick rubbed the sleep out of his face.

"You tired?" said Sam. "... you wanna do," he said, "to make the *party* go, study up on 'Landing Procedures.'" He handed Nick the flight manual.

"You been reading it?" Nick said.

"Not enough *pictures*," Sam said. "I *believe* I learn things visually." He took the thermos cup from Nick and drained it. "Gimme a sandwich," he said.

Nick reached back and to his left. He opened the top of the black briefcase, and removed two waxed-paper-wrapped sandwiches. In the bottom of the briefcase lay stacks of large-denomination bills. He took one of the packets and riffled through it. He replaced it, and handed a sandwich to Sam.

They had stolen the plane the previous afternoon, from the military side of the Tulsa Airport.

They wore the new Air Force blue uniforms, and Sam had, as a vanity, affixed his actual awards and ribbons to the blouse: the Distinguished Flying Cross, the Purple Heart, the wings indicating that he was a Master Pilot, and the bars of a Captain.

Nicky was dressed as an Airman First Class.

He drove the sedan. Sam sat in the back.

The car had been stolen two hours earlier, in the rain, from Base Housing.

The military weekend had begun, and two-thirds of the houses were empty, their occupants already partying at the houses of the remaining third.

Nicky had crossed the wires and driven the car away.

Its windshield decal proclaimed it the property of a Major, but the corresponding base pass was not found in the car.

"The *motherfuckers*," Nick said, "Will either probably be drunk, or inattentive."

"Or ... ?" Sam said.

"That's right," Nicky said. "Pee ess." He pointed at the rain, which was coming down in sheets. "S'gonna keep any policeman in the world in the Coop."

Sam knocked twice on the dashboard. They drove on.

The car stopped at the candy-striped barrier.

Inside the guard shack sat two Air Policemen in white helmets and brassards. Nick rolled the driver's-side window down as one of the air police rose. Nick made a show of reaching over and rummaging through the glove compartment. The guard opened the door of the shack and started forward, as Nick mimed searching for his pass. The guard stood half-under the overhang, in the now-horizontal, driving rain. He looked at the officer in the car's backseat. Nick held up a finger, indicating "Wait a moment." The guard glanced at the decal on the windshield. He raised the barrier and waved the car through. The car drove on.

"Fuckin world is *coming* to?" Sam said. He took the pistol from his lap, and returned it to the shoulder holster he wore under his uniform blouse. "Half a *mind,*" he said, "go back, tell that kid, this was a Security Check, he's *failed*, and he's busted back to civilian."

"You've never *flown* one of these before," Nicky said.

"This is a fuckin DeSoto," Sam said. "You ever drive one of these before?"

Nicky shrugged.

"Pee ess," Sam said, "*these* chickenshit motherfuckers, no *doubt*, have a flight manual in the cockpit, as specified under some fuckin 'order.'"

Nick leaned forward as he drove, the single windshield wiper struggling against the rain. Ahead all that could be seen was the faint outlines of the hangar doors, each of them in a small halo of overhead light.

Nick stopped the car.

"You tell *me*," he said.

Sam opened the rear door and hurried into the front seat. He looked at the row of hangars before him. He took the sketch of a map from his uniform pocket, and compared it to the numbers on the hangar doors. He pointed "forward."

Nick put the car in gear and drove on slowly. At the end of the row of hangars Sam directed him left, and they found themselves on the edge of the large open airfield, identifiable only by the weak blue points of the runway lights. They drove slowly, parallel to the nearest runway. At the end of a quarter mile they stopped. In front of them were five large four-engined bombers.

Sam consulted the scrap of paper. "Eight seven five Charlie," he said.

Nick peered through the windshield. "Farthest on the left," he said.

Nick turned off the car. The windshield wiper stopped. They sat as the rain pelted the car.

Sam reached behind him and took the black leather briefcase. "Well, *okay*," he said.

He and Nick left the car, slamming the doors behind them.

They ran past the row of planes and sheltered under the last plane's left wing.

Sam pointed left and right, at the landing gear, and Nick nodded. Sam worked his way, under the belly of the plane, to the nose. He opened the crew access hatch, threw the briefcase in, and pulled himself up and in behind it.

Nick removed the chocks under the left landing gear, and heaved them far clear of the plane. He moved under the belly of the plane, and did the same with the chocks on the right.

Sam was settling himself into the left-hand seat as Nick entered the cockpit.

Sam had taken off his wet officer's blouse and cap. Nick removed his short uniform jacket and used it to mop his face and hair. He balled it up, and threw it back into the plane. He slid into the right-hand seat. Sam removed a thick booklet from the pouch to the left of his seat, reached back, opened the briefcase, and took out the flashlight. He shone it on the booklet, which read, "USAAF-32104-A. Flight Manual, B-17, A4A, Extended Tanks."

Sam leafed through the manual, and looked from it to a bank of switches over the windshield. He threw one, and a small yellow beam came on over his head. He turned his flashlight off. He squeezed his eyes shut, shook his head, and turned the overhead light off. He threw the neighboring switch, and the small yellow light came on over the copilot's seat. He handed the manual to Nick and said, "Starting procedures."

"What if this motherfucker don't have any gas?" Nick said.

"Then our informant," Sam said, "is a bastard, and he ought to be ashamed."

"Well, okay," Nick said. He checked the index, and turned to the appropriate page. "'Having completed the *Walkaround ...*'" he read.

"Whaddaya want, *egg* in your beer?" Sam said.

Nick read out the starting checklist, and Sam followed his instructions. The instrument panel came to life.

Sam looked at the banks of instruments.

"Yeaaah," he said, "it's not that different."

Nick continued the checklist, and Sam followed it. After the third item the left outboard engine coughed and started. "*Okay*," Sam said. He raised a finger for Nick to stop reading. Sam then repeated the procedure and the Number Four outboard, starboard side, sputtered and caught.

"Where is the fuckin *nose* light?" Sam said, as he stared at the console. Nick checked the index and pointed to a switch. Sam threw it. The tarmac in front of them lit in a narrow circle of light, some twenty yards in front of them. The rain appeared to spurt up from the tarmac. Sam leaned forward.

"I can't fuckin see *anything*," Nick said.

"Tail-dragger," Sam said. "High nose. Now we 'S' it out." He checked his cheat sheet and pointed to his right. "Our runway should be over *there*," he said.

Sam threw back the sliding window and stuck his head halfway out. He released the brakes, and the plane started to move.

"What'd you tell the redhead?" Sam said.

"'The redhead?' I told her, 'See you later,'" Nick said.

"It's gonna say V-1." Sam pointed at the book. "That is the speed at which this plane, if asked, might lift off."

"V-1. One hundred twenty miles per hour," Nick read.

"Okay," Sam said. "And, so, you call out the speed," he pointed at a dial, "in ten-mile increments."

"Okay," Nick said.

The landing lights picked out a sign reading 185 L-5R.

Sam used the rudder to turn the plane onto the runway to the left. The two lines of blue markers became just visible as they made the turn, and then they were obscured by the high nose.

"How do you see?" Nick said.

"Well, I look out the fuckin side *window*," Sam said. He set the brakes. "*Show* me the fuckin thing." Nick passed him the manual.

"This is the landing gear," Sam said. He pointed to the lever. "These are the flaps. I say, 'Gear up,' you hit the gear. I say, 'Flaps up,' you hit the flaps."

He started engines two and three, and ran them up, watching the gauges before him. He pulled the throttles back, and synchronized the four engines, and listened, until they sounded as one.

"Well, *okay*," he said. He put his right hand on the throttles. He pushed the throttles forward. The plane began to shake. Sam watched the gauges as the sound and shaking increased. He nodded, satisfied, and tripped the brakes. The plane rolled forward. Nick looked out the starboard window.

"I can hardly see the lights—how do you keep it on the fuckin runway?" he said.

"I used to do it for a living," Sam said. "Call it out."

"Sixty," Nick said. "Seventy." A gust of wind started the tail sideways, and Sam corrected.

"Eighty," said Nick.

"The *idea*," Sam said, "that any fool cannot fly this plane alone is bullshit."

•   •   •

Nick stretched himself in the sun. He shivered himself awake. "Any more coffee?" he said.

"Naa, that's fuckin *it*," Sam said. "Pee *ess*. *Pee* ess: *any* straight, has got to have either a five or a ten in it."

"How is that pertinent?" said Nick.

"Because," Sam said, "Eighth Air Force. O Club, *English* motherfucker came in, some staff idiot. Play'n poker, flashes his hand, calls it a straight, *trashes* his hand, and starts raking the pot.

"'Straight what through *what?*' player says.

"'Oh, please,' says the fellow. Looks around. Everybody *saw* it. Trashes his hand, *ain't* no straight. Looking *back*, I should've done: gone through the deck. Counted the remaining fives and tens."

"Two disqualitive notions," Nick said, "to the *contrary.*"

"All right ..."

"The first: what about the other hands in the trash?"

"Two guys left in the hand," Sam said.

"Even so."

"And the second?"

"Other one, why was it your business?"

"Because," Sam said, "... hold on ..." He steadied the plane. He checked the piece of paper in his lap, and then he checked the compass. He keyed the mike. "Meriden Tower," he said, "this is ..."

He passed the paper to Nick, who read, "Two four five four Radio."

"Two four five four Radio. I am B-17, requesting VFR landing, your runway six-zero. Estimated touchdown, one five minutes."

The radio came back. "Five four Radio, you are clear to land. The winds are from the west at zero eight miles per hour, and my barometer is two eight point eight."

"Five four Radio," said Sam.

"Who is 'Five four *Radio?*'" Nick said.

"Us after we get repainted," said Sam.

"And why was it your business?" said Nick.

"The *straight?*" Sam said.

"That's right."

"No, it wasn't," said Sam. "But it *stayed* with me."

"Yeah, well, that's a case for the Padre," Nick said, "of incipient delusion, or some fuckin thing, of grandeur."

"'You tell *me*' is why I'm asking," Sam said.

Nick said, "Thing occurs like that, in the casino … ? Guy trashes his hand, the fuckin cards are dead. That's the first rule of Life, as I understand it."

"Tell you what. However, let's run through the landing list."

Nick picked up the flight manual.

·   ·   ·

"Tell me about the plane ride home," Weinberg had said.

"Planes stunk like shit, and vomit and gangrene," Nick said.

"Thought they licked that with Penicillin," Weinberg said. "Siddown."

Nick sat on the couch, and Weinberg sat across from him. He offered Nick a slim brown cigarette.

"I thought that they cured that with Penicillin," Weinberg said.

"*Some* of 'em," Nick said. "*I* dunno …"

Nick lit the cigarette and inhaled the smoke.

"They make 'em in New York," Weinberg said. "They'll *personalize* 'em, you want. Put your name on it. The broads? Various colors, for the broads. Pale pink, yellow. Various names. Perhaps *you* know 'em, having been to Europe."

Nick smiled.

"They taste? To me? Like face powder. Women like 'em, though," Weinberg said. He shrugged. "You, no doubt, would rather have one of your own. Hey? But you're in my office. So you're smoking mine."

The phone on the coffee table rang. Weinberg answered it. "Yes?" he said. He listened. He said, "All right," and he hung up the phone. "So, offer you one of *mine*? Thass a cheap trick," he said. "To determine *what*?"

"See, a guy says, 'Thank you, I have my own,'" Nick said.

"Which tells me what?" Weinberg said.

"Guy missed the whole point of the interchange."

"Well, that's right," Weinberg said. "Smoke your own, if you want to."

"Thank you," Nick said. He stubbed out the brown cigarette, and took a pack of Luckies from his jacket pocket. He shook one out and lit it.

"I was eighteen," Weinberg said. "*I* came back. Fuckin deck, so far below the waterline, Krauts took it in their head, stick a torpedo in it, *everybody* dies."

"I didn't know they torpedoed the ships going West," Nick said.

"Yeah, well," Weinberg said. "Fuckin ship. Painted white, big red cross into the bargain. *They* didn't give a fuck." He shook his head. "Whaddaya want to do?"

"Whatever I can do to make a living," Nick said.

"What'd you do before the war?" Weinberg said.

"A bit of everything," Nick said.

"What'd you do since?"

"… *you* know," Nick said.

Weinberg nodded. "I could put you on the *floor*," he said. "… I could put you on the floor … but I'll tell you what."

So Nick, after his probation, spent two years as Minister Without Portfolio from the Blue Room. During those two years he acquired a friend and the girl.

He'd met the friend out in the desert, at a murder site.

The victim had been found the statutory hundred yards off the highway, shot in the back of the head, his pockets full of chips from the Golden West. And so Nick, as its representative, was summoned, and he went.

He pulled onto the shoulder, behind the police cruisers, and walked toward the flashbulbs.

The lead Homicide detective was kneeling over the corpse, and looked up as Nick was ushered forward.

"You kill him?" the detective said.

"Yeah," Nick said.

"Why?" the detective said.

"I forget. Or maybe it was something he ate," Nick said. "Why'd you roust me?"

"Chips from the West in his pocket."

"I can't help with that," Nick said.

"Fuckin guy. Shot in the back of the head. The shooter doesn't take the chips. What does that look like?"

"It looks like a calling card," Nick said. "But we didn't do it."

"Then how do you explain the chips?" Sam said.

Nick shrugged. "You got to ask someone who's *guilty*," he said.

Sam straightened and brushed the dirt from his pant leg. He introduced himself.

"What's a Yid doing working for the cops?" Nick said.

"I'm striking a fuckin blow for *freedom*," Sam said. "Let's get a drink."

.   .   .

It had been Weinberg who had given Sam Nick's name, and Sam who had passed it on to the Old Man.

Their first meeting took place in Los Angeles, in the coffee shop of a Westside hotel. At the end of their half-hour meeting the Old Man had risen and said, "I'll take your answer next month. In Las Vegas. And it's going to be 'yes.'"

And it was yes, as the Old Man knew it had to be. And so they found themselves on the stolen plane, some forty miles Northwest of Meriden, Florida.

.   .   .

The inside of the hangar office was broiling hot.

Sam lay sweating on a cracked brown leather couch. Nick sat at a work table. On the table was an old brass paperweight marked "Curtiss Wright Radial Engines" holding down long-out-of-date flight plans. Next to it was a Hills Brothers coffee can holding a wooden ruler, a protractor, and various pencils and pens. Nick was leafing through a two-year-old copy of *Time* magazine. He was shaking his head over the story of a talking dog.

"Says *here*," he said, "dog in Great Britain. Capable of saying 'I want one.'"

"Of what?" Sam said.

"Well, that's the *question*," Nick said. "Is he barking it out randomly, or in response to his desires?"

Nick paged back through the magazine to the cover story, titled "Jerusalem: Who will Write the Judgment … ?"

"Says here *also*," Nick said, "there is an ongoing struggle in Palestine."

"I'm sure," Sam said, "that they will work it out."

Sam swung his feet onto the ground, and came to the table. He and Nick looked out through the filthy office plate glass, at the bomber.

The bomber sat in the hangar, and they could see the shimmering heat rising from its wings. The painter had already changed the tail number from the Army designation to the civilian N-2474R, and the Air Force rondels had been painted out. The painter stood on a scaffold on the port wing finishing the legend FIVE VETS PRODUCE TRANSPORT on the side of the fuselage. The original plane, bearing the legitimate tail number, had already been flown, without discovery or incident, overseas, and the organization had decided to continue to use the old identity until the ruse failed.

One of the Five Vets, a fat man in a guayabera shirt, came into the office. He slid a packet of documents across the desk to Sam.

"They Emmes?" Sam said. the man shook his head. "They *close?*"

"They're close *enough*," the man said, "for deniability. After-the-fact."

"Which means they stink like a cathouse towel," Sam said.

"That's right," the man said.

Out in the hangar two men were loading the plane, trundling large wooden packing crates up an improvised ramp into the fuselage.

"What're we carrying?" Nick said.

"Farm implements," the man said.

"… mean, they *catch* us, they'll bury us *under* the jail."

"That's right," the fat man said.

Nick and Sam leafed through the documents. They wore worn chinos and t-shirts. Their discarded uniforms lay in a corner of the room.

Sam took his dogtags from around his neck, and added them to the pile of decorations on his side of the desk. He pressed the pile toward the man, who nodded, and then looked at Nick.

Nick took out his wallet, and removed his identification. He passed it to the man, who took two worn green passports from the pocket of his shirt.

"Gonna take our pictures?" Nick said.

The man opened the passports. "S'close enough," he said. "Looks like 'two guys.'" He opened the passports to the photographs, and passed them across the desk.

Sam looked at the passports and then over at the plane.

"'Civilian plane,' they would've reconfigured, and disarmed it."

"Well, we pulled the *guns*," the man said. "Lashed 'em down, next to the Tokyo Tanks." He sighed.

"What they hold?" Sam asked.

"Thirty-six hundred gallons."

"Takeoff weight?" Sam said.

"You going *anyway*?" the fat man said.

"... yeah, *okay*," Sam said.

They looked out at the bomber. The painter had started on the outline of what would be a cornucopia.

"Five Vets Produce," Nick said.

.   .   .

The two men slept while the plane was serviced, painted, and fueled, Sam on an Army cot, Nick on the old brown leather couch, using the black briefcase for a pillow. Toward dusk they were awakened by their host, with coffee. He took a sheaf of papers from a clipboard and handed them to Sam. "Here's your Bill of Lading, and your Various Bullshit," he said. "And here's a copy of the flight plan that you filed for Costa Rica."

"... you the owner of the other plane?" said Nick.

"... and here's some sandwiches," the fat man said. He handed them a large paper bag. "And we refilled your thermos.

"... you *got* ..." he checked his clipboard, "thirty-six hundred thirty gallons. Which should set you down safe and dry. If not, thing's still equipped with the life raft." He turned to Sam. "What'd you fly?"

"How'd you know?" Sam said.

"Well, I could probably tell by your landing," the man said, "you fly a *tail dragger*, you probably want to knock fifteen miles per hour off your touchdown speed, and perhaps keep the nose high or, as we see, that fuckin beast wants to go bounding."

"Flew '25s," Sam said.

"Life raft's the same as in the '25s," the fat man said. "It's fuckin useless. And nobody's going to come to get you anyway."

.   .   .

They flew just North of East. At altitude Sam set the autopilot, and rose out of his seat. "Right back," he said. "Gonna check the tie-downs."

Nick sat alone. The control yoke in front of him moved minutely as the autopilot compensated for the light winds. The night was very clear and full of stars. The plane shook with a steady tremor.

Nick found himself thinking of a girl in Paris, then of the redhead, and then of the four years separating the two women. "Hell of a thing," he thought. "Hell of a thing."

The plane smelled of sweat and gasoline and vomit. Nick wondered if he could smell blood. He lit a cigarette.

Sam climbed back into the left-hand seat.

"… fucker was shot *up*," Nick said.

Sam ran his eyes over the gauges. "They were all shot up," he said. "That's what they were *for*."

Nick pointed to the row of six small aluminum patches, running, diagonally, down low, to the right of his feet.

Sam nodded. "Prolly shot the fucker's *balls* off," he said. "Good plane, though. Better than the '25s. Tougher missions, though, in these. Sit in the box, let the Krauts shoot at you? Where's the fun in *that* … ?

"The *armaments*," he waved his finger, indicating the plane's guns, "were basically just shark repellent."

"Tell me about that," Nick said.

"Life vests?" Sam said. "Pacific War? Canisters of shark repellent. They train the guy, 'You go *down* in *water*—pop the top. Shark repellent? Spreads out twenty-, thirty-foot circle, protects you, you get to the raft.'"

Sam took the cigarette from Nick's lips, took a drag, and handed it back.

"What's the joke?" Nick asked.

"*Joke* was, shark repellent's yellow die." He paused. "That's all—ton of shark? Sees you? You tell *me*. Even if there *was* a 'shark repellent.' Which there wasn't. Huh. It was food coloring."

"The flyers know that?" Nick said.

"Who's the Last to Know? His wife was cheating on him?" Sam said. "This is the power of the human mind."

"And the guns?"

Sam shook his head. "Crapshoot," he said. "Bottom-of-the-box? Tail-End Charlie? Engine failure? Flak gets you? You're straggling? That's all she wrote. One-nineties come through on a pass? It's your bad day? That's *you*, additionally.

"Fuckin guns, I say, better to leave 'em off. Give the plane extra ten miles an hour.

"I saw the *jet* one time. Flew through a box of '25s? Five hundred miles an hour. Driver was *this close*. I saw his face. Dead as he's ever going to be. Fuckin Krauts."

"What killed him?" Nick said.

"… fuckin Krauts … question occurs to me, they're building jets, they're building rockets, here we've got a plane originally built in 1933, we're flying it against jets. …"

"'How did they lose the war?'" Nick asked.

"Well, *yeah*."

"Fuckers with *rifles*," Nick said. "Went there and shot them."

Sam looked at his watch. He checked the map folded and stuck in front of the throttles, a bright red pencil mark running from Florida to the Azores. "F.B.I.," he said.

"It won't come down to that," Nick said.

"I'm just saying," Sam said.

"*Really?*" Nick said.

"For the record."

"Knock it off," Nick said. He stubbed his cigarette out. "Plane was designed in 1933?" he said.

"Yeah," Sam said. "They made it as a children's ride, Chicago World's Fair."

"What happened?"

"The children grew up."

When the dead man was found in the desert, suspicion fell first upon the Golden West, which, his effects indicated, had been the last place of his entertainment.

Sam Black took Nicky Greenstein from the murder scene to a small room off the bullpen at Police Headquarters. A uniform sergeant brought in a file, and placed it on the desk in front of Sam.

"What's in here?" Sam said to Nick.

"That," Nick said, "is the story of a life. Told by its major headings."

"What are they?"

"Chicago. The war."

"Tell me about the war," Sam said.

"The Hundred and First," Nick said.

"Tell me about Chicago," Sam said. He put a finger on the file.

"… *hey*," Nick said, which both understood to mean "the usual errors of youth."

"After the Army?"

"*In* the Army." Nick said, pointing at the file.

"Yeah, what?" Sam said. He looked at the Sergeant, who nodded and left the room.

"I sold, perhaps, a couple pair of stockings," Nick said.

"How bad did they say it was?" Sam said.

"They kept me late, and then they let me go home."

"With an *honorable*?" Sam said.

"*Almost*," Nick said. Sam waited.

"With a *general*," Nick said.

"'In Recognition of'?"

"I think," Nick said, "at that point that they were just tired."

"And so you went home."

"I went home," Nick said.

"To *Chicago*."

"To Chicago," Nick said.

"… to?"

"Well, come *on*," Nick said. "I got home late, I got home with a less-than-honorable discharge, and all I'd done before the war, of note, was to screw Anne Halloran, and run numbers."

"So?"

"I took up running numbers. And I did a favor or two for some people."

"… and?"

"Oh, come *on*," Nick said. "*I* didn't kill the guy."

"He had checks in his pocket from the West," Sam said.

"He also had, I'm sure, a driver's license. But you don't suspect the D.M.V.," Nick said. "What'd *you* do in the war?"

"I drove a B-25," Sam said.

"Hit anything?"

"Yeah. We turned Dresden into a parking lot."

They sat for a moment.

"So, Chicago seconded you to the Blue Room," Sam said.

"That's right," Nick said.

"*Look*," Sam said, "you *understand* … ?"

"Yeah," Nick said.

"You do that guy?"

"My duties. Do not extend *remotely* that far," Nick said.

"Where were you yesterday evening?"

"Noon to midnight? I was on the floor," Nick said.

"You usually on the floor?" Sam said.

"We had a pit boss down," Nick said.

"And afterward?"

"I was in the Lounge," Nick said.

"Business or pleasure?"

"I was gazing at the new girl," Nick said.

"I got to check," Sam said.

"Of course."

Sam sighed. He touched the file. "They hung a lot of tin on you, in the war," he said.

"They hung a lot *on* me, and they put a bit *in* me," Nick said.

"Uh-huh."

"… and I put a bit of tin in *them*," Nick said.

Sam stared at Nick a long while. He started to speak. Then he changed his mind.

"What?" Nick said.

Sam shook his head. "What happened to Annie Halloran?" he said.

"She married the regulation plumber."

Susie had asked, and Sam had told her he was going hunting with Nick. He had packed the small knapsack and dressed in khaki pants and a heavy t-shirt.

She stood in the doorway of their bedroom, watching him dress. He opened the top drawer of the bureau and removed a small glassine envelope. It held his pilot's license and certificates. He put the envelope into the inside pocket of the flight jacket, draped over the bedroom chair.

He took his holstered pistol from the same drawer. He removed the pistol and placed it on the bureau top, next to their wedding picture, a photograph of Sam on his graduation from Flight School, another of him and his wife at a nightclub, on their honeymoon in London, and a small framed snapshot of a smiling five-year-old boy.

Sam threaded a thick black belt through the belt loops, and into the holster, which now sat, tightly held between two belt loops, fitting snugly on his right side. Susie had resewn the loops to fit just before and just behind the holster, so that it could not move on the belt.

She had repeatedly resewn the middle buttons on his sportcoats, loosely, so that they broke free, should her husband have to clear and draw his weapon quickly; and she had resewn four shirts, ripped by the hammer of his .45, when he had had to do so.

Sam reholstered the pistol, and adjusted the weight on his belt. He took two loaded magazines from the bureau drawer, and put one in each snap-pocket on the front of his flight jacket. Susie watched him as he mentally reviewed his state of preparation.

The hunting rifle rested in a corner of the closet, and Sam went to open the closet door. Susie came up behind him, put a palm on the door, and gently closed it. She looked at him frankly.

"Well," he said, "you married it."

She took his face in her hands and gave him a kiss.

"Do you know how long?" she asked.

"I should be back in a week," he said.

"And is Nick going with you?"

"Nick's going with me."

That she resisted the questions "Is it dangerous?" and "Is it what I think?" touched him very much.

He took out his money clip and took a business card from it. He handed her the card, and she looked at it. It read, "Amalgamated International," and held an address and a telephone number in New York.

She shrugged, meaning, as he understood, "And it is not impossible this business card is what I will have in place of a husband."

"Susie …" he said. But she shook off her mood, and smiled.

"You know *what*?" she said. "*Actually*, it's not that different from an ordinary day."

"Do you want me to stay?" he said. She shook her head.

"What would we tell the boy?" she said. "When he's old enough to ask?"

He picked up his knapsack and his flight jacket, and she walked him to the front door of the tiny house. At the door, Sam stopped. He looked back at the living room. There was a cheap red rocking horse on the floor, and, around it, a few bright alphabet blocks.

On the coffee table, in front of the couch, sat Susie's mug of tea, her cigarettes, her matches, and a porcelain ashtray, marked "Souvenir of Brighton," commemorating their first night together, ten months prior to their marriage.

Sam looked back at Susie, his face composed into a mask of regret and reluctance bowing before Duty.

She shook her head and smiled. "You lying son of a bitch," she said, "get the hell out of here."

.   .   .

Sam disengaged the autopilot to feel the health of the plane.

"*That*," he said, "is one hell of a woman."

"*Susie?*" Nick said.

"Susie, yeah," Sam said.

"You tell her where we were going?"

"No, I didn't *tell* her," Sam said.

"… but she knew?"

"Yeah. She knew."

"They got those 'fifties lashed down tight back there?" Nick asked.

"You going to marry the redhead?" Sam said.

The plane flew Northeast. Behind them the sun began to set. Nick looked down at the copy of *Time*. Under the subhead "The Promised Land," was a photograph of Theodore Herzl and the legend "He organized the Return." Nick looked at his eyes. "Yeah, all right," he thought, "that's right."

Sam glanced down at the magazine.

"What'd you learn in the Army?' he said.

Nick closed the magazine. "I learned," he said, "you can polish your brass with toothpaste, and you can use the inside of a banana peel to shine your shoes. With a knife, always strike from below; and a couple of other things I forgot. But nothing I would tell my son. If I had one. If I have one. How's your kid?"

"He's fine," Sam said.

"Good."

"Well, *yeah*," Sam said. "What could be better than being fine?"

"Hunky-dory," Nick said.

"He is 'hunky-dory,'" Sam said.

"Good."

"Tell you what *I* learned, the Army, in addition to fly an airplane," Sam said

"What?"

"My kid? Grows up, don't let him go in the Army."

"Nah, he has to *go*, let him go in the Navy," Nick said.

"… that's right."

"… drive a *boat* around."

"You bet."

"Wear them white pants," Nick said, "and tuck your frikkin wallet in your socks. I ask you."

"I never *had*. Much use," Sam said, "the guys in the Navy. Tell you *why*: guys I met? O Clubs, joints in London? Were a supercilious bunch of goys. Loathed me, as an Army guy, *as* a Jew, and as my uniform was rumpled and had not been fashioned at Brooks Brothers, no, but purchased off-the-rack, in Lower Manhattan."

"How did you end up in Vegas?" Nick said.

"It's the Last Populist Refuge in this dreary world," Sam said. "Fuckin thing. Guys with a hose and a pail—scrubbing the ball-turret gunner out of the plane. You try *ammonia*, that don't work; you, we, tried baking soda, every fuckin thing. Paint? Smell won't go away. The shit and so on."

"Well, then, you sh'unt've gone into Homicide," Nick said, "as your life work."

"And I'll tell you what, I *wouldn't*," Sam said, "*probably*. Had I had a more relaxed war, which gave me a taste for danger and testing the limits of human courage. And what the fuck am I s'posed to do? Come home a Major and all, go to work driving a cab … ?

"I don't *think* … Here, you got, *Susie's* pregnant, come with me, Land of Opportunity. Child-bride, war-bride. *Okay*. Eighty-five million vets competing for ten jobs. She sees an advertisement, in the *Army Times*: looking for qualified men experienced with law enforcement. 'Susie,' I said, 'no. *Read it.*'

She says, 'It doesn't say experience *in* Law Enforcement. Haven't you ever been arrested?'

"'They're looking for a *homicide* detective,' I say. 'Look here, *Sam*,' she says. 'Buy a *book*. Someone's dead? I'll tell you *what*: somebody *killed* them. You find somebody who has a motive, and you go *arrest* them. How hard can it be?'

"The funny thing, she's not far wrong."

"Oh, my," Nick said.

"'*Susie*,'" Sam said, "I say, 'very funny, but, I go out there, I'm still gone have to sit down with the guy, no experience, and a blank résumé.'

"'Maybe,' she says, 'he'll be an Air Force fella.'"

"'That's possible,' I say.

"'Or a Jew,' she says.

"'I hardly think so.'

"'Isn't it *true*,' she says, 'that Our People run Las Vegas?'

"'*Some* of Our People,' I say, 'from the Purple Gang, and Murder, Inc. Also one or two, out of Chicago, and some Italian Friends. They are gangsters. They are *not* Las Vegas cops.'

"'All the more reason,' Susie says, 'which a smart man, you, would point out to a potential employer.'

"'Which is?'

"'You understand your Own Kind,' she says. She starts laughing.

"'What're you *laughing* at?' I say.

"''Cause you don't have to sell your résumé,' she says, 'you sell your *theory*.'

"'They're not my own *kind*.' I say. 'They're *gangsters*.'

"'Gangsters are Jews,' she says. 'Then policemen can be Jews. That's a good idea. Go out there and *tell* 'em.'

"*Susie*," Sam said.

"I'm crazy about her," Nick said.

"Why do you strike from below with a knife?" Sam said.

"Always strike from below the line-of-sight," Nick said. "*That* way, as was explained to me, the fella you're trying to kill, won't *see* you. Biiig fuckin Alabaman, or some fuckin thing. Ast me why I wasn't going to church?"

"And?"

"I told him. He beat the fuck out of me." Nick shrugged. "That's for *Jesus*."

"... this was where?"

"Jump school. I often fantasized about going back to kill him. Who's got the time?"

"Your guys do that fella in the desert?" Sam said.

"No," Nick said. "No. Only guys I ever killed, they were wearing these gray uniforms, and they fuckin stunk of cabbage—but thank you for asking. How'd you pass the interview?"

"The interview was simple," Sam said. "Captain *was* a flyer, in the *Big* war. Difficult part was the written test."

"Hard, huh?"

"No, not if you'd purchased the answers," Sam said.

"I'm gonna take a nap," Nick said.

"Well, then," Sam said, "I guess I'm going to have to 'meet you on the corner in a half an howah, meet you on the corner in a half an howah, meet you on the corner, in a half an ow-wow-wow-wow-*wuh*.'"

Nick started to compact himself into the seat. "What'd they bust you for?" he said.

Sam looked at him.

"Susie said, 'Haven't you ever been arrested?'"

"Well, *yes*, I got *arrested*," Sam said, "for beating the shit out of some guy."

"What'd the guy do?" Nick said.

"Asked for it." Sam held up a hand for silence. He listened for a while, and made a minute adjustment to the pitch of the third engine. He listened again. And relaxed, satisfied.

"Juvenile beef," he said. "Fielder's choice, cops gave me a stern warning, shined me on."

"What'd they do?"

"Broke my nose," Sam said. "I don't think that they meant to.

"*Susie*," he said, "First thing, I *met* her? London ... ?"

"... yeah?"

"I smiled at her. The park, what was the park?"

"I never got there," Nick said.

"Oh, yeah, you were fighting the war. Regent's Park. The Zoo? The frikkin *animals*, they trucked them out to safety." He grinned. "They left this girl, though. Such a pretty girl. I *smile* at her, I start to talk. First words? 'What happened to your nose?' I tell her, 'It's called a hook-nose, they give it to the

Jews.' She laughs, her eyes glint up. She looks at me a minute, and says, 'Fancy a cuppa tea?'" He looked at Nick and smiled.

"Cup of tea. Her folks. Got out in thirty-three." He shook his head.

"Cops book me as an *adult*," he said, "I never get into the Air Corps. No commission, never get to London, don't meet *Susie*. Big fat Irish Sergeant, looks me in the eye, 'Give'm a beating, let the kid go.' Conclusion of which, punctuation, 'Bang' with the day-stick, bridge of my nose." Nick yawned. "Get some sleep," Sam said.

·   ·   ·

Nick had met the redhead at the end of his first week on the job. He'd stopped into the lounge, where she worked, at the conclusion of each of the last three days' shifts, and spoke to her on the third day. She came over to him, straight and slim in her high heels, her face heavily made up and her hair piled on top of her head. She stopped in front of him, and put her drinks tray under her arm and waited.

"I know who *I* am," he said. "Who are *you*?"

"Talk to me in English," she said, and Nick was abashed.

"I beg your pardon," he said.

"That's all right," she said.

"Hello," he said.

"Hello."

"You're new?"

"Wouldn't you know?" she said.

"I'm new, too." The conversation stopped there for one long moment while he looked at her.

"Good God, you're beautiful," he said.

"I don't actually look like this," she said.

"What do you look like?"

"A farm girl," she said.

"... um," he said. "*Look* ..."

"All right," she said. And he looked hard at her to determine the depth of her agreement. And he saw it.

"Just like that?" he said.

"Yes. Just like that."

.   .   .

They sat on the patio.

"You know," Nick said, "I was never afraid of dying. I don't *think* that any of the guys were. My guys.

"Getting maimed, or so on, that was, of course, a different matter."

The patio was on the back of Sam's house. Right off the kitchen.

Susie and the redhead, whose name was Jen, were setting the kitchen table with red-and-white-checkered place mats and napkins. There was a sliding glass door separating the kitchen from the house. The door was open, and Sam and Nick turned to hear the sound of the two women laughing.

"Ain't that something?" Nick said, shaking his head.

Sam smiled. "Far ride from Rivington Street," he said.

"Yeah, well. How 'bout that?" Nick said.

They sipped their iced tea. Sam lit a cigarette. "Fuckin *heat*," he said, "I'm gonna tell you what: I love it.

"New York, other hand, basically, what you forget? It's an *island*. It's an is-land. Stuck in the Atlantic Ocean. It gets *cold*, it gets *cold*. And wet."

He nodded in deference to Nick. "Not like *Chicago*, of course."

"By what standard?" said Nick. "Seeing as how all the thermometers give up. And, fuckin guys? Don't happen to be *packing*? Come up to cops on the street? Midwinter? Beg the cops to *shoot* 'em."

"How are you doing out there?" Susie called.

"We're doing fine," Sam said. "Question *though* is: What are Chicago cops, the cold, doing, outside of the Coop?"

"… cops in the *coop*," Nick said, "good time for the mice to play."

Sam chuckled.

"Were it not so fuckin *cold*. Kids?" Nick said. "We were kids? Smash-and-grab? Turns cold? Bad time. No customers, you go in there, you stand out, *however* in-retirement the cops may be. Some store owner, a .38, gets into his mind, shoot the delinquent. Happened to an acquaintance." He took a cigarette from the pack on the low table. He lit it and inhaled and looked around.

"There *I* am: dead-to-rights, jammed up. Wiseguy comes around, talks a little tachlis, 'Come *in*; start you *right*.'"

"And you walked on that one?' Sam said.

"*That* one," Nick said. "Yes. Guy *sprung* me, used to run with Nails Nathan."

"Guy they shot his horse?"

"They shot his horse," Nick said. "Rode every day. Lincoln Park. Bridle path. Jodhpurs. Yellow leather gloves. Lincoln Park. Horse throws him, get this, into a *mailbox. He's* dead. Guys? That night? His guys? Go to the horse's stable, 'rat tat tat.' Fuckin horse. Medal of Honor at the Somme. Nails Nathan. Stone Jew. *Forget* about it."

"You know ..."

"*Here's* a story," Nick said. "Yom Kippur. Nails? Synagogue. Synagogue? Here they are, auction off the First Aliyah. Biggest deal of the year. Cantor? 'How much am I bid?' Nails, 'Eighty dollars.' Lot of money."

"Back *then* ... ?" Sam said. Nick nodded in agreement.

"'Eighty dollars is bid for the Honor of the First Aliyah?' Now: some macher stands up? 'One *hundred* dollars!' Nails comes back, 'One hundred *fifty*.' Nineteen twenty-two. '*Two* hundred dollars.' Nails rises, under his tallis, under his beautifully cut suitcoat, ivory-handled pistol in a shoulder rig. Jacket falls open, he turns, entire shul sees the piece. 'Five *hundred* dollars,' he says, 'and I'm *coming up*.' Up he walks."

"Fuckin *guys*," Nick said in admiration.

"Equally," Sam said, "*equally*. My brother? South Pacific. Short supply? The Marines?"

"... everything in short supply," Nick said.

"... you bet. A .45. Frikkin? Okinawa? .45? Forget about *that*. My Ma writes, 'What do you need?' 'Send me a .45.' *Home* front?"

"All the guns went to England."

"Went to *England*," Sam agreed. "Word, however, gets out? She? Mentions it, I dunno. Her, what is it? *Susie* ... ?"

"Yes, Sam," she called.

"Bunch of broads, club up at the Synagogue ... ?"

"'Ladies' Auxiliary'?" she said.

"Ladies' Auxiliary," Sam said. "She's working? In the loft? One day? Get this: Fella's a *button* man, his name is—"

"Are you ready to eat?" Susie called.

"Minute," Sam said.

"Button man ..." Nick said.

"'Rosenfeld,' something, deliveries. Ran the, all the deliveries, Garment

District. Coincidentally, numbers, broads, whatever you want, whores for the buyers, all-around guy ..."

"… uh-huh."

"Sinn at her sewing machine. Guy comes in? Same deal. Shoulder holster. Takes out his .45, lays it on the work table in front of her. 'For your son.' Walks out."

"How'd she get it to him?" Nick said.

"How she *got* it to him. *Mind* you, this is an *immigrant*. In Poland? Spoke eight languages. Never learned English. She, I'm over there, no man to ask. Figures it out, she ships the piece, APO? No *way* that pistol is ever getting to the South Pacific. What does she do?"

"What?"

"What she *does*," Sam said, "what she does? Saves up. She buys, get this, a portable Philco radio. Fits the pistol into it, ships it to Okinawa. Nobody steals it. Why?"

"No electricity."

"No electricity. Okinawa? Guys on a rock? Where they going to plug it in? It *arrives*. Package from home. He unwraps it? 'What the fuck is *this* … ?' Guys laughing, 'Yiddishe Mamma.' A note, however, telling him to look inside."

"He wasn't concerned, somebody reads the note?" Nick said.

"Note was in Yiddish," Sam said. He spread his hands. "Some landesman's going to steal her present to her son … ? No."

"He bring it back?" Nick said. "The gun?"

"No, he stayed on Okinawa," Sam said. He shook his head.

"Your Ma still with us?"

"No, she died," Sam said. "*But*: she met Susie."

"Your Dad?"

"My Dad," Sam said, "truth to tell, actually left us. We were one year over here. Two years."

"He ever show up?" Nick said.

"No, he never showed up." Sam shrugged. "What the hell. I was *blessed*, you know," he said, "to have a mother who—"

"Boys," Susie called, "the dinner's on the table."

They rose from their lounge chairs, and stretched.

"… reason I always, in addition to I'm crazy about them, loved her family," Sam said. "I ever tell you how they got out?"

"How'd they get out?" Nick said.

The two men walked into the kitchen. Jen was carrying a large, flat bowl of pasta to the table, and she smiled at them.

"*Bobby*," Susie called. "*Bobby*: come *down* here."

"They knew some *people*," Sam said. "Early thirties."

"Bobby, come *down* here. Don't make your Father go upstairs to get you."

"… who, who," Sam said, "emigrated to Palestine."

"… and?" Nick said.

They sat at the table.

"Who wants what to drink?" Susie said.

"We want another beer," Sam said. He turned to Nick. "I want you to meet some people," he said.

Sam had told him the man's name, and enough of his history for Nick to understand the recital was incomplete.

Sam introduced him to Nick in the coffee shop in Los Angeles. The man was in his early sixties; small, and muscled, somewhat overweight. His face was tanned a dark mahogany. He sat at a booth with Sam and Nick. One of his bodyguards sat at the counter, watching the room; the other lounged outside the door, watching the hotel lobby.

The man had been the head of the postwar European operation called Aliyah Bet, the clandestine resettlement of the Jewish remnant of the Holocaust in Palestine.

He had come to this position as a senior member of the Palmach, the fighting arm of the Haganah, which was the underground Jewish Army in Palestine under the British Mandate.

Sam had told Nick that the Old Man had served, before the war, in the Night Squads, protecting the kibbutzim from the Arabs, and, in the war, as a Sergeant in the Jewish Brigade of the B.E.F., the British Army in Europe.

Sam did not tell Nick that, in conjunction with his duties as Commander of Aliyah Bet, the Old Man had supervised the ongoing operation known as NaKumah, meaning Revenge.

This unit was tasked by the Haganah with the discovery and the execution of Fascist war criminals; and Sam had been recruited, after the war, but before his repatriation, into its ranks. In his year with that unit, he had shot seven high-ranking Nazis. Some of them had been "de-Nazified," or cleared, by Allied tribunals. Some were discovered in hiding, having assumed new identities. Each had been identified by the unit's detectives, and each had been killed by one shot to the head, the shot preceded by the proclamation "I execute you in the name of the Jewish People."

Sam had mentioned these activities to no one. Both his work and his silence had drawn the attention and the admiration of the Old Man.

In the coffee shop, Sam introduced him to Nick. Though he had conveyed it before, through an intermediary, he recited Nick's war record, and a brief history of his accomplishments, his antecedents, and his crimes.

The Old Man sighed. "I need you two to steal a plane," he said.

. . .

Nick awoke, after his first night with Jen, in her bed. Her room was small, and sparse, and perfectly neat.

The clean white muslin curtains flapped once in the light morning breeze, and Nick smiled. He sat himself up against the headboard. Jen opened her eyes and turned on one shoulder, to look over at him. She smiled.

"*Desert,*" he said. "Desert? Comes alive at night." Her expression didn't change. She didn't comment or respond. She just smiled, and Nick found himself smiling back at her.

Some weeks later, they had gone riding in Nick's car, the top down, out through the desert at night.

He'd pulled off the highway onto a dirt side road, and then off that, and out into the desert.

Jen had brought a bottle of wine.

Later, they sat, naked, Jen wrapped in a blanket. Nick was looking at the stars. He felt her question and turned to her.

"Who was the man?" she asked.

"Guy in the desert?" Nick said. "He …" She leaned over and kissed him and began to dress.

"He, and I adore this guy, dead-as-he-is. This group was hitting the Strip at Blackjack?" He began to dress.

"*Funny* thing, I show up on the job. Blue Room is apeshit, Hold at Blackjack. 'What's going on?' My first job, figure it out.

"After my first week? Weinberg calls me in, 'Thank you thank you.' Reason has been restored in the Law of Averages, Hold is back up to eighteen percent, all is right with the world. 'I don't understand what you *did*,' he says, 'and I don't want to know. Chicago is grateful, I am grateful, and this would be an *envelope*.'"

"What was in the envelope?"

"Five grand," Nick said.

"What *did* you do for it?"

"For them? Didn't do anything," Nick said. "Weinberg? *Wrongly* intuited I'd shot the guy. The desert? Who, it turns out, was, indeed, the cause of it all." Nick cleared his throat. "… that I had *shot* him."

Jen nodded.

"Don't you want to say, 'Did you?'" he said.

"Nope," she said.

"I didn't," Nick said. "But, coincidentally, as I said, he had, in fact been, you might call it the Mastermind—save he got shot—of the crew who *were* hitting the Strip."

"How'd they do it?" Jen said.

"*All* right," Nick said. "How they *did* it: they were switching out the shoe."

Jen nodded.

"You know what that means?" Nick said.

"The Dealing Side," she said.

Nick grinned. "*So*," he said, "Desert Inn? Gold Rush, the West? *Everybody's* down five, ten percent, on the Hold, Blackjack. Four nights in a row. Blue Room. I show up? 'Go solve it.' Okay. I figure: Counters? No."

"Why not?"

"Too much dough. Too regular. Some what, some dealer, four, five clubs? Somebody's going to notice. One of the Eyes, out front, it's Counters, s'going to spot the guy. It's not Counters. More possible is collusion. I jump in the dossiers, the dealers? I reach out, through Weinberg? Dealer's bank statements. 'Anybody buy a boat?' And all the vanilla things, you know, you do *first*.

"In the process? This guy? Washes up dead. What's he got? Chips in his pocket from the West."

"But …" she said.

"*Absolutely*," Nick said. "If *I* shot him, I'm going to … ?"

"Clean out his pockets," she said.

"Clean his *pockets* out, *salt* him with checks, somewhere *else*.

"Homicide? Brings me in … ?"

"Sam," Jen said.

"*He* knows. Some guy? Turns up dead, chips in his pocket, the West? *Last* place that did him is us."

"*Unless* …" she said.

"You get the gold ring," Nick said. "Yes. Unless *we*, in a prodigy of under-standing, are one move out *ahead* of the cops."

"And why not?" Jen said.

"Be, because, this requires two things. *Before* a guy. Makes a move that elab-orate, he cannot make it in the dark, but only in response to his understanding of the thinking processes of his opponent."

"In this case, Sam." Jen rolled up the blanket, and sat on it. She shivered once, and draped Nick's leather jacket over her shoulders.

"Sam the cop," he agreed. "Or else, here I am, *new* guy, fresh on the job? I have no basis to anticipate some *unknown* policeman—the level of whose understanding is, of necessity, quite literal—will look at our chips, the guy's pocket, and think, 'Aha! Some Evil Genius planted them there to distract me from the *real* shooter, who, of course, must be somebody else.' Police work? Art of the obvious. I'm new. *I can't know*, some cop, comes across the chips, knows *I* am that smart.

"So Sam the cop takes me in."

"To see if you are that smart," she said.

Nick shook his head. "To see if I am that *stupid*," he said.

"First proposition? Prove a guy's intelligence? Hard to judge by appear-ances. Here's how you *do* it. You've got to see what he *did*. What he's done, did he *fool* you; did he fool someone you respect? And, of course, you look him in the eye. Why? *Lack* of intelligence, *if* a guy's sharp? Is hard to approximate. Sam takes me in to see if I am *dumb* enough to think that I can fool him by salting my own chips on the guy."

He finished dressing. He gave her a hand, pulling her up from the ground. She handed him his leather jacket.

"No," he said, "*you* wear it."

"I'm not cold," she said.

"Missing the point," he said. "American guy? Offers a girl his jacket? Sport-coat? What is she required to do?"

"Drape it around her shoulders," she said. "Thank you."

"Well, I *guess*," he said. "Well-brought-up girl like you … ?" He put a hand on her shoulders. With the other hand he unzipped a side pocket in his jacket, and removed the small automatic. He tucked it into his belt, butt forward, on the left.

He took her hand, and they walked toward the car.

"… farm girl, you must have brothers. Don't you got no brothers?"

"Two," she said.

"They come back?" he said.

"Yes," she said. "They came back, thank God."

"Like to meet 'em someday," Nick said, and Jen hugged his arm around her.

"What do you do, if the other fella *is* smart enough?" she said.

"To fool you?"

"Yes."

"Playing dumb?"

"Yes."

He smiled. "Well, then you got to pay him off," he said.

One pair of headlights sped down the highway, a quarter-mile away.

Nick took the girl's arm from his shoulder and motioned her to stop. Their car sat some hundred yards away. Nick swung wide around it, to the left. Jen watched him, as he disappeared, making a circuit of the car. After a moment she could no longer see him, save once, as a momentary movement in the dark.

She gave a nod of appreciation.

He appeared at her side, took her elbow, and walked her quickly to the car. He started the engine. Threw it immediately into gear, and sped off onto the dirt road, and down the dirt road onto the highway. He turned onto the highway, and drove, quickly and intently, a half-mile before turning on the lights.

"You want to *hit* someone," he said, "nighttime? Best time. Let 'em get in the car, turn on their lights. Kills their night vision, night vision's gone, *hearing's* gone, they turn on the engine. *That's* the time."

They rode quickly on the blacktop, Nick with his right arm draped around her shoulder.

"How did they switch the shoe?" she said.

"Real good *diversion*," he said. "*Move's* the same, *diversion's* different each night.

"One time, God bless 'em, they got? Old couple? Pitches a fight. Old people screaming." He smiled in approval. "Woman? Calls him something? He turns around, bam. Coldcocks her, she goes down, he's standing over her, about 'she ruined his life' eighty-year-olds. I love it. Everybody's looking. Other side of the floor? Switch out the shoe.

"*Next night*: the West?" he said. "Young woman. Goes crazy. Strips off her blouse, her bra, gets up on the table, breasts bouncing, screaming obscenities. *Meanwhile* …"

Jen didn't answer. He looked over at her. She opened her eyes sleepily and drew herself closer to him.

"… meanwhile …" she said.

"Meanwhile, *meanwhile*," he said, "fella in a wheelchair. Overseas cap. American Legion. Purple Heart, Silver Star. Pinned on the cap." He paused for a moment. "Fellow in a *wheelchair*. Other side of the room. Switches out the shoe."

"How did he do it?" she said.

"How he did it: *cold* shoe's hidden underneath his seat. Curtained compartment. We understand …"

She nodded. Nick shook his head. He blew out a breath.

"Diversion, other side of the floor? Everybody looks away. *Dealer* looks away. Looks back? Deed is done. Dealer looks back? Wasn't s'posed to look away, but what could happen? Wounded vet sitting there. Dealers? Can't do enough for him."

"I *remember* him," Jen said. "A wounded vet. Ginger hair, ginger hair, wore a cross around his neck … ?"

"You saw him."

Jen nodded.

"And now he's dead. I *suppose*, *whoever* hit him, thought he took us off, reason they whacked him, for the money, of course, but *primarily*, for pulling it off as a wounded vet. *I* might've. *Otherwise*? Traditional penalty, tune him up, make him make right the dough, give him the Warning.

"*Sam* figured, guy who whacked him? Someone on the Strip. A combat record, son, a brother, got killed. Took it personally. "

"… Sam …" she said sleepily.

"Followed his nose, the guy, whatsisname, the Gold Rush."

"No, I don't know his name," she said.

"*Who*, way I understand it, *sees* the guy, walking out of his room, Motel, Stop-Inn Motel, out on the Fourteen."

"They didn't bust the guy, Sam?"

"What guy?" Nick said.

"The guy who shot him?"

"*Sam* …" he said. They drove on.

"This *guy*," he said, "I *understand* it, would've got away clean, and the whole crew. *Save* our friend from the Gold Rush? Sees him walking out of the motel room. He remembers the guy as the wounded vet. But now he's walking. *Our* guy. Pulls over, and, by way of education, beats the guy rather viciously. First backing him up into the motel room. Finishes the beating. Looks around? What does he find. Wheelchair, Blackjack shoes, five casinos on the strip. And bags of chips.

"Only mistake the guy made. Walking five feet from his motel room to the trunk of his car." He shook his head.

"What is the Warning?" Jen said.

"'Don't Come Back,'" Nick said. "You *sure* that you are from Texas?"

·   ·   ·

The pitch of the propeller changed, and Nick woke up.

"Leaning it out," Sam said. He pointed at the fuel gauges. "… leaning it out," he repeated to himself.

Sam glanced at the chart, folded and marked with a course and notations.

His face took on the Pilot's Look: "What have I forgotten?" He nodded, unfolded the chart, and draped it over the small clipboard, strapped to his right thigh. The penciled course still ran East-Northeast from Meriden, Florida, to the Azores. Sam took two pencils from the sleeve pocket of his flight jacket. He contracted his brow for a moment, and used one of the pencils as a straightedge for the new line, which ran to the Azores from New York. He wrote over this line, "E by S, and then 101½ degrees Mag =." He worked out the declination in his head, and added ".135/True, on Final, approx."

He turned the pencil over and erased both the accurate and the false course. He then tore off all but the final segment of the chart, balled up the remainder, slid back the small window to his left, and threw the chart out into the wind. He forced the window closed. He raised his left hand a bit, then let it fall. Nick murmured his agreement: if it came to that, it was too late.

If they were impounded in the Azores, it would be by the F.B.I., who would, then, have apprehended them in the commission of various crimes, including filing a false flight plan, submitting a fraudulent manifest, altering the registration of an aircraft, all in aid of the international smuggling of arms, and in violation of both an International and a Federal embargo against the supply of arms destined for the Jews in Palestine.

Their apprehension would result, at the least, in the revocation of Sam's pilot's license, and, most probably, in the forfeiture of their American passports. The latter would ensure Sam's cashiering from the Police Force, and, not improbably, in felony convictions and jail time for them both.

The black briefcase held thirty-five thousand dollars, destined for the Portuguese Officialdom of the Azores. It all would be required to refuel and service the plane, and induce the Portuguese officials to perjure themselves to the effect that they had inspected the aircraft and its cargo, and found it, as advertised, farm equipment, and approve and endorse their continuing flight plan indicating that their destination was Spain, all the while knowing that the plane and cargo were destined not for Spain, but for Jews in Palestine on the verge of war; and that their connivance, if discovered, would be most severely censured both by the United States, and by the Government of Portugal.

"You know *what*?" Sam said. "I'm beginning to like this plane."

"Yeah? *Why*?" Nick said.

"… and you better," Sam said, "hand me the *booklet*, and let me review how to land it."

Nick handed the manual to him. "How long you think?" he said. Sam squinted, and looked forward, over the nose.

He leaned to his left and looked down at the waves. He ran his eyes over the airspeed indicator, the compass, and the fuel gauges. "Three hours," he said, "one way or the other."

.   .   .

The preparations needed for the landing were minimal. Sam reviewed the bomber's flight manual, and rehearsed the landing checklist several times with Nick. They engaged in some unnecessary patting of pockets and tightening of straps, and Nick drew the black briefcase closer to him.

"You talk to Susie?" he said.

"I did and I didn't," Sam said. "I left. I went out? Susie's standing in the doorway. Here I am, walking, to the car. There's the kid's tricycle on its side. I put it upright, I look back at the house."

"Never look back," Nick said.

Sam nodded. "Yes, but you're not married. There she is. Little wave. I go back to her. '*Susie* ...' All she says, 'What would you tell the boy, he's old enough to ask?'"

"She understood the deal," Nick said.

"I didn't *tell* it to her," Sam said, "because, *why*? *And* ..."

"... the deal goes South, Feds got a handle on you, 'Give it up or we whack your wife as an accessory,'" Nick said. "That's their idea of getting their knees brown."

Sam rubbed his face. He took the thermos, and shook it to find it empty.

"My brother," he said, "went in, Pearl Harbor. That Monday. Dawn. Line twice around the block. He's standing there, spare pair of BVDs, left jacket pocket, spare pair of socks in the right, candy bar, pack of Luckies, and his birth certificate. *This* son of a bitch was *mad*. His farewell speech, 'Ma? Good-bye.'"

"Eloquent."

"Yeah, you know?" Sam said. "Yes, it was."

.   .   .

Sam checked his chart against his watch, and began a long descent.

"Frikkin Arabs," Nick said. "North Africa, Goums? Working for the Krauts.

"Our guys told us, their favorite trick? Slip in your lines in the night. Two guys in a tent, cut the one guy's head off, stick it on a stake, other guy wakes up, starts screaming, and here he is 'mental.'"

"I heard that," Sam said.

"… all his life, supposedly, he wakes up screaming. Eighty years old. '*Marge* … they cut my buddy's *head* off …!'"

"Very frightening," Sam said.

"Except two things," Nick said. "First being, we? Didn't have tents. The second? *My* Platoon, *nobody's* walking up on us, the dark or otherwise.

"*And* I'll tell you what: the *Arabs*? Can take their public relations campaign and tell it to the Marines, for *Arabs* …."

"Hold on," Sam said. He reached for the flight manual, hesitated for a moment, then nodded, and moved his hand to the bank of fuel switches. He switched the two marked "Left Wing," "Right Wing," to "Centerline," and made a notation on the chart.

"… Arabs …." he said.

"*They*," Nick said, "are nothing but a bunch of guys. Here's the difference. Movie, one time, guy says, 'An American will fight for three things.'"

"… a girl," Sam said.

"Yes. A *girl, himself,* or *to save the world.*"

"I endorse it," Sam said.

"Arabs? However? Fight for fun, for pay, for loot, and then forget it. *We* realized? All you have to do is make it less than enjoyable? Home he goes." He lit a cigarette.

"… what do you think?" Sam said.

"What do I think, 'the Eretz'?" Nick said.

"Yes."

"I think the Brits, anti-Semitic cocksuckers, one and all, will do all they can to poke us in the fuckin eye, then go fox hunting. The Arabs? I think we can beat 'em."

"*All* of 'em?" Sam said.

"Well, *yeah*," Nick said. "If we have to, yeah." He turned in his seat and looked back at the arms and ammunition behind him.

"Susie's *folks*," Sam said, "thick German accents. Thirty-three, they got out. No English. Susie is, what? … eight. She tells me, two months? She's speaking perfect English. Golders Green. Reads, writes, sings, and dreams. Like a Limey. Kicker? Try her out today on German … ?" He shook his head. "Gone with the wind."

"What's Golders Green?" Nick said.

"Jewish North London. Nice place."

"Yeah?"

"Yeah. I hook up with Susie. First three-day pass? They take me in. Her house. My own room."

"You balling her? At the time?"

"Yeah."

"At her parents' house?"

"Yeah. I can't keep my hands off her."

"Parents know?"

"What they *know*," Sam said, "is: I am a Nice Jewish Boy, and an American officer, *wacky* in love with their daughter, which is mutual. I'm going to spend my life with her."

"And if you get knocked on the head?'

"Her old man sits me down," Sam said. "'I'm going to marry your daughter, Max,' I say. He waves it aside. What he wants to *say*, there's a *child*, they'll raise it as their own.

"I'm screwing his daughter, and he's reassuring *me*."

"Got lucky," Nick said.

"... fuckin *Max*, the conversation's half in Yiddish. Fuckin guy ..."

"He the one, get you together with Our Friends, after the war?"

"He's a noncombatant," Sam said, "V.E.-plus-two, I'm in London. Eh? Outside the O Club. Brit soldier comes up. Tells me my name. Shoulder flashes. Jewish Brigade. Sergeant. 'Can I talk to you?'"

"Palmach?"

"My *brother*?" Sam said. "Pearl *Harbor*? Wouldn't even come home. Calls my Ma from Penn Station. 'I'm going to Parris Island.' 'When?' 'Tomorrow. Four a.m.' 'Come home tonight.' 'No, Ma. I got to go.' Click."

"You go see him at the station?"

"I did," Sam said. "There he is, off in a corner. Butts all around his feet. Sitting there, shaking his head. '*Jerry*,' I say.

"'There's a recruiting booth on Times Square,' he says. Yeah. *Huh*. Offered him a battlefield commission, the 'Canal."

"He take it?"

"It was in the Reserves." Sam laughed. "Jerry, he says, '*Sir*. This Marine would rather be a Private, the United States Marine Corps, than a General in the fuckin Reserves, *sir.*"

"How'd he end up?"

"Gunny Sergeant, and half-a-belt of Nambu in the chest, Okinawa," Sam said. "Marry the redhead."

·   ·   ·

The bomber touched down at the end of the long runway at Lajes in the Azores.

Sam saw the jeep detach itself from the tower compound and pace him to the end of the runway.

He finished the rollout, turned the plane, and the jeep took up station in front. The placard proclaimed in Portuguese and English, "Follow Me," and Sam did, running slowly down the mile-long runway, back toward the tower. "Well, *okay*," he said. "You want to be Mutt or Jeff?"

But Nick was gazing at the tower. "How long's it going to take to turn this plane around?"

"About an hour," Sam said. "But."

"I'll talk to them," Nick said. "You stay with the plane. What do you figure, flying time to Tel Aviv?"

"Got to check the weather," Sam said. "Calm winds, six, seven hours flying. They got a *shower*, though, I'd love to take a shower, get some sleep, here."

"Tell you what," Nick said. "Stay with the plane, I think. You're good to fly? I'll top us up on water, food, cigs, deal with the Gendarmes, and let's get out of here."

Nick took the wallet of forged documents from his jacket pocket. He held out his hand and Sam placed his own, false, passport in it.

The jeep stopped, its soldier-driver dismounted, and motioned the plane onto the hardstand next to the tower. The soldier gave the cut-neck sign, and Sam cut the plane's engines. The plane kept ticking, in the silence, as the engine heat dissipated.

"*Well*," Nick said. He undid his shoulder harness, and began to stretch himself out of his seat. Half-out, he realized that he was still tethered by the intercom connection to the headset around his neck. He took the headset off, and tossed it onto the seat.

He looked out the starboard window. Two middle-aged men in uniforms walked toward the plane.

Nick hefted the black briefcase onto the seat.

"What do we do if they don't bite?" said Sam.

"Well, that's a good time to punt. Money, however," Nick said, "has been found, down through the ages, to improve all things."

Nick peered out of the window, as did Sam, for a clue as to their reception in the attitude of the officers approaching the plane, in the lack of activity in the adjoining building, and on the airfield.

One small two-engine plane was taking on fuel from a fuel truck.

Sam kept looking out the window, sweeping as much of the airdrome as he could see. It was evident he didn't like it either. The engines had cooled and the ticking stopped.

"What're *you* looking for?" Nick said.

"I dunno. Other plane from the States … ? Government plane, something," Sam said.

Nick looked at the plane being refueled. It was a six-passenger commercial plane in Portuguese livery. A man in coveralls stood on the wing, filling the tank from a hose which ran down to the truck.

"How much fuel, flying time, we got left?" Nick said.

"Hour." Sam shrugged. "Maybe an hour. Maybe."

"What's the closest land?"

"Uh-*huh* …" Sam said.

The two-man delegation stopped, some twenty yards from the plane. One man gestured to the soldier by the jeep, who reached a pair of chocks from the back, and started toward the plane. The official walked toward the plane.

"Closest land's Madeira, five, five hundred miles, and change."

"We got enough to get us there?"

"Nope."

There was a rap on the fuselage door.

"Look here. Okay, okay," Nick said. "Fire it up, take it to the fuel truck. Fire it up now, *do it* …" Sam turned in his chair and started the number one engine. The man with the chocks retreated from the plane.

Nick opened the black briefcase, and took out a sheaf of bills. The wrapper said, "Five Thousand Dollars." He handed the money to Sam. "Get the plane fueled. Just enough to *get us there*. Taxi it down to the end of the runway. Wait for me there."

"*Really*," Sam said.

"May not *come* to that. In the *event*? *Eh*?"

"They don't need the plane that badly."

"Fuck the plane. They bust me, that ain't nothing. You? Don't you get caught here. Gimme your .45."

Sam put the sheaf of bills in the inside pocket of his jacket. Nick took the pistol from Sam's holster.

"... I ..." Sam said.

"Just take it out," Nick said.

"You shoot that guy?"

"I don't remember," Nick said.

He tucked Sam's .45 into his belt at the small of his back. He carried back the briefcase through the fuselage, past the arms crates, labeled "Farm Machinery," past the plane's strapped-down machine guns. He opened the fuselage door, and swung out into the glare of the airfield. Nick closed the door behind him. He pounded on it twice, and the plane began to taxi toward the fuel truck.

The senior officer handed his clipboard to an underling and stepped forward, expostulating. Nick smiled, and held up two hands in peace. One held the briefcase. The officer came forward, speaking in Portuguese, and pointing at the plane. Nick stopped before him. "Anyone speak English?" he said.

"This *plane* ..." the official said to Nick.

"I couldn't agree *more*," Nick said. "And I've *got* something for you."

The plane continued slowly toward the fuel truck. Nick put the briefcase down, between him and the officer. "What we have in *there*," he said, "is thirty thousand dollars. And *these*," he took the documents wallet from his jacket, "these are official forms, and manifests, sufficient to impress even the most meticulous officials with our right to continued passage."

The engine noise had ceased, and Nick glanced back over his shoulder. He saw Sam swing down from the nose hatch, and call over the man from the fuel truck. When Nick turned back, he saw that the junior officer was glancing back toward the terminal.

"Thirty thousand dollars," Nick said. The man took off his cap, wiped his brow, looked down at the briefcase, and back up at Nick.

The fuel truck operator had pulled his truck up beside the bomber, and was climbing up onto the port wing, carrying the hose. Sam stood on the wing, and he was looking beyond Nick and the Portuguese, at two men in dark suits and crew cuts, who were walking toward Nick. Nick saw them, and looked back at Sam. Sam cut his hand across his throat, as a question. Nick shook his head. Sam turned back to the fuel attendant. The gas was already flowing into the wing tank. Sam looked at a gauge on the hose. He bit his lip.

The two men in suits, one middle-aged, one young and fit, stopped near Nick. The senior Portuguese official handed Nick his documents, then he and the other man drew back, leaving the briefcase sitting on the tarmac.

The two Americans looked for a moment at Nick.

"Howdy," Nick said.

The younger man moved a few paces to the side, his eyes, unmoving, fixed on the plane. He had a webbing rifle sling across his left shoulder.

The middle-aged man held out his hand, palm up, and Nick placed his documents wallet in the palm.

The man looked cursorily at the documents. He took a leather-mounted badge from his left-hand pocket and showed it to Nick.

"Federal officers," he said.

"Okay," Nick said.

"You are in violation of Federal and Civil Aviation statutes, various International Agreements, the International Arms Embargo, and the illegal shipment of arms. Your plane is impounded, and you are under arrest."

"You guys are on the wrong track," Nick said. "As you *see*," he pointed at the documents, "we have a valid Commercial Transport License, our *manifest* ..."

"Are you armed?" the man said.

"I have a small-caliber sidearm," Nick said. He put his hands on each side of his jacket and stopped. The agent nodded at him to open it.

Nick drew the sides back, revealing the little Walther pistol tucked on his left side.

"Thumb and forefinger, left hand," the agent said.

Nick removed the pistol as instructed. The agent stole a quick glance down at it.

"Nazi gun," he said.

"They're wonderful craftsmen," Nick said.

"Place it, on the ground. Pointed away from me," the agent said. Nick did so, and the agent used the side of his foot to brush it away. It clattered over the cement.

Nick turned to the sound of the fuel truck engine. The truck began to pull away, and, as it did, the bomber's first engine came to life, and the plane began to taxi toward the end of the runway.

When Nick looked back, the younger man was in the process of slinging the Thompson gun from behind his back, forward. Nick drew the big Colt from the small of his back, snapped down the safety, and leveled it at the two men.

"Let's hold it right there," he said. "*You:* just let the Tommy gun drop. Let it drop. Just take your hand off it, and let the sling take it."

"Pal," said the older man, "that's thirty years in Leavenworth."

"Just take your hand off the stock," Nick said, and the younger man did so, letting the sling hold the gun.

"Thank you," Nick said. To run the permutations in his mind took less than a second. He sighed.

"Lads," he said. "All it is? Let's just stand here, until the plane takes off. Then I am yours."

"Put your weapon down," the older man said.

"After the plane takes off."

The bomber had reached the end of the runway. Sam turned it into the wind, and ran each of the engines up.

The engines now were running smoothly. And Sam gave them two bursts, signaling to Nick.

Nick shook his head. He raised his left arm, and pointed it, toward the far end of the runway. Sam signaled again. Nick turned his thumb down, and pumped it twice.

Nick never took his eyes from the two men. The bomber did not move. Nick gestured again, emphatically, for the plane to take off.

After a long moment, the pitch of the engines changed, and the plane began its takeoff roll.

"All right," Nick said.

He safed the big pistol, and placed it on the ground. As Nick stood, the agent in front of him drew his revolver. He nodded to the younger man, who stepped to the side for a clear field of fire, knelt, and brought the submachine gun up, taking aim at the approaching plane.

As Nick went for the pistol on the ground, the older agent shot him dead.

The slugs from the Thompson gun stitched up the starboard side of the plane's nose, but they missed the pilot.

The plane gathered speed and passed the shooter, who emptied the magazine at the retreating plane, which was now not a vulnerable target.